SACKETT SURROUNDED

I leaped to my feet, and Bauer came up, knife in hand. Diana tossed me the poker from the fireplace.

From outside the noise of fighting had ceased. Bauer's smile was cool. "It is too late now," he said. "My men have won. Give Diana to me and you shall go free and we'll not burn your fort. After all, there are other women."

My poker held ready, I made no reply. His knife was not a small one. The poker, for all its usefulness, was unwieldy, and if his wounds bothered him, there was no evidence of it. He was an unusually strong, agile man and obviously was no stranger to hand-to-hand fighting.

Suddenly Diana screamed, *"Kin!"*

Lashan was in the doorway, pistol in hand. As my eyes caught him, his pistol was lifting to take dead aim at me . . .

THE WARRIOR'S PATH

Bantam Books by Louis L'Amour

Ask your bookseller for the books you have missed

BENDIGO SHAFTER
BORDEN CHANTRY
BRIONNE
THE BROKEN GUN
THE BURNING HILLS
THE CALIFORNIOS
CALLAGHEN
CATLOW
CHANCY
CONAGHER
DARK CANYON
DOWN THE LONG HILLS
THE EMPTY LAND
FAIR BLOWS THE WIND
FALLON
THE FERGUSON RIFLE
THE FIRST FAST DRAW
FLINT
GUNS OF THE TIMBER-
  LANDS
HANGING WOMAN
  CREEK
THE HIGH GRADERS
HIGH LONESOME
HOW THE WEST WAS
  WON
THE IRON MARSHAL
THE KEY-LOCK MAN
KID RODELO
KILLOE
KILRONE
KIOWA TRAIL
THE MAN CALLED
  NOON
THE MAN FROM
  SKIBBEREEN
MATAGORDA
THE MOUNTAIN
  VALLEY WAR
NORTH TO THE RAILS
OVER ON THE DRY SIDE
THE PROVING TRAIL

THE QUICK AND THE
  DEAD
RADIGAN
REILLY'S LUCK
THE RIDER OF LOST
  CREEK
RIVERS WEST
SHALAKO
SILVER CANYON
SITKA
TAGGART
TUCKER
UNDER THE SWEET-
  WATER RIM
WAR PARTY
WESTWARD THE TIDE
WHERE THE LONG GRASS
  BLOWS
YONDERING

Sackett Titles by
Louis L'Amour

1. SACKETT'S LAND
2. TO THE FAR BLUE
   MOUNTAINS
3. THE DAYBREAKERS
4. SACKETT
5. LANDO
6. MOJAVE CROSSING
7. THE SACKETT
   BRAND
8. THE LONELY MEN
9. TREASURE
   MOUNTAIN
10. MUSTANG MAN
11. GALLOWAY
12. THE SKY-LINERS
13. THE MAN FROM THE
    BROKEN HILLS
14. RIDE THE DARK
    TRAIL
15. THE WARRIOR'S PATH

THE WARRIOR'S PATH

Louis L'Amour

BANTAM BOOKS
TORONTO · NEW YORK

THE WARRIOR'S PATH
A Bantam Book / July 1980

2nd printing .... July 1980   4th printing .... August 1980
3rd printing .... July 1980   5th printing .... September 1980
                6th printing .... June 1981

Photograph of Louis L'Amour by John Hamilton—
Globe Photos, Inc.

ISBN 0-553-20418-1

Published simultaneously in the United States and Canada

Bantam Books are published by Bantam Books, Inc. Its trademark, consisting of the words "Bantam Books" and the por-
trayal of a bantam, is Registered in U.S. Patent and Trademark
Office and in other countries. Marca Registrada. Bantam
Books, Inc., 666 Fifth Avenue, New York, New York 10103.

PRINTED IN THE UNITED STATES OF AMERICA

15 14 13 12 11 10 9 8 7 6

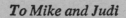

To Mike and Judi

Author's Note

The Shawmut, where Diana takes refuge, was, of course, a part of what is now known as Boston. The Reverend Blaxton (sometimes written Blackstone, but in the one signature I have seen, it is Blaxton) was much as he appears here. The same is true of Samuel Maverick, who was helping to establish a family that has contributed much to our history, to say nothing of having added a word to our western vocabulary.

Contrary to general opinion, slave raids from Africa to the coasts of Europe were not uncommon. The raid on the village of Baltimore, a town in West Cork, Ireland, took place in 1631. More than one hundred people were carried away into slavery.

The Warrior's Path led, with many branches and offshoots, from the far south to the towns of the Iroquois and even farther north. The Iroquois used it to attack the Cherokees, Creeks, and so on, and vice versa. The route was also used by traders and other travelers, as it was undoubtedly the best, following the contours of the land through areas in which there were water, fuel, and game.

THE WARRIOR'S PATH

Chapter I

What I hoped for was a fat bear, and what I came up with was a skinny Indian.

It was lonely on the mountain, and I had been watching the sun crest the peaks with light. There was some mist lying in the valleys, and all around me the rhododendrons were in bloom, covering the flanks of the Blue Ridge and the mountains nearby. Seated among them, their petals falling across my shoulders and into my hair, I watched the path below.

It was an old, old path, old before the coming of the Cherokees, old before the Shawnees hunted these hills, as old as the first men on these mountains.

All through the afternoon there had been no sound but the twittering of birds, but I knew something was coming up the trail yonder, for I'd seen birds fly up from time to time, marking its progress along the path, which was visible only at intervals.

What I wanted was a fat bear, for we were needful of grease, and my ribs were showing. When a body lives off the country around, fat is the hardest thing to come by. Fresh meat was no problem, but it was lean, mighty lean.

An Indian was the last thing I was wishful of seeing. We had good friends among them, but when a body becomes friendly with one nation, he naturally becomes an enemy of their enemies whether he is wishful for it or not. Moreover, a friendly Indian could eat us out of house and home, and we were shy of meat and corn flour.

1

Next to a fat bear it was Yance I was most anxious to see, for he was coming across the hills with fur, which we would soon be packing for trade in the settlements.

This Indian was old, and he was hurt. When I put my glass on him, I could see that. It was pa's glass, one used by him during his seafaring days and a right handy contrivance.

Sitting among the blooms of rhododenron, all pink, purple, and white, and scattered among them the pink of mountain laurel, I watched him come. Scrooched down in the brush the way I was, it was unlikely he'd see me.

The old man was reaching for the end of his rope. He was worn out and in need of help, but I'd had dealings with redskins since I was knee-high to a short duck, and Indians could be mighty sly. That old Indian might be a decoy to get me to show myself so's I could be bow shot or lanced, and I was wishful for neither.

He seemed to be in perishing bad shape. Coming to my feet, I must needs take the shortest way, which meant right down the steep cliff through the rhododendrons. It was all of three hundred paces back to where our path turned off, and that old man was hurting.

This here was our country, leaving out a few Indians who might argue the point, but I'd see no man die whom I had not personally shot.

He was still a-coming when I slid into the trail before him, but he was weaving a mighty weird path and was ready to drop in his tracks. I was close enough to catch him.

He wasn't only worn down from travel, he was gun shot.

Getting an arm around him to keep him from falling, I took time to slip his knife from its sheath for safety's sake. Then I walked him to where I could lead him through the brush to our cabin.

We'd built, Yance and I, well back in a niche among the rocks with a cliff overhanging from above. We had a fine field of fire on three sides in case of attack, which happened whenever a passing war party took the notion. This was the place we built after the Senecas killed pa and Tom Watkins in the mountains above Crab Orchard.

When I put that Indian down on the bed, he just naturally passed out. Putting water on to boil, I unlaced the top of his hunting shirt and found he'd been shot through the top of the shoulder with a musket ball. The ball was still there, pressed against the skin at the back of his shoulder. Taking my hunting knife, I slit the skin and oozed it out. The wound was several days old but wasn't in bad shape.

Sakim often commented on the fact that wounds in high country did not fester as often as they did in crowded cities. Sakim had come to America with pa, but he had been a physician and surgeon in central Asia, a descendant of a long line of scholars from the great age of medicine. Pa had met him after pa was kidnapped aboard Nick Bardle's ship where Sakim was also a sailor. He'd come aboard Bardle's pirate craft by shipwreck or capture, and when pa made his escape, Sakim was one of the two who chose to leave with him.

When we were youngsters at our small settlement on Shooting Creek, he had been our teacher. A noted scholar among his own people, his education far surpassed any available in Europe at the time. He taught us much of the sciences and of history but also of sickness and the treating of wounds, but for all his teaching, I was wishing him with us now.

The old man opened his eyes while I bathed his wound. "You are Sack-ett?"

"I am."

"I come Penney."

The only Penney I knew was Yance's wife, whose name had been Temperance Penney when he took her to be wed. She was back on Shooting Creek, waiting our return.

"Miz Penney say me come Sack-ett. Much trouble. Carrie gone."

3

Carrie? That would be Temp's baby sister, of whom I'd heard her speak.

"Gone? Gone where?"

"Pequots take him. Bad Indian. All much afraid of Pequot."

Right now I was beginning to regret this old Indian. Had it not been for him, I'd have been shagging it down the Cherokee Path to find ol' Yance, who was behind time in his coming. There was always the chance that he'd rounded up too many Indians.

Of course it took a few to be too many for Yance, and I had mercy for anybody who cornered him. I'd done it a couple of times when we were youngsters and was lucky to get away with my hair. Yance was bull strong, bear tough, and he could fight like a cornered catamount.

Yance was casual about most things, but pa had pressed it upon us to be prompt. It was a rule amongst us to be where we were supposed to be and no nonsense about it. We knew it was often the difference between life and death.

"Miz Penney say you come. Much bad Indian. Take two girls."

Taking up my musket, I moved to the door, standing where I could watch the path to our clearing. If Yance came running and was hard pressed, I might take down at least one of them. I mind the time he came to the door with a big she-bear about two jumps behind him. It was a nip-and-tuck thing getting him in the door and keeping the bear out, and just having freshly mopped the floor, I was almost minded to shut the door and let them fight it out.

"All we want is the hide and the tallow," I advised him later, "not the whole bear."

"Did you ever tote a fresh-killed bear or even a bear hide and its tallow over three ridges in a boiling hot sun? I figured to let him bring it right to the doorstep."

"What happened to your musket?"

4

He blushed. "I was fixin' for a shot when he came for me. I'd no choice but to allow for distance betwixt us, so I taken out running."

This time Yance would be a-horseback with pack horses, which would hold him to the trace and no chance to take to the woods. He was an almighty stubborn man and I knew he'd not leave his horses and furs for some Indian.

"You wife Penney?"

It took me a minute to realize he'd mistook me for Yance. What had he said before? Two girls gone? Taken by Indians?

He'd come a far piece if he'd come from Cape Ann or the nearby country, and those girls were long gone now. Still, I'd heard of a swap being made, goods for girls, or whatever. Anyway, she was kin by marriage to Yance. We'd never let them down. Whatever we could do would be done.

It must have taken that Indian a week to get here. Even more, it was likely. I'd never been up north, for it was Yance who'd gone girlin' up there to find himself a wife. Only I think he was just looking around when he saw her and took to her first sight.

Putting my musket close to hand, I put water on and began slicing meat into it for a stew. I added some wild onions and other herbs from the forest, for we did with whatever was to hand.

There was no question of not going. My corn crop would suffer from lack of cultivation and from varmints, but crops were a chancy thing in this country. There'd have to be grub got ready and packs. Whilst the stew was shaping up, I set to gathering what we'd need.

The old Warrior's Path would be the fastest route even though we might encounter war parties along the trail. Yet we must travel fast. Indians were notional about prisoners. They might want them for slaves, for torture, or for trade. They might want them simply to exhibit and then kill, but if they whined and carried on

5

or got weak so they could not travel, the Indians would surely kill them out of hand. It had happened before.

Temperance Penney had been living in a settlement nigh to Cape Ann when Yance found her. We Sacketts were a free-roving folk, and now and again we boys would take off across the country to see what might be seen. Often one of us went alone, or sometimes two or three would venture together.

We had visited Jamestown a time or two, and Kane O'Hara from our settlement had gone down to the Spanish villages to the south. It was there he found his wife. We'd heard tell of the Pilgrim folk to the north, but Yance was the first to traipse off thataway.

Yance was curious as an Indian as to how other folks managed, and he lay up there in the woods watching their village until he had seen Temperance.

She was sixteen then, pert as a kitten and feisty, with the woman in her beginning to show. Already her good spirits had gotten her into trouble. Her neighbors were good folk but serious minded and with a set way about them and not much time for play or merrymaking.

Yance had only to look one time to know what he'd come north for, and come night, he'd taken a quarter of venison down, hung it outside her door, and rapped sharply on the door; then he skedaddled and laid low.

Now few of those northern settlers were hunters. In the England of their time all the game belonged to the king or ran on a few of the great estates, and unless they poached, they got none of it. Nor had they weapons about except during time of war. Fresh meat was hard to come by, and when they reached America where game abounded, they had no skill as hunters and were uneasy about taking game, for here, too, the game was said to belong to the king. A haunch of venison outside the door was a likely treat, so they took it in and were grateful.

If Temperance herself had any ideas, she wasn't talking about them, just going about her churning, weaving, and gathering as though she paid no mind to anything. After they were married, she told me she'd seen Yance on the slope and in the woods a time or two from a distance, so she had her own ideas where that venison came from.

A few night later Yance came down from the trees bearing another haunch and was made welcome.

He was a bearer of news and from another colony as well, although, being one of us, I don't imagine he was too free about saying just where he came from. Yance was a good talker, that being the Welsh in him, for the Welsh are like the Irish in having a feel for the language and a liking for the sound of their own voices. He done a sight of tale telling, but he never once looked at Temperance, but she needed no telling to know whom he was talking to, and for.

Now a pert and feisty girl like Temp, with a shape like hers, had taken the eye of every man in the settlement, not to mention occasional peddlers and tinkers who passed. Some of the local sprouts had ideas about her, and then here comes this stranger in wide-brimmed hat and buckskins. They liked nothing about him.

Moreover, Yance had been brought up like all of us, free thinking and free speaking. Pa had believed in us using our minds, and he believed in freedom and in expressing ideas, nor was Yance one to keep his mouth shut. He stayed on, a-courting Temperance, and it wasn't long until he had crossed the ways of the folk, and he found himself in the stocks.

It was the way of the time to pitch rotten fruit or clods at whoever was in stocks, and as the boys and men cared little for Yance, and as he was a stranger in buckskins, like an Indian, he caught more than his share, good though he was at ducking. He had taken it, biding his time. He knew he would not be there forever; moreover, he had a good idea what Temp would do, and she did it.

7

Somehow or other she contrived to get the keys, unlock the stocks, and set Yance free. Being wise for his years, Yance just naturally left the country; being doubly wise, he had taken Temperance with him.

He might not have taken her, having respect for her family and all, but she wasn't to be left behind. Moreover, she had been doing some thinking beforehand and led him down the country where they could rout out a preaching man. He wasn't of a mind to read over them until she told him she'd go with Yance without it, and he got right to it.

From time to time after she came to us, she sent word home by traders or travelers, so they knew she was honestly wed and cared for. Now they were in trouble, and they'd sent for Yance.

This was 1630, and folks had been living in that Massachusetts Bay colony for ten years or so, but most of them were latecomers, innocent as babes about Indians and such.

Nobody needed to tell us about Pequots. We'd had no doings with them, but word is carried on the wind, and other Indians had told us of them. They were a strong, fierce people, unfriendly to the whites.

It was in my thoughts that it was Temp's mother who sent for Yance. She was a righteous, churchgoing woman, but she knew a man with hair on his chest when she saw him.

"Who took those girls?" I asked the old Indian again.

"Pequots."

Had he hesitated there just a mite? Or was that my imagination? If they were not already dead, trying to get prisoners away from the Pequots would be a hard-bought thing. Yance was suddenly in the yard, astride that big red horse he favored, his pack animals loaded down with fur. It took only a minute or two for me to lay it down to him.

"I'll go. No need for you to lose your crop."

Well, I just looked at him, and then I said, "Pa always said, 'I want it understood that no Sackett is ever alone as long as another Sackett lives.' Besides," I added, "you will need me to keep those Pilgrim folk off your back whilst you take out after the Indians."

"Don't figure the Pequots will be easy. Any time you take after them, you've bought yourself a packet, Sackett."

"What about him?" I gestured toward the Indian. "He's old, and he's hurt."

"I go." The Indian spoke quickly. "You go, I go. You no go, I go, anyway."

"You fall behind," Yance warned, "and we leave you."

"Huh." He glared at Yance. "You fall behind, I leave *you!*"

Yance put up his horses and then went to eating. On horseback, we would make good time up the Warrior's Path. We had meat, and we had cold flour, so there would be no need to stop for hunting.

"That other girl," I asked, "the one with the Penney girl, who was she?"

It was a full minute before he spoke. "She Macklin girl. She plant woman."

Why the hesitation? What had happened up there, anyway? What was wrong with their own men? Of course, few of them were woodsmen, if any at all. In the old country they had been craftsmen, weavers, woodworkers, and their like, and the Penneys knew Yance was a woodsman, knowing the ways of wilderness travel and of Indians.

A plant woman? What did that imply? That she gathered herbs, perhaps, or was knowing about them. Such a girl would be at home in the forest.

"We'd better hurry, Kin. I think we'll have this to do alone. Those folks aren't going to look for Diana Macklin."

Something in his tone made me look up from the packing. "No? Why not?"

"Because they do be saying she's a witch woman. They'll be saying 'good riddance,' and they'll just walk away."

9

"But what about the Penney girl?" I protested.

"Too bad for her that she was in such company. I tell you, Kin, they will do nothing. Unless it be us, the girls be lost—lost, I say."

Chapter II

Come daylight, we had distance behind us. We took a back trail up through the rocks behind our cabin so no chance watcher would know we had gone, winding through the rocks and the rhododendron. We were all mounted, and it was the first time I'd ever seen an Indian a-horseback. The old Indian's name was Tenaco.

Horses were scarce in the colonies, and we had bought ours from a Spanish man who wished to return to Spain and had to sell what horses he owned. The Spanish men of Florida were not permitted to trade with the English, but people will be people, and we had much they wished for, so the trading was done. We paid in gold, of which we had found a little, and had more we kept by us from pa's dealings.

There was Indian country before, behind, and all about us, and any stranger was fair game for any Indian. Yet some of them were moved by curiosity and the desire for trade, and we were wishful of no trouble.

It was far we had to go, through terrain wild with strange trees and vines, a country of lonely paths, and the awareness of death rode with us, Tenaco no less than we, for Indian forever killed Indian long before the coming of the white man.

We rode the Warrior's Path, three mounted men and a pack horse to carry our necessaries.

A witch woman, they said! Well, I put no faith in witches, although both Welsh and English had stories

11

enough of witches, elves, gnomes, and haunts and such. Pa had the gift, it was said, and to some it was the same thing, but not to pa or to me or to Lila, who was said to have it, too.

Yet being thought of as a witch would be held against her, and it was unlikely any would wish to go to the rescue of a witch even if the child with her was liked. It was likely they'd feel the Indians got what they deserved when they took her.

We saw no fresh track of moccasin or boot. We passed among the dark leaning poles of the pines into the shadows and beyond, wondering what memories these slopes held and what peoples might have been here and gone before our coming.

Half of our teaching had been from Sakim, the scholar from far-off Asia, and Sakim lived with the awareness of lives he had lived before.

We carried long bows made English style, for pa and several of the others amongst our lot had understood the bow. It was a saving of lead and powder, which now we mined for ourselves or made. Also, it was silent hunting and left no echo upon the hills for unfriendly ears.

How lonely were these silent hills! How reaching out for the sounds of men, for I believe a land needs people to nurse its flesh and bring from it the goodness of crops.

As we looked upon the shadowing hills, I saw a red bird fly up, a bit of the sunset thrown off by a soundless explosion, and then there were a dozen flying, then gone.

"It is an omen," Tenaco said. "There will be blood."

"Not ours," Yance replied grimly. "It is Temperance's sister they have taken."

"Do you recall her, then?" I asked.

"Aye, and a lovely lass. She would be ten now, I think, perhaps eleven. Gentle, sweet, and graceful as the wind. She was the first of them to accept me—after Temperance, of course."

"You knew the other girl?"

"Ah, she is almost a woman, that one! A woman? But of course! She was strong, quiet, remote." He looked at me. "You would like her, Kin, witch or no."

"I put no stock in witches."

"You will when you see her. There's a strangeness about her and a difference. A kind of stillness and poise. She has a way of looking at you that makes you uneasy, as if she could see all you were and were meant to be. Yet there's a wildness in her, too."

He chuckled suddenly. "The young men are afraid of her. She sews well, spins well, does all things well, but she looks on them with no interest, and lovely as she is, they become speechless when with her."

At night we left our cooking fire and went on, then bedded down to a cold camp in the woods, not all together so we might not all be taken at once if the worst came.

Day after day retired behind us, and night after night we gave our smoke to the sky. We left tracks and dead fires behind us, moving on into the days, knowing there was little time and at the end, the Pequots.

We had fought other Indians, but these had a bloody name, a reputation for fierceness. Yet a man cannot think of death at such a time; he simply tries to do what needs to be done. Women of our kind had been taken, women of our family, since Yance was wed to Temperance.

I thought of the other one. The silent one who stands alone in the wind. There was something in the way Yance looked at me when he spoke of her.

We wore buckskins and wide-brimmed hats and Indian moccasins, for they were best for the woods, and we had not been back to Shooting Creek for some time. There was one of us there who could make boots, but we thought them not as well for the forest.

In a moccasin a man can feel a twig that might crack before he puts his weight upon it; he can feel the

13

rocks with his feet, take a grip with his toes if need be. And each of us was skilled, as were the Indians, in the making of moccasins, which was essential, for they wore out quickly.

Each night we plied Tenaco with questions about Plymouth, but he knew little of it. He had been there but spent most of his time with white men at Cape Ann or some of the outlying settlements or farms.

There was peace with his people, the Massachusetts. Before there was any settlement in his country, there had come a terrible sickness, which men called the plague, and it swept away most of his tribe, leaving them helpless before the attacks of their deadly enemies, the Narragansetts. Knowing their lands would be taken from them bit by bit by the Narragansetts and that his people would be destroyed, the chief of Tenaco's people went to the white men and invited them to come and settle in his land, and he gave them choice land between his people and the Narragansetts.

It was a cool, clear night when we came at last to the edge of the settlement. There were only a few cabins. "Show me their house," I said to Tenaco. "I will speak with them."

He showed me the house. It looked square, strong. "It's built of stone," Yance said. "Her father was a stonemason in England."

"Watch for me, but stay out of sight. I don't want you back in the stocks again." A thought occurred to me. "Tenaco? Do the others in the settlement know they sent for us?"

He shrugged.

We squatted on our heels, watching the houses. Our horses were well back in the forest, picketed on meadow grass.

All was still. Nobody moved. It was not a good thing to go among such houses at night, particularly wearing buckskins, which Indians wore up here but no white man. It was a risk to be taken.

"All right," I said, and was gone.

The Penney house was the garrison house, built

with a slight overhang to fire upon Indians who came to the doors or windows or tried to fire the house. Here was where the others would gather if trouble came.

A few chinks of light showed where other houses were. Doors were barred now, shutters closed against the night. I saw few corrals, a few fenced gardens. Walking swiftly, I came to the door and stepped lightly on the two boards that did for a stoop. I tapped lightly.

There had been a murmur within, suddenly stilled. Behind me in the woods an owl hooted. Nothing moved, then a faint rustle of clothing.

The latchstring was not out, nor had I expected it to be. I waited, then tapped again.

"Who comes?" A man's voice, low and a little shaken.

"Sackett," I said, and I heard the bar lifted. The door opened a crack, and I stepped quickly in.

"You be not Yance." The man was heavyset, not tall but a solid-looking man with an honest, open face.

"He waits," I said, "with Tenaco."

"Ah!" The man let his breath out, in relief, I thought. "We heard he was dead. Killed by the Pequot."

"He was shot," I said, "I cut out the musket ball myself. Do your Indians have muskets, then?"

"Not many." He turned, gesturing toward a bench by the table. "Sit you. Will you have something?"

"Whatever," I said.

"We expected Yance," the woman said. She was a pleasant-faced woman, but there were lines of worry on her face now.

"He came, but we suspected all might not make him welcome, so I came down."

"There would be risk for you, too, if they knew you were here."

"I shall not be long," I said, "if you will tell me what has happened."

"They went to the woods," the woman said. "Carrie was much with Diana Macklin. Diana was teaching her the herbs for medicine, and they went a-gathering.

"It is only a little way, a meadow yon. Diana often went to the woods and meadows and was not afeared, and Carrie was much with her."

"I never wished it," Penny said irritably. "That you know."

"I don't care what they say!" Mother Penney replied somewhat sharply. "I like her. It's just that she is independent and speaks her own mind."

"It is not that alone," Penney said. "There's the dark look of her, the knowledge of herbs, and the books she reads."

"Macklin reads. You do not speak of that!"

"He's a man. It is right for a man to read, although I speak no favor of the books he reads. Blasphemous, they are."

"Let's get on with it!" I spoke irritably, for they wasted time. "They went a-gathering, and they did not come back, is that it?"

"Aye," Penney said, "and the bloody Pequots have them. Dead they are by now, or worse."

"Maybe not," I replied. "This Diana you speak of sounds to be a shrewd woman. Such a one might find a way to survive, and for your daughter, also . . . Carrie, is it?"

"It is."

"And Pequots, you say? Were they seen? Or their tracks?"

"No, but—"

"Then why Pequots? There are other Indians about and white men, too."

He stared at me, aghast. "White men? You wouldn't for the world suspect—?"

"I would," I said. "I know not your people, but there are ships along the shore, and all of their sailors be not angels from heaven. It may be Pequots, but if we are to find them, we must know."

"Pittingel was sure. He said it had to be Pequots. He is a man with much knowledge of the world."

"Good!" I replied. "Does he also know Indians?"

Penney looked uncomfortable. "He is a very important man. A trader," he said, "a man with ships of his own and a place on the council."

"Good!" I said. "Why haven't you gone to him?"

"Well, we did. He tried to help. He looked, and he had his men out in the woods, searching high and low. They found nothing."

And tramped over every track or bit of sign, I told myself, but then I said, "There was an organized search, then? The village turned out?"

Penney flushed. "Well—"

"Tell him the truth!" Mother Penney spoke sharply. "Nary a bit would they do but talk, talk, talk! And all they would say was 'good riddance,' and not for my Carrie, mind you, but for Diana Macklin!"

"We had better know each other," I said. "I am Kin Ring Sackett, brother to Yance."

"I am Tom Penney—my wife Anna." He paused, looking uneasy. "Others are coming."

"Others?"

"Joseph Pittingel will come here himself. And Robert Macklin."

Anna Penney looked at me. "Carrie has been gone for days upon days. We know not if she be alive or dead."

"If she is alive," I said, "we will bring her home. If she be dead, we will find where she lies."

"I believe you will. When Carrie disappeared, it was Yance Sackett of whom I thought."

Tom Penney interrupted, a shade of irritation in his voice, which led me to believe this had been much discussed and that he had not approved. "No doubt he is a hunter. But he is only a man. What can he do that we have not done?"

Ignoring him, I said to her, "You have had Indian trouble?"

"No, not recently. You see, Joseph Pittingel has much influence with the savages, and he has kept them from us."

17

"Then he is the man to get them back, and by peaceful means. A voice lifted in their councils might be all that is needed. Or, failing that, a ransom of goods."

"We would pay," Penney said, "although we have little to offer."

"Oh!" Anna Penney put a hand to her mouth. "How awful of me! You have not eaten!"

"I am hungry," I replied, "and the others are, also. If you could put something up, I'd carry it to them."

She began putting dishes on the table. A bowl of hot stew and a mug of cider with fresh-made bread. I fell to, listening to Penney as he grumbled. Even as he talked, I could sense the fear in the man, fear for his daughter coupled with the helplessness of a man who knows not which way to turn.

There was a sharp rap at the door and an exchange of words, and the door opened. I felt the draught but did not look up.

Two men had come in, and I identified them at once by their voices. Pittingel's was that of authority, of a man assured of his position and a little contemptuous of those about him of lesser station or what he conceived to be so. The other man's voice was quiet, his accents those of an educated man.

"Sackett?" I looked up, then stood up. "This is Joseph Pittingel—and Robert Macklin."

"Kin Sackett," I said, "up from Carolina."

"A brother to Yance Sackett, I believe," Pittingel said. "A difficult man, your brother."

"A very able man," I replied coolly, "with perhaps ways that are different than yours."

"It is regrettable," Pittingel said, "that you have had your long march for nothing. All that could be done has been done. We made every effort, but by now they are far, far away, and the Pequots, well, they are a hard and bloody people."

"I hear much talk of Pequots," I said, sitting down again, "but nobody seems to have seen them."

"Of course, they were here. I am told one does not often *see* Indians."

"Too true," I agreed. "And it might have been them."

"A frightful people!" Pittingel said. "A vicious, murderous lot!"

"Nothing seems to prevail," Macklin said quietly. "I am afraid our daughters will never be found, as the others were not."

"There have been others?"

"I see no connection." Pittingel dismissed the idea with a gesture. "No doubt they wandered off into the woods and were lost. There are swamps. Even hunters have been lost. And the last one was almost a year ago."

"How many others?" I insisted.

"Three," Macklin replied.

"All were maids?"

"True," Penney said, "although I had not thought of it so. I thought of them as children——"

"Tomorrow," I said, "I would like to be taken to where they were last seen."

"They were gathering herbs," Macklin said. "Diana knew much of herbs and their worth as food, medicine, or dyes. She was teaching the young miss——"

"It was a mistake," Pittingel said sharply, "for which you have yourself to blame. You were warned. The Macklin girl was not fit company."

Robert Macklin turned sharply around. "Joseph," he said quietly, "you speak of my daughter."

Pittingel flushed angrily. "Aye! Your daughter, Macklin, yours by birth, but whose in reality? The devil's own, I say, spawned in your wife's womb, but the devil's own!"

Macklin's features had stiffened. "Pittingel, you have no right——"

"Here, here!" Penney interrupted. "Let's not become heated over this. Argument will not get our girls back, and Joseph Pittingel turned out his whole lot, every mother's son of them to search! We owe him that, Macklin."

"You are right, of course," Macklin said quietly. "If you will excuse me—"

"No, it is I who must leave," Pittingel interrupted. "I have business elsewhere.

"Sackett, if there's aught I can do, call on me. I have many men here and a ship due in any day now with her full crew. Anything I can do for my good friend Penney will be done."

He went out, and the door closed behind him. For a moment there was silence.

"You should not incur his anger, Robert," Penney warned. "He is a man of much influence with both the church and the council. It was only he who prevented them from having Diana up before the assizes. And with the evidence they have against her, it would mean burning."

"Evidence!" Macklin scoffed. "They have not a paltry bit of evidence. Diana is a good girl, and a God-fearing one."

"She was seen gathering mandrake," Penney reminded, "and she walks alone by night. How much do they need? Did not Brother Gardner's cow go dry after he spoke angrily to Diana? Did not—?"

"Nonsense!" Macklin said. "Purely nonsense!"

"Nevertheless," Penney said sharply, "that is why they will not look, Macklin, and you know it! They do not wish to find Diana, and my Carrie must suffer because of it! I was a fool to—!"

"Talk will not bring her back," Anna Penney interrupted.

Pushing back my empty bowl, I got to my feet and drank off the last of the cider.

"If they can be found, Mistress Penney," I said, "I shall bring them back, with Yance's help." I put down the mug. "One more thing. Do the Pequots have muskets?"

Penney looked around. "Muskets? I think not,
20

although there was talk of some selling of arms to them. Why do you ask?"

"Tenaco," I said, "the messenger Mistress Penney sent for us, was shot. He was shot only just after he left here, shot by someone who both had a musket and who did not want him bringing help."

I lifted the latch. "Now who do you suppose would do that?"

I stepped out into the night and pulled the door shut quickly behind me. Instantly I rounded the edge of the house and stood quiet to let my eyes grow accustomed to the darkness.

A moment I listened. Someone, some*thing* was out there. Out there in the darkness, waiting.

Chapter III

Waiting or watching. The night was a secret place, but the keys to the secrets were the senses. Edging a little along the cabin wall, feeling the rough stone at my back, I listened.

There was a pile of cut wood stacked in cords nearby; beyond it was a lean-to. Crossing swiftly to the stack of cordwood, I waited an instant, then moved to the lean-to and around it. Nothing.

In a moment I was at the edge of the woods, and there I waited, listening. Whoever was watching, and I was sure someone had been, was back along the path to the woods down which I'd come. Somebody had laid out in the woods, watching for me.

The night would be none too long, and I was wearied with travel, so I made out to pass through the woods, stepping light and easy. We boys had played so much in the woods and hunted with Indians back yonder that we'd become like ghosts when in the forest.

It had taken an hour, but I was back in the woods, and Yance came out from nowhere.

"Tenaco's gone."

"Gone?"

"I was rustling cooking wood, and next thing I knew he had disappeared."

"He'd done his job. He found us, brought us here. It's no fight of his."

We moved off together to where the horses were. The moment Tenaco was gone, Yance had shifted camp. Not far, but far enough for safety, or whatever safety there was in a hostile land where even the white people would be against us.

We slept, trusting to our horses to warn us and to our own senses. At dawn we ate some of the meat I'd brought from the Penneys' and drank some of their cider. Then we moved the horses to a hidden meadow, a small place cozied down among the oaks; then I went back to watch for Penney.

When they came, Penney and Macklin, there were two other men with them. I looked to my priming.

One of them was a powerful big man, and it was not a thing that pleased me, for I'd expected them to come alone.

The night before there had been much talk while I was at table, and taking no part in it, I listened nonetheless, for a trail is followed not only upon the earth but in the minds of those one pursues or the minds of those whose thinking is similar.

It had been talk of local affairs and happenings, events or persons of which I had no knowledge. There was much talk of sermons, also, and I gathered from this, as well as what Yance had told me, that sermons had much to do with shaping of thinking. These were a stiff-necked, proud folk, not easily persuaded to any course not dictated by conscience, yet conscience could be a poor guide if accompanied by lack of knowledge.

Yet now I thought of what must be done. Lack of knowledge of the Pequots was my greatest problem, for little as I knew of Indians, I had learned from dealings with those I knew that there were great differences in them, and to speak of a redskin as being Indian was like speaking of a Frenchman or an Italian as a European.

If I knew little, I at least knew that I knew little. My experience had been largely with the Eno, Catawba, Occaneechi, Seneca, and Cherokee. There were differences, and the differences were important.

They came up the path together, Penney and Macklin in the lead.

The house Tom Penney built indicated much of his character: solid, built for security and comfort, not a hasty habitation thrown together for mere shelter. It had two rooms, the large kitchen–living room and a bedroom adjoining. There was a loft where the girls slept, warmer because of the rising heat. Everything in the house showed the hand of a man with a love for work and for his materials.

Diana Macklin, seventeen and unmarried, was obviously a maid of independent mind, accustomed to the woods and the search for herbs. Not likely that she would wander off with a child and become lost, although even woods-wise men occasionally did.

When they were near, I stepped into their path. "You can take me to where they were last seen?"

"I can." Penney pointed. "It is ten minutes. No farther."

Macklin said, "Diana would not become lost. She had played in the forest as a child."

"This knowledge of herbs? She had it from Indians?"

He hesitated ever so slightly, and I wondered why. "She learned it in England, and more from a woman here, and some from the Indians, also."

"She spoke their tongue?"

"She did. She had a gift for languages."

Surely an unusual girl and one who, if she kept her wits about her, might make a place for herself even among Indians and could protect herself and Carrie.

The big man was Max Bauer, and he was both wide and thick. There was about him an air of command that surprised me. He did not appear to be a man who would be second to Joseph Pittingel, which had me wondering if I had not underestimated Pittingel himself.

"Ho!" Bauer thrust out a huge hand. "So this is the woodsman!"

The instant our hands met I knew he meant to crush mine to show me who was master, so I met him grip for grip and saw his confidence fade to irritation, then to anger.

"You have come far? From Virginia, mayhap?"

"Far," I said.

"You will find nothing! The earth has been trampled so that no tracks are left!"

"Not even on the first day?"

He brushed off the suggestion. "I was not here the first day. When my boat came in, I went to study the ground. It was hopeless."

The hollow where the girls had come to gather herbs was a pleasant little place, a meadow beside a small pool with reeds all about the pool's edge and forest encircling the hollow itself. There was a wide variety of plant life and a well-chosen place in which to look for herbs.

The earth had been badly trampled, the grass pressed down, reeds parted where men had gone to the water's edge. Any sign one might have found had long since been destroyed.

"There's nothing here," I said.

"Agreed!" Bauer spoke loudly. "It is a waste of time! In any event, by now the Pequots are far from here."

"Pequots? You saw them?"

"I did not. But they were here. I have a feel for them. They were here."

We had seen nothing of Yance, nor did I expect him, but I knew he was out there, watching and listening. We had been so much together that each knew the other and his thinking, and right now he was beginning to do what I would have done in his place. He was casting about in a wide circle to pick up sign farther out, where the grass had not been trampled.

Now we had to place ourselves in the minds of the maids or their captors and try to decide what they must have done. The search would not have progressed far on that first attempt, for undoubtedly few of them were armed; fewer still would know anything about tracking.

These people were city folk or from good-sized towns. In England they had been craftsmen for the most part, gentry some of them, and the parks or woodlands of England were vastly different from these primeval forests, or so I heard from my father, Jeremy Ring, and the others at our settlement on Shooting Creek.

We went back to the settlement. The man with Max Bauer was a small, quick-moving man with sandy, tufted eyebrows and a quick, ratlike way about him. His name was not mentioned, and I deemed him judged of no consequence, yet I did not feel so myself. It is such men of whom one must be forever wary, for they live in the shadow of greater or seemingly greater men, often eaten by jealousy or hatred, not necessarily of those whom they serve.

We stopped at the Penney's, and the rest went on, but Macklin and I went in and sat down to a glass of cider, cold from hanging in the well.

Anna Penney was filled with questions about Temperance, so I told her much of our life at Shooting Creek. "Our settlement is at the foot of the mountains. The water is very clear, cold, and good there. We have a dozen cabins, a stockade, and several of us are good farmers. So far the crops have been good, and there are berries in the forest and many roots. All of our men are hunters, and there is much game."

"Your family is there?"

"My father was killed by the Senecas, and my mother is in England. She was wishful that my sister not grow up in the wilderness, and my brother Brian wished to read for the law.

"You must not worry about Temperance. She is much loved and is one of us. We do not have a church, for services have always been conducted in our homes. I fear by your standards ours are not much. Rarely do they last longer than half an hour.

"She has good friends amongst us. Jeremy and Lila Ring are there. They came with my family. Jeremy was a soldier and a gentleman."

"I have heard of Jamestown. It was to Virginia the first settlers here were going, but they came ashore sooner than expected."

"Jamestown is far from us. We came up the rivers through Carolina."

She left the house, and Macklin and I sat alone. He seemed uneasy. Several times he cleared his throat as if to speak. He was a tall, quiet, scholarly-looking man.

Putting down my glass, I said, "Tell me about your daughter."

He looked at me strangely, but he did not speak for a moment. Then he said, "Why? What is it you wish to know?"

"To find them I must understand them. A track is not only marks upon the earth. If she is a prisoner, she must do what she is told, but if she is not, or if she gets away, I must understand her thinking. She may have been taken. We know nothing."

"Do you doubt it?"

"All is surmise. Nobody *saw* Indians take her."

He took a swallow from his mug, then wiped the back of his hand across his mouth. "She is a fine girl," he said, "a fine, honest girl."

"Most maids of her years are already wed," I commented.

He looked straight at me, his eyes hard. "She had many offers. Why Joseph Pittingel himself—"

"He wished to marry her?"

"He spoke of it. Joseph Pittingel is a wealthy man."

"She refused him?"

"She did, in a way. She just, well, she just looked at him and walked away."

I decided I liked Diana Macklin.

"Yet there was little search made for them. Was something wrong?"

He sat silent, his lips firming in a stubborn line. He liked not the trend of the conversation but seemed to realize my need to know. "After all, you will hear it soon or late." He looked around at me. "There is always talk in these small settlements when someone is different. She liked none of the young men, although she was gracious and sweet to the older ones. I suspect it was that only which saved her from being called up. Some said she was a witch! My daughter, a witch!"

"I have no faith in witches," I replied, "nor in the devil, for that matter."

"Be careful of what you say," Macklin warned. "It is well nigh as sinful not to believe in the devil as not to believe in God!"

"Could she have gone away of her own free will? Seeing the attitude around her—and she seems a girl of uncommon intelligence—could she have decided to go and simply not return?"

He considered that, then shook his head. "No. Had she been alone, she might have gone away, but she would not take Carrie with her.

"Carrie loved her like a sister, and they were much together, but Diana would never have taken her from her family. Also," he added, "Diana would have waited until spring. Midsummer is not a good time to begin such a journey, and Diana is a girl to think of such things. She was never impulsive but very cool. She thought things through to their conclusion."

"What of Diana's mother?"

"Diana's mother is dead. She died in England when Diana was a small child."

Someone approached the door. Anna Penney returning from wherever she had been. I got up. "Shall we go to your place? We must talk more of this."

Reluctantly, he got to his feet as Anna entered. She came at once to me. "You will find my Carrie for me? You and Yance? When she was gone, the others would not look, and I knew what they believed, yet I have always loved Diana. I never believed any of the things they said. It was just that she—"

"She what?"

"She loved the night. Our parson has said that witches love the night, that they meet in the forest in old caves, ruined buildings, and that they keep to darkness and the shadows."

We crossed the lane to Macklin's cabin, spotless in its neatness. We sat at the table, and he looked out the open door.

"Our house is empty without her," he said. "I have been much alone, and she cared for me. I—have some small skill with tools, but I am happier with my books. She read them, also, and we talked—long hours."

My eyes went to the small row of books. *The Compleat Gentleman,* by Peacham, stood beside Barrough's *Method of Physic* and Michael Dalton's *Country Justice.* Although I knew them by name only, I had seen them in Jamestown. Bacon's *Essays* and his *Advancement of Learning* I knew well. They had been among the last batch of books brought up from the coast. "I see some old friends yonder," I said.

His expression changed. "You have read them?"

"Bacon," I said, "and much else. My father was a reader of books, and our teacher was a very great scholar. He was Sakim."

"An infidel?"

"Some would call him so. I would not."

"How can you hope to find them? Not even Max Bauer could, and he is our best in the woods."

Slowly I got to my feet. I knew much that I had wished to know. If Pequots had the girls, they might be dead by now, but I did not believe it.

"Those others who disappeared? All were girls?"

"Yes, but that means nothing. A lad would have found his way back. But a girl?" He shrugged.

"Diana, they say, was very much at home in the woods."

"She was different."

I walked to the door. "I will find them, Macklin, but what of you? Should you stay on here? There is

29

suspicion, and if what I hear of your people is true, she would be risking much to return."

He looked at me, then shook his head. "How far can one go? And where can one stop? Is there no place in which to rest?"

"You've been through this before?"

He shrugged. "It is ever the same. And it is my fault. She was reared by me. I could have made her another way, and she would have been like other girls." He frowned suddenly. "But I was a fool. I did not want her like others. I wanted her to be like herself."

"And like her mother?" I asked.

The eyes he turned toward me were the eyes of a man who had been through hell. There was pain there and fear, anger, resignation—I knew not what, only that he was a man suddenly without hope.

"So you know? I guess I always knew there would be a time. I knew someone would come who knew."

He stared at me, then the floor. "My God, what will we do *now?*"

Chapter IV

A thunderous knocking on the door interrupted whatever might have been said. Macklin went to the door, and I stood back, expecting anything.

There were four men, and they brushed by Macklin to face me. "You are Sackett?"

"I am."

"You are to leave—*now*. We do not need your godless kind in this place. You are to go, and you are not to return."

"I have come only to help," I said coolly.

"We do not need your help. You must go—or suffer the consequences."

"It seems that help is needed whether you believe it or not. Two girls have disappeared. Perhaps they have been taken by Indians, and you do nothing to find them."

"That is our affair. It is none of yours. One of you was here and ended in the stocks. Make sure that does not happen to you."

I smiled at them. My musket was in my hand, and in my belt were two pistols. "I must ask your pardon, *gentle*men, but be sure I do not end there. If I should be put in your stocks for no more than coming to your town, I can promise it would cost you much.

"I have come only to do what you yourselves should have done. I shall not leave until I have accomplished what I have begun. You are, no doubt, good enough men in your ways, but those ways are not mine.

"Two girls are missing. I understand others have disappeared before this."

"Others?" They looked startled. "But that was long ago. It was—"

"Last year," I answered. "Are you so careless, then? Have you not asked yourself why it is girls who vanish?" I knew nothing myself. I was but giving them that on which to think. "The forests are wide and deep, but are they selective?"

"I do not know what you mean," the speaker said. Yet he was disturbed. Had he, perhaps, thought of this, also? "It is true—"

"You have suggested I leave. Very well, I go. But I shall not leave until I know what has happened here. You no doubt think of yourselves as Christians, as God-fearing men, yet you call off a search and condemn those girls to death in the wilds, perhaps, just because of your foolish superstition."

"Be careful!" The spokesman's face lost its look of indecision. "You do not speak of superstition here! What we have seen is the work of the devil!"

I shrugged. "I go now." I stepped around them but did not put my back to them. "I shall do what I can do and what you did not do."

"We could not." One of the others spoke for the first time. "There were no tracks."

"There were tracks, but badly trampled tracks, yet any Indian could have found the trail. Any tracker could find it."

"We have one of the best. He could not!"

"Could not? Or did not?"

Stepping through the door, I closed it behind me. I was angry, and I knew the folly of that. Anger can blind one too easily, and thoughtlessly and foolishly I stepped away from the wall. There was a sudden *whoosh* in the night and a thud. A knife quivered in the log wall behind me.

I lay on the ground. I had dropped a moment too late, for I had been narrowly missed by a thrown knife but in time to avoid a second. I had not merely hit the ground but had moved swiftly off to one side, then farther. I could see nothing.

The night was dark, but there was starlight, and already my eyes were growing accustomed to it. An attempt to kill me because I was here? Or had somebody listened to what was said inside?

Ghosting away, I reached the forest and slid into its dark accepting depths. In less than an hour I was near where our camp had been; it was there no longer.

Yance was there.

"Had trouble?" At my assent he added, "I figured so. There was some coming an' going in the woods about, but I moved my camp yonder.

"I found tracks," he added, "far out where nobody took time to look."

"Indians?"

"White men, wearin' moccasins, like you an' me." We moved off into the darkness, traveling swiftly for some minutes. When we slowed down again to listen, he said, "You see that Pittingel again?"

"Others."

"When I was in the stocks, there was a sailor man in them right beside me. He'd been drunk and roisterin' about, but he was sober enough in the night, and we talked some.

"I've been recallin' things he said, like this Pittingel now. He owns a couple of ships, sends timber to England, corn to the West Indies, and he brings back sugar, rum, and coffee, but that wasn't all.

"After everybody was asleep, we talked a good deal. It wasn't very nice, settin' in those stocks, unable to move more than a mite. He told me Pittingel was a trickster. He said Pittingel had some of his ships lay off the coast until they were all scrubbed down and aired out, but that wouldn't fool him. He knew a slaver when he smelled it."

"Slaver?"

"Blackamoors. From Africa. They buy them from the Arabs. Most of the slave dealers are Arabs and some Portuguese. He sells them in the Indies.

"Folks here don't take to slaving, so Pittingel lets nobody hereabouts guess, but he's slaving, all right."

We were quiet, each thinking his own thoughts. Yance said suddenly, "Macklin will miss her. According to what Temp had to say and from what I saw, Diana spent most of her time with her pa. She read from his books, and they talked about what they read."

Anna Penney had put by a little food for us, and Yance ate, taking time out, here and there, for the cider. We talked a little in low voices about the country around, and then we moved off to a place he'd found, and there we bedded down for the night. Yance was soon asleep.

A long time after he slept, I lay awake, looking up at the stars through the leaves and listening to the horses tugging at the grass. The woods were quiet, and the town, if such it could be called, was far enough away that we heard nothing. Yet the settlement would be quiet after dark; anyone out after dark would be suspect.

It was but ten minutes' walk to the hollow from which the girls had vanished. It was plain enough that many men had been here, for the grass was trampled. It was no more than we expected.

It was a pleasant enough place, a small meadow surrounded by woods, and on the edge of the woods a small pond of an acre or more. Reeds grew about, and a few marsh marigolds grew here and there. On the pond floated lily pads. On the shore, back at the edge of the trees, there were violets. It must have been an idyllic spot before the searching parties trampled it out of shape.

The east side of the hollow I dismissed at once, for there was a dense thicket of blackberries there. No man in his right mind would have attempted to get through that mass of thorns when other ways remained.

We stood still, looking all around, trying to take

in the complete scene, trying to picture what must have happened here. Yet as we stood looking and listening, there was a sound of men coming along the path from the settlement. Yance vanished.

The first I saw was Max Bauer. "Miles away by now," he was saying. "An army would be needed for the searching, and it is sad, for they were so young. Yet we can try an approach to the Pequots. I am sure that Joseph Pittingel . . ."

Deep within the forest, an owl hooted. My eyes were on Bauer, and I saw him pause, head turning slightly toward the sound. It was no owl, and I believed he guessed as much, although the difference was subtle.

Yance, telling me had found something.

Penney left Bauer's side and crossed the meadow to me. "You will seek them, then?"

"I will. You go home now, and leave it to Yance and to me. Remember, Yance is wed to Temperance, and although we are not of one blood, their children will be. Kinship is a strong thing between us, Penney."

"Sackett, we, Anna and I, we thank you. We—" He choked up, and I turned my eyes from his embarrassment.

My hand touched his shoulder. "Go, man, go home to your Anna, and trust in us. If she be alive, we will find her."

He turned back to them. Macklin hesitated as if he would speak, then turned away with Penney. Bauer lingered. "If there is aught I can do, call upon me, but I fear you waste your time."

"It is only a trail," I said, looking straight at him, "and we have followed many such from boyhood. Where a hound can follow, or an Indian, there we can follow, too."

There was a dark look upon him, and I liked it not, but the man nettled me with his assurance. Of Max Bauer I knew nothing but that he was employed by, or seemed to be employed by Pittingel, but I trusted him none at all. There was power in the man but evil, also. I knew a little of fear as I watched him go, and it angered me. Why should I fear? Or Yance? Who had ever defeated us?

Yet all men can fail, and each man must somewhere find his master, with whatever strength, whatever weapon. So we must be wary, we must use what guile we had, for it was upon my shoulders that nothing we had ever attempted or done was so fearsome a thing as this we now would try.

I knew not why I believed so, yet believe it I did.

Through the dappled light and shadow of the forest I walked on gentle feet, knowing only that Yance had come upon something.

Of course, it would be no great thing. If the ground is trampled, one has only to cast about in a great circle, an ever-widening circle, for when those who were here left this place, they did not make tracks only in the meadow but in the leaving of it.

Yance was squatted at the foot of a huge old chestnut awaiting me. When I squatted beside him, he said, "Old tracks." He paused. "Five or six men ... two of them barefooted."

"Barefooted?"

"Aye, an' they've gone barefooted a lot. Feet spread wide." He paused again, throwing down the twig on which he was chewing. "Looked to be carrying heavy. Deep prints."

We were silent together, each thinking it over. "It ain't likely," Yance said, "that any folks native to this country would go barefoot. The Indians didn't, and certainly those Puritan folk or Separatists or whatever they are, they hold to boots."

We straightened up, looked carefully about, and listened; then we moved off. He pointed the trail, and it was as he said. Five men, two of them barefoot.

The trail was not an easy one, but we hung to it. At times, rains had washed it away entirely, but we were helped by the fact that these folks did little hunting, and most were afeared to go into the woods alone, so after the meadow nobody had messed up what tracks there were.

We saw deer tracks, too. There was game here if a man were to hunt it down.

We lost the trail.

In the morning we found it again, just a few tracks where they had crossed a stream and one of the barefooted men had slipped. A few hours later we found what we both had been watching for. A camp.

We studied it carefully before we moved in, and then it was only I who went in, and Yance began hunting the tracks made when they left.

He came up to the edge of camp. "Still going north," he said. "Find anything?"

"All three have muskets," I said.

"*Three?*"

"Two of them, the barefooted ones, are not armed."

"Slaves," he said.

"Maybe . . . likely," I added.

"That Pittingel now . . . that man I was in the stocks with . . . he thought Pittingel was a slaver."

"He *thought*. We know nothing, Yance, and it doesn't pay to decide anything without we've evidence for it. The man may be a fine Christian gentleman."

Yance snorted.

Then I said, "What else?"

"It's the girls, all right. I found their tracks, only a couple of them, for they weren't allowed to walk about. One set of smaller tracks, the others a shade larger. Then they were tied up and dumped on the ground. There was some cooking done."

"Slave?"

"No, one of the others." We sat together in the dappled shade of a tree, alert for sound. "It's an old camp, Yance. Been used two, three times before. Several times, I think.

"They had more than one fire, some old smoke-blackened stones, some fresh. Found where ashes had been beaten down by rain, then a fire laid atop that. Not so large a fire."

We rested, chewing on venison jerky. "No Indians made this trail, an' those girls were carried in a litter, looks like. No Indian ever done that."

Yance looked across his shoulder at me. "What do you make of it, Kin?"

"Same as you do. Somebody else has taken those girls and blamed it on Indians."

"Slaves?"

"Why not? Read the Bible. There'd been whites held as slaves for several thousand years before the blacks were enslaved. The Egyptians had Hebrew slaves as well as others. The Romans had Greek slaves as well as slaves from England and Gaul.

"Jeremy told me about raids on the coast of England and Ireland by slavers from Africa. One whole village, Baltimore, on the Irish coast, was carried off in one raid."

After a moment I said, "Young, pretty girls, they'd bring a price in Africa or to some planter in the West Indies."

"They'd have to have a way, a ship. They'd need a ship."

"And the ship would need a cove or a bay, somewhere to come in either to tie up or lie at anchor."

Yance got to his feet suddenly. "Let's get away from here!"

We had no need to talk of it, for each had the same realization. If the men who had taken the girls were slavers, then they must be careful not to be found, and we were searching for them. That meant they must find us, and that meant we must be killed.

Once within the woods, we moved swiftly, keeping a few yards apart to leave a less distinct trail. We found an open meadow and skirted it, running swiftly. We had left our horses, and we had to approach them now with care. We would have been better served had we left them with Penney, for in these woods and along the shore that lay not far off upon our right there was little need of them.

We found the horses alone and safe, and we moved, riding swiftly away and putting miles behind us, turning away from the shore and into the deepest forest. When we slept that night, I lay long awake, listening to Yance's easy breathing.

I thought of my sister Noelle, far away now, in England, and I thought of her being a prisoner, as they were, hoping but scarcely daring to hope.

Frightened they would be, and Diana Macklin trying to give courage to little Carrie, and those strange men close by. As they lay bound, they could look into the future only with dark, trembling fear. They could not believe they would be found.

"Yance?" I whispered.

He was suddenly awake. "Aye?"

"We've got to find them, Yance."

"We will." He turned on his back. "You think of something, Kin? That Joseph Pittingel? He had a ship. It was overdue."

Chapter V

Diana Macklin opened her eyes and looked up into the leafy pattern above. It was not yet day, but already she heard one of the slaves stirring about. They were the first black Africans she had seen, and at first she had not known how to think of them or speak to them. Indians she had known, but these were different.

So far there had been little opportunity, for the three white men were always about, always suspicious, trusting nobody, yet one of the slaves, she sensed, was at least sympathetic. The two slaves, although both were black, were utterly different in nature and appearance.

She had no illusions. Nobody at the Cove would try very hard to find her. Carrie was another question, for the Penneys would try. Her father would do what he could, but he knew less of the woods than she, and the people of the Cove would promise, but they would not carry out much of a search. If she and Carrie were to escape, they must do so themselves, and there was little time left.

Her captors were irritable and frightened. She had sensed that as the days went by they grew more and more worried. Obviously they were frightened at the prospect of holding two white girls prisoner on this shore. Although few of the Puritan folk of Plymouth, Cape Ann, or the scattering of small settlements in their vicinity were given to wandering in the forest, there were a few who were looking for new sites with commercial advantages, and that meant somewhere along the shore. And the ship that was to have picked up the girls and themselves was already overdue.

Lying quietly, Diana thought of what she must do. Her only hope was the slave they called Henry.

He was a tall, strongly built young man with regular features. That he had been a warrior was obvious both in the way he carried himself and in a few scars she had noticed. The other slave was shorter, stockier, more subservient, but she had gathered from talk among the others that he was an excellent fisherman and boatman.

She sat up and began brushing herself off and arranging her hair. Henry passed near her, gathering twigs. "Soon," she said softly, "it must be soon."

He made no reply. Had he heard? Had he understood? If he had understood, would he help? Or would she fall into even worse hands? She thought not, but was that only hopeful thinking?

No matter where they went, what they did, one of the three white men was always present, always watchful.

Henry, she was sure, planned to escape. Yet in all the time they had traveled together, she had heard him use but one or two English words. He usually spoke in Portuguese to one of the white men, the tall, thin one, who spoke it well.

"If you helped us," she spoke softly again as he came to her side of the fire, "you would be welcomed."

The fat, dirty-looking white man sat up, staring at her. "You talkin' to him?" he demanded.

"What?" Her face was innocent. "If you must know, I was complaining. I am tired of sleeping on this dusty earth."

He leered at her. "Aye, but ye'll be sleepin' elsewhere soon, y' can bank on that."

The camp stirred to life, yet within her was developed the resolution. *No matter what, it must be today, or at the latest, tonight or tomorrow.*

She bathed her face and hands in the stream. After their capture they had walked westward for two days. Twenty miles? Possibly. Then for two more days they had walked north, following an old Indian trading path, and then they had walked east, toward the coast.

They were within a short distance of the seashore now. She could smell the salt air. The stream flowed east. Washing her face, she tasted the water. It was tidal water, she was sure. Not fresh water, certainly.

They were awaiting a ship, a slave ship. Very coolly she considered that. Once aboard a ship there would be small chance of escape. And the ship would come, so it must be soon.

She had risked speaking to Henry because it was a time for risks. So far they had not complained, not made any attempt at escape. They thought she was frightened, and they knew Carrie was.

Somewhere along the coast to the north of Cape Ann, that was as close as she could guess. Once free, they must go south—south.

Or west, for they would pursue, they must pursue. They would expect them to go south.

West.

Diana Macklin was seventeen at a time when most girls of fifteen and sixteen were wed. She could scarcely recall a time when she had not known responsibility, and long since she had learned that a certain coolness, aloofness, bred respect and some hesitation on the part of too aggressive males.

Their capture had been simple. She had knelt to pick some leaves from a plant and arose to see a man holding Carrie with a knife at her throat. Now, looking back, she wished she had just screamed. There was a good chance the men would have fled, but she was not the screaming type, and by the time she thought of it, a man had a hand over her mouth, and it was too late.

For three days they were hurried, almost running, until when night came they could only fall to the earth, utterly tired, utterly whipped.

Very quickly she decided they could not escape by running away, for their captors could run faster and longer. Nor would crying and pleading help. Carrie tried that.

They must first escape; then they must hide, and once free, they must never again be caught. Meanwhile, she thought, planned, and discarded plans, watching every chance, noticing everything. What she wanted most of all was a hiding place, somewhere they could go immediately and keep out of sight and just wait. She saw hollows under fallen trees, overhangs half hidden by brush, hollows among the rocks, and caves. None looked right; on none dared they take a chance.

Carrie got up and bathed her hands and face, then straightened her clothing, brushing off the dust and fragments of dried leaves and bark. Then she straightened her hair, and Diana combed it for her and helped her braid it again

"Never," Diana had warned her, "give up, and never let down. Keep youself just as neat as you can, for if you respect yourself, they will respect you, also."

"Do you no good," Lashan had said. "Whoever gits you will fix you up the way he likes."

She had not replied, ignoring him, which was far better than exchanging comments in a war she could not win. She must seem to be going along, seem to accept until the moment came.

Now she watched Lashan as he stood by the fire. He was tall, thin, almost emaciated, yet she knew he was strong, with a strength far beyond what it seemed possible he could have.

Suddenly he looked up at her. "Be you a witch?"

Carrie turned her head, half frightened, to look at her.

"They say that I am," she said. Suddenly she knew all present were looking at her. Both the blacks had looked around. Henry was curious; Feebro stared at her, suddenly arrested in movement.

"Ain't much of a witch," Porney commented, hitching his pants to a more secure position with hands that needed washing, "or we'd never ha' taken you."

She turned her head and looked right at him. "It isn't over yet, is it? Give it time to work."

Suddenly frightened, Porney came to his feet and moved back from her. "Give what time to work? What? What've you done?"

"Be still!" Lashan's voice was a whip. "She's making a fool of you."

"No pains yet? None at all?" She was still looking at Porney. "I thought you looked a little stiff when you got up this morning." She was smiling. "But give it time."

"All right! Be still!" Lashan held a willow switch in his hand. "Any more such talk, and I'll . . ."

Diana merely looked at him. "You, too, Lashan. You, too."

He struck with the switch, a vicious cut across the shoulders. She stood very still, her face white. "If I am damaged, Lashan, there will be questions. He who buys us will wish us unblemished."

Lashan stared at her, his eyes ugly. "You're not aboard ship yet, lass, an' don't y' forget it. Many a bit can happen afore we make it, with Injuns about an' such. Y' push me too far and I may sell y' to the Injuns m'self."

There were no more words, but she had done what she wished and had made the others, at least, wary of her. She put her hand on Carrie's shoulder and felt her cringe a little. That was the worst of it; she had frightened the child. Of one thing she was sure. The others might be wary of crossing her, but Henry was the only one who might help; because he was thinking of escape for himself.

Under the trees they waited another long, slow afternoon. Lashan paced restlessly, irritably. At any moment some Indian or some men out searching for good land on which to locate might discover them.

Even a fisherman along the shore, for it was nearby. Already the ship was two weeks overdue.

"You must not be afraid, Carrie. Not of them or of me. I am no witch, but let them think so if they wish. It may frighten them."

She spoke very softly that they might not hear, yet her words did not allay her own fears. And she was frightened. No matter how much she might reassure Carrie, she knew that nobody was coming; there would be no rescue.

Vern went away through the trees again. He was a small, well-made man with a narrow face and a pointed chin. He wore a stocking cap with a tassel, and a wide leather belt held up his canvas pants. The others she had not seen before, but she remembered Vern, for she had seen him one day at Shawmut when he came ashore from a shallop.

He had not been among the group that kidnapped them but had been waiting for them here, probably with the news the ship was delayed, for Lashan had cursed viciously after they talked.

She had seen him an instant before he saw her, so she had let her eyes sweep past him with no sign of recognition. Yet he had recognized her, and his eyes lingered on her from time to time.

None of them talked to her but Lashan. The fat one, whose name she had heard but could not remember, had spoken to her but once, that very morning. Lashan did not like it, and she was sure he was under orders to permit no such thing.

They slept, awakened, let the fire burn down. Vern came back, helped himself to a swallow of cider, then went away again.

It was very still.

She was good in the woods. She could move quietly, and she had endurance beyond most of the men she knew, but none of them were woodsmen. She could escape, but what of Carrie? Could the little girl run fast enough, keep quiet enough, endure enough?

Yet there was no choice. They must try. With or without the help of Henry.

He was quiet, respectful, and well-mannered. He carried himself with dignity and with some assurance. Moreover, she had noticed him in the woods, and he moved like a woodsman.

Slowly the afternoon waned away. Vern came in, sat by the fire, and dished up food for himself from the pot Feebro had prepared; it was some kind of stew of wild plants and wild meat. She had seen turtle meat, some pieces of rabbit, and some bits of fish go into it. It was good, very good.

They would soon be fed, and then they would be tied up for the night. She had already seen the sharp points of a broken stump where the tree had blown down, breaking off to leave the ragged stump. It was close by. If she could get close to it, she could use those sharp points to pick at the ropes that bound her wrists; she could pick the strands apart, given time. And it would take time.

She had chosen her route out of camp, between two close-growing trees—no brush there, no leaves, no small twigs that might break.

Vern lay down to sleep. The fat man went away to watch by the shore.

Wind and wave being what they were, ships were often overdue, sometimes for weeks. And sometimes they never appeared.

Lashan had settled down. He had lit his pipe and was smoking. Henry got two bowls, filled them with the stew, and brought them over. As he handed one first to Carrie, then to her, he whispered without looking at her, "Ship's coming. I saw the tops'ls."

The ship was coming! It was here! Then—

"Tonight," he whispered, rising from his knees to return to the fire.

Lashan was staring at them. He could not have heard, but had he guessed?

Tonight? How?

Chapter VI

The silver of moonlight lay upon the leaves; overhead a few fluffs of cloud drifted behind an etching of treetops. We lay among the maples, listening to the night.

"We're nigh the sea," Yance whispered. "There's a taste of salt on the air."

"Aye, and a ship offshore. I hope we be not too late."

"She's not up to anchor yet."

"I see that. Do we fight the whole crew of them, then?" Yance inquired irritably.

"She's your kin," I replied coolly, "but if we must fight them, we will. She has no more than twelve guns, and we have two."

Yance snorted his disgust. He was about to speak when we heard an angry shout, then another and a deal of cursing. "Gone!" Somebody shouted the word. "Gone, you fools! Who was on watch?"

There was a murmur of talk. "Get after them, then!" The voice was strident and angry. "They cannot have gone far! Get them, or by the Lord Harry, I'll—!"

"They've gotten away," Yance said complacently. "Ah, she's a broth of a lass, that one! She'll be backing up for no man."

"How far will they get? A lass and a child, and in skirts, yet? In the forest?"

"They'll get far enough, I'm thinking, and there will be us to help."

47

"To help, I'm willing," I said, "but *how?* They will be off into the woods, and those men will go tramping after, breaking down the brush, trampling the tracks. Ah, they be a pack of fools, then, and they'll see what they have done when morning comes. Far better they'd be to sit tight by the fire until day breaks. How far can two girls go?"

Standing up, I listened for small sounds, for the great oafs down there were crashing about like so many cows drunk from corn squeezings.

A soft wind stirred the leaves, and I tried to set myself in her shoes to figure what she might do, but nothing came to me. She was a canny one, they said, and that might help, but she'd not travel so far with a youngster to hand.

Away from the sea. That was as much as I could guess. Along the shore they'd be seen from the ship and would be out in the open too much. Inland there were Indians to fear, and these girls had been raised up with Indians always a threat.

We moved back, deeper into the woods, holding to a fairly straight line away from the sea.

For an hour or two we heard them threshing about in the woods, frightening the game, causing the birds to fly up, and never a thing did they find. We kept our weapons convenient lest they come upon us, but somehow they did not, and with morning we had a problem.

Where would they go now? The girls had fled, but to where?

We moved away from our camp at first light, and keeping a short distance apart, we began hunting sign. Nobody needed to tell us we were in trouble, for there was no telling where those girls would go.

"Look," Yance said, squatting nigh a tree, "we got to give them credit for brains. They ain't simply going to run wild in the woods. That Macklin girl is smart, real smart. She'll head inland."

"It's closer to help if they go south," I suggested, but I agreed with Yance.

"Closer to help but surely the way they'll be expected to go. The way I see it, they'll head north, hoping not to meet Indians, and when they are well back from shore, they'll circle around."

"So what do we do?"

Yance shrugged. "We can try to pick up their trail, but that way we might lead those who are following right to them. I say we strike inland. We go due west, and after the first day we start working north."

It was what I had been thinking, and it offered our best chance. I had no wish to get into a shooting fight if I could avoid it even though the people who had been holding those girls supposedly knew nothing about us.

We started fast, hitting a dim trail and taking it at a dog trot. We'd been hunting the woods our lives long; like the Indians, we could run all day if need be and often had.

As we ran, I was doing some thinking. The girls must have escaped some time after midnight. Say one or two in the morning. That meant they had been gone anywhere from a few minutes to an hour when their escape was discovered.

They would have fled straightaway, then hidden until the immediate search was over. Then they would have taken off again. Traveling in the woods by night would not be easy, but having much at stake, they'd try to keep going.

Give them, to use a figure, two miles before discovery of their escape, maybe four since then. I slowed down.

"Yance? We better listen. They should be turning south soon."

He drew up. "How do you figure?"

"I've been remembering that big river we heard tell of. Remember? He told us that river came down from the north, took a big bend, and flowed kind of east-northeast to the sea? That river mouth was a natural harbor, kind of protected from the sea by sandy islands just like the sounds back in Carolina.

"The way I see it, those girls are headed west, and they are going to come to that river or sight it, and then they'll have to turn south.

"Remember that sailor man we talked to in Jamestown? He drew us a diagram in the dust about that river, said it was a natural trade route to the Indians up country without being bothered by those folks around the settlements."

We ran no more. The forest was of oak and maple, with hillsides here and there covered with the graceful white trunks of the birch. It was very still. A woodpecker tapped busily somewhere not far off, and we saw a small flight of birds holding close to the ground, flying into the brush around a small meadow.

On moccasined feet we moved with no sound, and at brief intervals we paused to listen. Sound carries for some distance, and our ears were now attuned to the natural sounds of the wilderness, so we would quickly detect any sound foreign to the forest.

We came up the side of a knoll, moving among the trees. Leading the way, I topped out between some oaks alongside a clear space. We were high enough to have a view all around, and my eyes caught the movement just as Yance's did.

"Kin?"

"I see 'em."

Merging our bodies with the trunks of trees beside which we stood, we watched six men coming along a trail behind us. There was no mistaking the man in the lead, for surely there could be no two men of that size who moved as he did. It was Max Bauer.

"Well, what d' you know?" Yance whispered. "Would you guess they was coming to help?"

"Not much."

"Trailin' us," Yance said. "I got a notion—"

"No," I said, "but we can make it hard for them. Not all at once or they'll know we've seen them. Let's just let our trail kind of fade out."

Several miles ahead we could see another such knoll. "See that? We'll meet there."

Yance was gone into the brush like a ghost. I swear, that brother of mine could move soft as a cougar, and he was just as mean to tangle with.

I let him go, then slipped off on the other side of the hill, leaving plain enough prints. Then I saw a hard old deadfall lying across some others like it. The bark had peeled off this one leaving the surface bare and smooth as a naked limb. I stepped up on it and walked its length, switched to another, then to a couple of rocks. From there I went into a stream and walked for a quarter of a mile in the water, which was murky from rain runoff higher up.

Coming out on a shelf of rock, I stood still to let most of the water run off me, then followed the rock along the shore. Coming up on several deer, I threw a stick at them, and they ran across a small meadow into the trees, leaving a trail for each. Chuckling, I circled one side of the clearing. They would have to check out each deer's trail to be sure it had not been made by or followed by a man. It would not hold them long, but it would slow them down.

Reaching the knoll almost an hour later, I scrooched down close to a tree and gave study to the country about. Far off to the west and north I could see there was a sort of gap in the trees, which must have been that river that came into the sea up the coast from Cape Ann. That it curved around some, I already knew.

By now, if the maids were still moving, they would be somewhere only a few miles to the north or west of us if we'd been guessing right. Yet the men who were following our trail were tracking *us*, not the girls. Yance joined me.

"Wonder if they know about that river?"

"Doubt it. They wouldn't meet up with many hunters or the like. Wouldn't be fit company. Of course, that Macklin girl was a listener. What I mean

51

is, she paid attention to folks when they talked, and when I was tellin' Temperance about our country, she asked a passel of questions, all of them right canny. Still, not many of those folks get far from the settlements, and she might not."

It was a worrisome thing, for in the thickness of the forest we might pass them within a few yards and know naught of it, for knowing nothing of our presence, they would be still if they heard us, suspecting we were enemies.

Near as we could figure it was about fifteen miles from the shore of the sea to the river at the point where we now were. Yet the maids seemed to have headed west and then would turn south, and the area in which they now could do that could be less than five miles, probably less than three.

We gave study to the country, trying to figure how they might travel. Yance gestured toward it. "Hard to believe, with folks needing land that all this lies empty and still."

"I like it wild," I said, knowing he did, too. "But think of all the poor back in the old country who would like to have even a small bit of it."

"Aye." Yance swept his eyes across the country, alert for any sign of movement, any suggestion of travel. "And I am thinking they will come, Kin. They will come. It is a vast and lonely land now, but it will not be so long."

We came to our feet and moved away. "You work slowly across to the westward," I suggested. "I shall go swiftly west and scout the country toward the great river."

We parted. It was our way to do so when hunting, and we had bird calls or sounds we could use to signal one another; we often worked apart, but we worked as a team.

We must work swiftly now, for those coming behind us would soon know their slaves had escaped and would be coming for them, seeking them out, and us.

What happened within these woods no man would know, and many had died here, unmourned and unknown, and so would it be with us if we erred even slightly.

I had gone scarcely a mile and had paused to listen when I heard the faintest sound; turning my head, I looked into the eyes of a girl, and she into mine.

For a moment neither moved or spoke. She stood slim and graceful as a tall young birch tree, and she looked straight at me, and then she smiled. Others came up behind her, a smaller, younger girl and a tall young black man. He carried a spear and, at his belt, a knife.

"It is all right, Henry," she said. "He is a Sackett."

"What," the black man asked, "is a Sackett?"

She smiled with sudden humor. "Who knows, Henry? It is some strange sort of beast that comes up from the south and brings fresh meat and steals young girls from their homes."

"I can see," I said quietly, "why one might steal a girl, although the idea had never occurred to me before."

"All girls are not easily stolen," she replied. "But we have been, and now we try to return again home. You will help us, sir?"

"Your mother sent for my brother," I said. "We both came. But we had best move. Others are behind us who would keep us from helping you."

"There are those behind us, also," she said. "You are alone?"

"Yance is here. He will join us soon, I think."

My eyes went to Henry. "I was also a prisoner," he said.

"He helped us," Diana said. "Without him we might not have been able."

Turning southward then, I led the way into the forest, but first I paused and sent into the sky the call

53

of a lone wolf hunting. There would be no answer, but Yance would know, and he would come.

The black man, and Diana as well, looked lean and fit. Carrie Penney looked a little drawn, a little pale, but there was no time now to think of that. Nor was I worried about Yance. By now Yance would be moving south to join us.

I led off swiftly, moving like a ghost through the close-standing trees and thick brush. Behind me, Diana was astonished by the way I found openings in the brush where there seemed to be none and how I automatically chose those routes calculated to leave the fewest tracks.

During our frequent pauses she studied Kin Sackett, for this was the man who suddenly had all their lives in the hollow of his palm, up to a point. Diana looked upon him with some skepticism despite the confidence she felt, for she was not one to trust easily. She had liked Yance when she first met him, and her sympathies had been completely with Temperance when she fled the community with him. This new Sackett was taller, quieter, and an altogether more thoughtful man, one, she suspected, of cooler judgment. Despite that, she was wary. Diana Macklin was not one to give herself completely into the hands of anyone.

At the same time she knew her danger and, moreover, the danger the Sacketts entailed by helping. If captured, they would be killed. She and Carrie would be enslaved, but the Sacketts would be killed, and they had nothing to gain.

They started on and had been going but a short distance when Carrie stumbled and fell. She got up, frightened. "Di! Don't leave me!"

"We won't leave you," I said. "Here, let me give you a lift." I swung her to my back. "Put your legs around my waist and hang to my shoulders."

I started off again, walking as if unburdened, and they followed.

Yance was hanging back, bringing up the rear,

keeping his eyes open for trouble. I did not look around, knowing he would be there; if there was trouble, Yance would give me a signal.

We were deeper into the forest now. All about us were huge old maples and clusters of oaks, some of them seven or eight feet in diameter. Here there was less undergrowth, and we could move with greater speed. I was almost running now, weaving a swift way through the forest.

She watched me constantly, and well I knew her reasons, for he is naught but a fool who trusts himself too lightly to a stranger. Now the land was changing; there were more low, rolling hills, and suddenly we topped out on a rise and caught a glimpse of blue beyond.

The river? No. The look of the water was not right. A lake, then, or large pond. We came down to the shore among the willows, and I let Carrie slide from my back. She was not heavy, yet even with my strength the carrying of her was tiring.

Yance came in. "Had a glimpse back there. They gained on us."

Carrie looked up at me. "Can't we go home now? Is it far?"

"Not far, Carrie," I said, resting a hand on her shoulder, "but we cannot go there now. There are men close upon us. They are between us and your village."

Yance disappeared in the woods, scouting a way. I lay down, resting, letting all my muscles relax completely and giving way to complete rest. It was something I had learned to do to conserve strength. Through the willows I could see the water, hear it lapping.

Resting, I was. Yet thinking as well. From the glimpse I had, the lake was a large one, and we had to go back to the east and then south.

Diana came up beside me and sank to the ground nearby. "We are due east of the Cape, I think?" she suggested.

55

"We are."

"We cannot go east?"

"There are men coming toward us. Evil men, I think." I paused. "Do you know Max Bauer?"

"What of him?"

"He is one of them, I think."

She was silent for several minutes. "He is Joseph Pittingel's man."

"Who has a ship that is overdue."

"Maybe he is coming to help?" she suggested. "He was often in Carrie's home. She knows him."

I shrugged. "They are saying in the settlement that Pequots took you. Pittingel says it. Bauer, also."

"They are not eager to find me, I believe." She spoke calmly. "I am sorry for Carrie that she was with me when they came."

Yance came suddenly, soundlessly, from the willows. "Indians," he said. "A lot of them, I think."

Chapter VII

Following him, I looked past his pointing finger at a thin column of Indians, all of whom seemed to be warriors, advancing along a trace from the southwest. Within the range of my vision, judging by their spacing, there were at least forty in the group.

"Wait," I suggested, "and let them pass, then cut back behind them. It is our only chance."

If we could do it. Leaving Yance to watch, I went back and explained quickly. "No sound," I added, "and then when I say, we must move quickly and quietly."

We waited then, watching them come. I knew not the clothing or the paint these warriors wore, for it was different than any I had seen. Were they Pequots? Mohawks? I held my musket ready, knowing that its one shot could mean but one enemy dead. I had pistols, and there might be a chance to reload.

My throat was tight, for fear was upon me. We were but three men against forty, and if they rushed, we should have small chance indeed. Two musket shots, then our pistols and knives, with Henry's spear, and I yet knew nothing of Henry, whether he could fight or even if he would. Yet he was stalwart, and he carried himself like one who knew his way with weapons.

Where they came from we had not yet been, so there were no tracks of ours, and if they held to the trace they now followed, they would still see no sign left by us. But—I smiled at the thought—if they held to the trace, they would surely come upon Bauer and those with him.

We held still, making not the slightest move, scarcely daring to breathe, and the first of them came abreast of us and not fifty yards away, flitting through the forest with scarcely a sound.

They were slim and wiry men rather than muscular, yet a few among them seemed powerful, and no doubt all were strong enough. They carried spears, but bows and arrows as well as the tomahawk were much in evidence.

Slowly they passed us by, and my first guess had been close, for I numbered them to be thirty-two and no signs of battle among them, so if it was a raid they were upon, it lay before them.

No sooner had the last of them disappeared in the forest than I straightened up and beckoned. We went down the slope, past some pines, and took the very trace they had followed, retracing their steps back to the way from which they had come.

We passed the lake, keeping it close on our right, and a half-dozen miles farther we made camp in a pleasant nook among giant oaks where we swiftly gathered some fallen twigs and branches and built a small, warm but almost smokeless fire. Hidden as we were in a deep place among the trees, the fire would not be seen beyond our circle of trees.

In a dish, hastily made of birch bark, we sliced up some venison; then, when it had been simmering for a half hour, I added a couple of handfuls of cattail pollen. Diana watched us curiously and somewhat skeptically, I thought, but she made no comment.

Yance put together two cones of birch bark and plugged the bottoms; then we filled each with the soup. One went to Carrie, the other to Diana. Carrie hesitated, looking doubtful, but hunger overcame the squeamishness at trying something new. Meanwhile, I mixed up more of the soup, adding to what had been left.

Glancing over at Henry, I said, "You've been in the woods before?"

"They were different."

"You move like a woodsman."

He looked at me, his head up. "I was a warrior in my own land. I led men in battle."

"Looks like you may get a chance for battle," I commented. "Was it in Africa?"

"I am Ashanti," he said simply.

"A slaver?"

He shrugged a shoulder. "There was war. When the war was over, the victor had slaves, or he killed them so they could not attack again. Some of the slaves we sold for guns or cloth."

"How'd you become a slave? Did you lose a war?"

"No, we took slaves aboard the ship, and there were not enough slaves for the ship, and then the wind started to come up. Suddenly I was pushed from behind, and I was a slave, also."

"So now you know how it feels."

He shrugged again. "Some win, some lose. I lost then; now I win. I am free; I will stay free." He stared at us defiantly.

I smiled. "Why not? We are not slavers, nor are we owners of slaves. We do our own work."

His look was disdainful. "A warrior does not work!"

"No? If you stay with us, you will help. You will work, and you will fight. Otherwise"—I pointed toward the woods—"there is freedom out there. Take what you will of it."

He did not move; hands on hips, he stared at me. "I have told them I would help," he said. "My promise is my blood. I will stay until they are safe."

"Good! We can use you."

A few minutes later Yance asked, "What did he mean, he was pushed from behind?"

"Pushed down a hatch, probably. It has happened

before. Men who take slaves are not particular who they enslave. I had much talk of this with Sakim, who had once traveled from Cairo to Timbuktu."

We gathered wood for the fire, and Henry did, also. We kept it low, and every now and again one of us would move out into the woods, away from the fire and even the low sound of the voices there, to listen.

That night we stood watch, Yance, then Henry, finally I. At dawn we moved out, and I let Diana set the pace. Cape Ann and the settlements were east of us and a little north of east now.

We traveled slowly, for Carrie's strength was waning, and I feared for her. If Diana Macklin tired, I did not know, for she walked proudly, quietly, making no complaint but thoughtful always of Carrie Penney.

When we had two hours behind us, we again neared a small stream that ran northward into the river. There we stopped to rest, and Henry wandered down to the river. We found huckleberries growing in a few patches near the stream and busied ourselves with picking. Yance wandered about, restless and uneasy.

Glancing through the leaves, I could see Henry had rigged a pole and was fishing.

Yance paused near me. "Think we should try for the settlement? Can't be more'n nine, ten miles across there."

I had been giving it thought but worried that we knew nothing of Max Bauer or where he was, or of the others, coming south with Lashan.

Had they given up? I decided they had not. The girls were precious to them, for such a girl as Diana would bring five or ten times what a stalwart young black man like Henry would bring. Also, they dared not let us escape, for once it was known that white girls were being taken, they would be hunted down.

The woods were thick, but there were streams to cross and meadows. Somewhere over there were the Indians who had passed us and no doubt Bauer and his men. Yet it must somehow be done.

I went to where Diana picked huckleberries.

"Know you of any settlement on the great bay south of Cape Ann? It might be easier to reach."

"My father has a friend at a place they call Shawmut. He is the Reverend Blaxton. He lives alone there, I think, with one servant."

"Is he the only one?"

"There is another at Winnesimmet. Samuel Maverick has a fortified house there, a place with a palisade and several guns mounted."

"A good man?"

"Yes, he is. A very kind, genial man, but he has great physical strength, and he is said to be absolutely fearless."

"He knows you?"

She hesitated. "He may remember me. My father helped with the raising of some of the beams of Maverick's house, but I met him but once when I was a little girl."

"It is good. We will try for his place."

"We would be safe there if he would take us in, for they would fear him. Or be wary of him, at least. He is a man of reputation, well known in the colony and in England, and I think even Max Bauer would hesitate to face him."

We picked berries a little longer. A thought came to me. "He is a married man?"

"He is. He married the widow of David Thomson, a very good woman. I have spoken to her."

Henry came up from the edge of the stream. He had six good salmon and a large pickerel. "I will fix them," he said. "It is better to eat them and carry the weight inside than out."

We were eating the fish when Yance returned. He had gone off suddenly into the woods, and he squatted beside me when he got back, taking a piece of the fish, baked in the coals. "Found a trace . . . old one. Runs off south by east."

"A likely way?"

"Aye. There be deadfalls here an' yon, but we could make two, three miles . . . maybe more."

We moved out at dusk, taking the dim trace, and once we had gone into it, I left Yance to lead and fell back. At the campsite I studied it with what light was left; then I began carefully cutting out the tracks of two people.

There was no way to choose whose tracks, so I simply took those tracks of which there were fewest. Carrie had moved around mighty little, so with a little brushing here and there and then a sifting of dust and broken leaves, letting the slight breath of air dictate where it fell, I left behind a camp that showed only three people: Diana, Henry, and myself.

A really fine tracker, if he took the time, could read the true story, but they were going to be moving fast, and I wanted to mislead them. They had lost the trail, I was sure of that. Now they would find it again, but of only three people. Where were the other two? Or where was the other one, Carrie, and who was the stranger in moccasins, which was I.

At the entrance to the trace and for some way along it, I erased all sign of travel, scattering a few twigs, some bits of bark. Then I started running, a long, easy stride to overtake them, but it was full dark before I did, and when I felt I was close to where they might be, I slowed my pace to come upon them quietly. They had covered almost two miles and had stopped briefly near a small stream.

We moved on into the night, pausing frequently so that the girls might not tire too soon. At one stop I sat beside Diana.

"I liked your father," I said.

She turned her face toward me. I could see the faint whiteness of it in the shadowed place. "He is a good man. I do not think shaped for this life, nor this country."

"To make a country we need all kinds. He is a thoughtful man, and such are needed. He reads, he thinks. Too many of us are so busied with living that we do not."

I gestured about us. "A man must think, but he

has not enough to nudge his thinking. From morn 'till night we are busy with finding game, hunting food, cutting fuel, shaping wood for houses. Ours is too busy a world, and there is no time for considering."

"I know ... even father. There are days when he has not the time to touch a book. There is no market where one can go and buy what is needed. It must be hunted, gathered, or made with the hands."

"And at night," I added, "a man is too tired. I fall asleep over my books, but we must read, not only for what we read but for what it makes us think. Shaping a country is not all done with the hands but with the mind as well."

We were silent, and she dipped water from the stream and drank, then again.

"How will it be," I asked, "when you return?"

She was quiet for a minute, and then she said, "It will be the same, I think. Perhaps worse. If it were not for my father, I would walk away one day and never look back."

"Why don't you ..." I caught myself, not wishing her to misunderstand, "and your father come south to Shooting Creek? You would like it there, I believe, and there is a place. One of our farmers was killed by Indians, and his cabin is a strong one. It is empty."

"Thank you."

She gave no sign that she thought it a good suggestion or not, so I said nothing further. After a moment we started on, walking steadily into the night. Yance carried Carrie for more than a mile, and we stopped again.

Henry was impatient. "It is foolish. We cannot escape. They will surely find us."

"Would you leave them?" I asked.

He threw me a disdainful glance. "Of course not, but we will all be taken." He paused a minute. "You do not know them. They are vicious, and they are cruel."

"Whose slave were you?"

"A ship's captain. He has been much along this

coast, and he has made swift attacks on Indian villages and carried some of them off for slaves. I was his servant."

He turned his head toward me. "To lie in the hold of a ship was not good, and there was no chance for escape. So I let them hear me speaking English and telling another slave that I was once servant to an Englishman. It was not true, but it worked as I hoped it would, and the captain sent for me. I became his servant and henceforth was upon deck. Then I taught him to trust me."

"And how did you get ashore?"

"Lashan needed a man, and there was no other, so for this one time they left me ashore to help him. It was what I had been waiting for."

"If we get through this, you will return to Africa?"

He was silent, thinking about it. "I know not," he grumbled. "I have seen much since then. Perhaps there is a better life here."

"There are slaves here, too."

"There are slaves everywhere. Many are slaves, one way or another, who do not realize they are, but I shall not be a slave. There is opportunity here even among white men."

"You are not worried about your color being a handicap?"

"Worried, no. In some ways it will work against me, and in others it will work for me. You wonder why I speak English as I do? I learned it from an Englishman who was a slave in my country. He was captured when a party came ashore from a ship. He began as the lowest of slaves, but it was discovered that he knew something of treating illnesses, although he was not a medical man. Then he became my teacher, also. Soon he was my father's adviser and confidant. When my father died, he returned to his country and returned with gold and diamonds my father had given him.

"He stood upon the shore with me before his ship sailed, and he said to me what I should remember, that any man can be a slave, and a few men, if they will it, can become kings. He put his hand upon my shoulder and told me that in the world were two kinds of people, those who wish and those who will, and the world and its goods will always belong to those who will.

" 'When I came to your land, I was a slave, but I shouldered whatever burden was given me. I looked for other burdens, and for those who will shoulder a burden there will always be many burdens to carry. Finally I helped your father, whose burdens were growning too heavy for him, and your father rewarded me, first with freedom and second with wealth.' "

Well, it seemed to me it was time to move along, so I got up. "Henry," I said, "it looks to me like you had a good teacher."

"Yes, it is so, although it took me much time to learn it. What he taught was good, but what his life showed me was even better."

The day had not yet come when we stopped in a hidden place in the midst of a thick stand of young pines. It was the side of a knoll where the ground broke steeply off, then shelved to a narrow bench. There we bedded down and were instantly asleep. This time we felt secure, and all slept, and deeply, too.

The sun was not yet up when I awoke. For a moment I lay still, listening to the forest sounds, identifying each as my ears came upon it. Rising, I went to the edge of the bench where we had slept and looked all around. A moment, and then as I started to turn, I heard the faintest *clink* of metal on metal.

My breath caught and held; then slowly I exhaled and looked in the direction of the sound.

There not thirty yards away was a camp! And in the camp, striking flint against steel, was Vern, about to light a fire!

Chapter VIII

Very, very carefully I stepped back. When out of sight, I turned swiftly and awakened Yance. Accustomed to trouble and knowing me, he was instantly awake and alert. He moved to awaken Henry, and I went to the girls.

Gently I touched Diana's shoulder and put a finger across my lips. Her eyes flared open; there was an instant until she realized, and then she moved quietly to awaken Carrie. My gestures toward the enemy camp were enough to warn her.

Swiftly, quietly we moved away through the woods, going directly away from their camp. Somehow we made it, or seemed to.

The leaves were wet with dew, or perhaps there had been a whisper of rain during the night, but there was no sound as we moved quickly along. That they would find our camp was without question, for once they started to look about for dry wood, they would undoubtedly come upon it. The first problem was distance, the second to leave no trail, yet it was distance of which I thought at first.

Max Bauer had not seemed to be with them, so perhaps the two groups had not come together. Or it might be that Bauer was too shrewd to allow himself to be found with the men who had actually been holding the girls. And it was he who worried me most, for I doubted the tracking skill of Lashan or Vern.

"If aught goes amiss," I warned Diana, "go at once to Samuel Maverick. From what you have said, he seems a good man and a solid one. Go to him, tell him all, and trust to his judgment. If he knows your father, he will get word to him."

The war party of Indians, I believed, had gone off to the north of us, raiding some other Indian people, I suspected. Bauer should be close by, but I suspected he was now behind us, as was Lashan. With luck—and mentally I crossed my fingers—we should have a clear way to Shawmut.

We moved well through the long morning, and when it came to high sun, we were upon the banks of a goodly stream, one flowing north into that great river that I assumed to be what the Indians called the Merrimack or something of the sound.

"This must be that river called the Musketaquid," Diana said. "Father came once to its shores and fished here while with other men who looked for land for the future."

The river worried me. It was a good hundred yards wide and perhaps more, and we had to cross it. Yance and I could swim, and no doubt Henry could, but I doubted the girls could, for it was not often a woman has the chance to learn, and Carrie was young.

Leaving Henry with them, Yance went downstream, and I turned up, for well we knew that Indians often conceal their canoes along the banks after traveling, hiding them against the next crossing. There were places where canoes were left for years, used by whoever came and left hidden on one side or the other.

We found no boat, it not being our lucky day, but Yance came upon several logs lying partly in and out of the water. They were of modest size, and there were others nearby.

Choosing dry logs, we found several of the proper length and bound them together with vines. The river moved with incredible slowness, and while we worked, we studied what currents we could see so as to know how best to control our crossing. Meanwhile, the girls ate huckleberries picked from bushes along the shore.

When the raft was complete, and a pitifully small

thing it was, we had the two girls climb aboard, and with them we put our muskets and powder horns.

Henry came suddenly from the woods. "They come now!" he said.

"Yance?" He looked up at my question. "You and Henry. Get on with it. I'll wait a bit."

I kept one pistol with an extra charge of powder and ball laid out close to hand. And I had the bow and the arrows. They shoved off. Yance being a powerful swimmer, I knew he'd do his part, but Henry proved just as good, and the two of them, with tow lines, started swimming for the far bank, letting what little current there was help them along.

They weren't more than a dozen yards out when somebody yelled, and I heard crashing in the brush. The first one I sighted was the fat one, and he slid to a halt and lifted his musket to fire. It was no more than thirty yards, and I wasted no lead on him but put an arrow into his brisket.

His musket went off as he staggered, the ball going into the air, and he lost hold on his musket and grabbed the arrow. It was buried deep, and I saw him tugging as he fell.

Slinging my quiver to my back, I took up the pistol. There was more crashing in the brush, and somebody called a question. The fat man had fallen out of sight behind some brush, but I could hear him groaning there.

Suddenly a tall, thin man appeared in view, looking about. I lifted the pistol, but he saw me and dropped from sight. A quick glance showed me the raft was a good sixty yards into the stream and no longer a very good target, as the girls were lying flat, and you could see nothing of Yance or Henry but their heads and occasionally the flash of an arm.

There was more movement in the brush, and I took a chance and fired at the sound, knowing I'd best get going. Then I hastily reloaded, and taking the pistol in hand, ran along the shore until I reached a bend large enough to give me some cover. Then I tied my pistol to me and went into the water. When I was a dozen yards out, I went under and swam some twenty good strokes before coming up for air.

I was downstream of them, and I heard a shot but no other sound, and when I cleared water again, I turned my head for a look back, and there were three men on the shore, two of them getting ready to swim and a third running along the bank looking for me. He spotted me just as I took a breath and went under, but I changed direction and went downstream and swam a good thirty strokes before I came up again, just shy of midstream.

Looking back, I could just barely see what I believed was the raft, and it was close to shore. I swam toward the bank then and came out on the bank among some deadfalls. There was no sign of the raft or of my people, but I could see at least two men swimming.

Shaking the water off my pistol, I swore softly, bitterly. I had no more powder with me, and my bowstring was wet. All that remained was my tomahawk and knife.

Taking a quick look along the shore again, I went into the trees and started toward where my path should join theirs. There was a thick stand of maple with occasional oak and in spots a pine tree or two. Nobody looked to have wandered these woods, but there was not too much brush, and I moved quickly, running through the trees.

My one thought was to rejoin Yance and the rest, and what followed was brought on by pure carelessness. I jumped a deadfall, leaped up to another, and ran along the top of it for thirty feet or so, then dropped to the earth and broke through the brush and found myself looking into the end of a musket held by a grinning redheaded man with a scar across his nose.

He has another one there now, for my reaction was instantaneous. Seeing the musket, I threw up a hand and grasped it, jamming it back into the man's face. He staggered, but another leaped on my back, and

I went down into the leaves, bucked hard, and almost threw the man off. I came to my knees, swinging a fist into the nearest face, for there were three at least, and then I lunged up with a man still clinging to my back.

A broken-off tree, felled by some wind, was near, and I slammed myself back against the tree and a stub of a broken branch that thrust out from it. The man on my back screamed and lost his grip, and I lunged away from him and into the brush. Somebody shouted and swore, a gun blasted behind me, and the lead hit bark from a tree near my head, but I was running again, weaving a way through the forest that would show them no target for shooting among all those tree trunks.

That I was a good runner served me well, for I had run much in the depth of forests before this, and leaping some obstructions and using others, I ran as never before, thanking the good Lord and all my ancestry for the long legs of me.

I had escaped by merest chance and because I had come upon them almost as suddenly as they upon me, and they were ill prepared for what followed. Fear helped me much, and I ran, bearing off toward the river again and hoping my brother and those with him were already to the east of me.

When I slowed down, I felt for knife and toma-hawk. Both were with me. My quiver had been thrust around and was still across my shoulders with my bow. Luckily he who leaped upon me had wanted my throat and nothing less.

Suddenly I came upon the tracks of Yance and the others and made haste to scatter leaves across them and to drop a dead branch along the trail as though it had always been there. Then I walked away into the woods.

As the crow flies, it was likely no more than fifteen miles from where we now were to Shawmut, but by the route they would take and that I must take, it would be no less than twenty. In the wilderness there is no such thing as traveling in a straight line, for one turns aside for trees, rocks, embankments, cliffs, and what not until one may cover half again the distance a straight line would require. Also, such diversions, no matter how small, can lead one far astray unless the traveler is alert.

The land over which I moved was strange to me but very familiar. Strange in that I had never before traveled over it but familiar in that it was wilderness country, and in the wilderness I was ever at home.

My moccasins made almost no sound on the damp leaves, and in most places I could, by twisting and turning, avoid the dry whisk of leaves and branches as they brushed my clothes. My buckskins, stained by travel and by lying on grass and leaves, merged well with the foliage and tree trunks through which I moved.

What worried me most of all was that for the time I was virtually unarmed except for combat at close quarters. If seen, I should have to use every skill to avoid offering a target, and among these woods were enemies who knew every trick of woodcraft.

When there was a path, I ran, taking the usual easy pace of the Indian or woodsman in the days before horses were commonly used, for at this time there were no horses in the Massachusetts Bay area and few elsewhere aside from the Spanish colonies of the far south. Our own horses we had left in a secluded pasture where Macklin could from time to time attend to them.

I had no food, yet often had I gone without food for several days at a time and could endure. Nonetheless, I kept a wary eye for huckleberries or whatever the forest might offer and soon came upon a thick patch at the edge of a meadow.

There were bear tracks about, but I saw none, although it was a likely place for them, and I picked and ate for nearly an hour before I started on. Huckleberries were tasty enough, but I had need of meat.

Suddenly coming upon two red deer and having a goodly chance at the one, I measured the distance with my eye and let fly with my tomahawk. Many a time had I hit such small marks as the end of my thumb, but this time the fates were not with me, for the unkind beast turned his head, and I missed. The deer ran off, and I went hungry to my tomahawk and returned it to my belt, mumbling a few unpleasantries the while.

No longer running, for I had come into an area of low hills, scattered rocks, and much fallen timber, I went carefully. It is a thing a man must forever guard, that he not twist an ankle badly or break a leg, for to be down and helpless is often to die. There was no sound but the wind in the leaves, no movement but small animals or birds. It had become suddenly warmer, and I tried for a look at the sky, but the foliage was thick, and I could see naught but patches of low gray cloud.

Several times I sat to think, to try to imagine where Yance and the others might be, but all I could surmise was that they were north of me and but a few miles off, yet I hoped our enemies were following me instead of them, and, rising, I went on.

Of Shawmut I knew nothing. It was not a settlement, merely a place, and of it I knew only that two or three men lived there. That it was close by to the sea and that a fair harbor was near, I did know, and some among those to whom I had talked at Jamestown or Williamsburg had suggested it might in some while become an important place. Such things are commonly said of this place or that along a coast newly discovered, always to be taken with a grain of salt.

Throughout the sultry afternoon I plodded on, lonely and a bit weary, my thoughts forever returning to Mistress Macklin, from whom I tried in vain to draw them away, at first by force and then by trickery. Neither would suffice.

Why should I think of her? I scarcely knew her. A likely maid, of course. Downright beautiful, when it came to that, and a lass of some poise and presence, and no more of a witch than most girls of her age, who are all up to some trickery or other.

Yet who was I to talk of women? I knew less of them than of deer or beaver, and they were much more chancy things from all I had heard.

Noelle was but a child when she left for England, so the little I knew of women was by observing the wife of my brother or those of my friends, and they were not helpful. A woman who has trapped her game has a different way about her than one who is still on the stalk.

My ignorance of women I covered very well by a seeming indifference and by keeping my opinions to myself, most of which, had they been expressed, might well have been wrong. It was easy enough to see why the young men of the Cape Ann area might be doubtful of Diana, for she had a disconcerting way of looking at a man.

Yet aside from her beauty there was much in her to admire, for she was a quietly capable person who did not scream, faint, or cry so far as I had seen. She looked matters in the face and did something about them, and my mother had been such a woman, and Lila even more so.

The Indian girls I had seen among the Cherokees or Catawbas and the white girls I had met in Jamestown were much alike. They all knew how to move, to sit and to bend to show their figures to the best advantage, and I was used to that. Diana, with a better figure than any of them, did nothing of the kind, or did she? In some more subtle fashion? It worried me that she seemed innocent of guile, that she seemed only concerned with what was at hand. So I came to avoid her, while thinking about her.

Yet I was being foolish and very vain. Why should such a girl think to use such wiles on such as I? Who was I, after all, but a tall young woodsman from a strange wilderness to the south, a man without any of the graces of which I had heard women speak.

I was much too serious. Yance was full of laughter and fun and great at dancing. Kane O'Hara, who had won a Spanish wife, was a gifted talker, a storyteller, and a man with a ready smile and eyes that twinkled with merriment. Jeremy, my father's friend and Lila's husband, was every inch a gentleman. He carried himself with style and knew much of the world. People, and women especially, listened when he spoke.

And I? I talked little and at the dances sat along the wall and watched, more at home in the forest than among people. No doubt I would live alone forever, for what woman would find me attractive? Who would want a tall man with high cheekbones and a face like a blunted wedge who knew nothing but hunting and tracking?

I would think of Diana no longer.

Chapter IX

When at last I came to Shawmut, it was to a cove inside of what was called Fort Hill, and I came by canoe with a friendly Indian who would accept no gift for the favor.

"There are good men here," he said, and left me standing on the shore at the foot of a path that led to Beacon Hill.

Here all was still, a peaceful place indeed, with some trees off to the south beyond some sand hills and poor grass. On the ridge of Beacon Hill, before me, there were a few cedars and what appeared to be elms. Only the cry of sea birds gave sound to my hearing, and I walked along in my wet moccasins looking for the house of the Reverend Blaxton, which I heard was close by.

By some he was considered eccentric, for he wished only to live quietly here beyond the reach of too many voices and to walk along his hill, down by the sea, or to read his many books. A good life, I told myself, a very good life indeed.

The path wound along the hill, and no doubt he knew I was coming for some time before I reached his gate. A Pequot woman served to keep his house, and he had a sturdy man who had come to help from time to time. The house itself was of logs flattened a bit on top and bottom to fit more snugly and well thatched with flags, rushes, and sedge from the swamps below the hill and along the shore.

He met me at the door, a grave but pleasant

young man of about thirty years. "You are Reverend Blaxton?"

"I am."

"I am Kin Ring Sackett from Carolina. My brother and I have been searching for the two maids who were lost."

"Taken by Indians, it was said."

"Indians are suspected of too many things they have not done," I said, "nor were any Indians involved in this."

He hesitated a moment, then said, "Will you come in? I entertain but rarely here."

"It is a lovely place." Indeed it was, with wild flowers all about a fine view of shore and bay. Walking up the hill, I had seen a profusion of plants. Blueberry, blackberry, strawberry, and wild grape vines seemed to abound everywhere. "I envy you."

The comment seemed to please him, and when we stepped inside, it was quiet and cool. The floor had been paved with flagstone, neatly fitted, and there was a fine hearth and fireplace, with a small fire burning, enough to warm some soup.

"From Carolina, you say?" I was looking at his books. "It is far."

"We are in the western country," I said, "far out on the frontier. Beyond us are naught but Indians, although we hear of Frenchmen and Spanish wandering there."

He glanced at me as I stood looking over the titles of his books but made no comment in that respect. "Why have you come to me, then?"

Turning, I said, "For advice, in part. Secondly, not to lead those who follow me too quickly to the house of Samuel Maverick."

Then, accepting a cup of warm broth, I explained all to him. How Mistress Penney had sent for us and how we had come swiftly to help, how our efforts had resulted in finding the girls already escaped and in company with a black slave who was helping them and escaping himself.

"It is a serious matter, that," Blaxton said. "I look upon slavery with no favor, but to help a slave escape is looked upon almost as thievery, for you deprive a man of property."

"Aye, but they did not help him."

"It will not be seen in that light. They were white. It will be assumed that because he left with them they aided him rather than otherwise."

He sipped his broth, as I did mine, then asked, "They are with Maverick now?"

"I hope so. I had a brush with those who followed them and tried to lead them down the wrong path. They would have come along swiftly, for my brother Yance was with them."

"Yance? Yance Sackett?" He smiled suddenly. "I have heard of him. Heard nothing good but much that I admired. Although I am a man of the cloth, the people of the congregation and I do not always agree." He gestured. "I find it more pleasant here."

After another brief silence he said, "If they were not taken by Indians, then by whom?"

"There were three white men, men of the sea, by all accounts, and two black slaves, one of whom helped them escape . . . a fine young man."

"White men?"

"Slavers," I said, "and obviously awaiting a slave ship to pick them up. The ship was overdue."

"You did not see such a ship?"

"There was a ship offshore. She seemed to be coming in. We were at the mouth of the Merrimack," I added, "a place used by traders and such."

"I have heard of it. But you only saw a ship offshore. *Perhaps* it was coming in. You assume very much."

For that matter he was correct. I sat, turning it over in my mind. It was true, we knew nothing. Even the maids assumed much, and we had only what Henry could tell us and what Diana believed.

"We believe Max Bauer was leading those who tried to intercept us," I suggested.

He put his bowl down hard on the hearth. "You *believe!* If you are to mention such men, you must know."

It nettled me, yet he was right. The girls had been taken away, the girls had escaped, but for whatever we suspected, we could prove nothing. We knew nothing; we had nothing.

"One of the men," I added lamely, "was seen working on the shore for Joseph Pittingel."

He smiled, an ironic smile. "You are, indeed, an innocent," he remarked. "Joseph Pittingel is a man of many interests. He gives largely to the church. He is often called to advise in matters of the colonial administration. I fear the best thing you can do, or the girls themselves, for that matter, is to be still about what you surmise."

He refilled my empty bowl. "I must speak to Samuel of this," he commented. "He is a thoughtful and a knowing man. I am afraid the young miss is in trouble, also, this maid of Macklin's."

"That she is suspected of being a witch? Surely you put no stock in that?"

"I do not, nor will Maverick, yet there will be others who will, and we must think of them." He looked at me suddenly. "You have spoken with her. What kind of lass is she?"

"Beautiful," I said quickly, "and sensitive, but she thinks. She has a good mind, an excellent mind, and far beyond her years in good sense."

He chuckled suddenly, and I did not know why, but he glanced at me slyly. "It is not often I hear a young man comment on a woman's *mind.*"

"She is worthy of comment for her beauty," I replied stiffly, "but among us a woman's mind is important. On the frontier a man and his wife are two. They walk beside each other. To survive, the two must work as one, sharing thoughts as well as work. It is not the same, I hear, in the cities of Europe."

"You must guard your tongue," Blaxton advised. "Joseph Pittingel is a shrewd and dangerous man, skilled in the usages of power. He can have you deported, sent back to England."

"Back?" I shook my head. "He could not send me back. This is my home, this is my country."

He looked at me sharply. "This is your country!" He shook his head as if astonished. "It is the first time I have heard that said. 'This is my country!' It has a nice sound, a fine sound, but most of us, you know, are English."

"I was born here. I have not seen England. To me it is a land far off where a king reigns."

"He reigns here, also," Blaxton reminded. "It is not good to forget that."

"Where I live," I said, "is beyond the mountains where only Indians are. I do not think the king reigns there nor has power. It is a man himself who rules himself, and it is people working together. Perhaps you may think us wrong, but we do not often think of the king."

He considered that, then smiled. "To tell you the truth, we do not often think of him, either, yet it is not well to forget. You can be sent home to be tried by his courts, sent to his prisons, or executed by his officers."

We finished our broth and sat there in silence, enjoying each the company of the other. Finally he nodded to indicate the books. "Do you read, then?"

"I do. In our home there are many books, and my teacher was a good one." I glanced at him. "You might not approve. He was an infidel, a Moslem."

He shrugged. "I would say this to none but you and perhaps to Sam Maverick, but I have myself read a book by a Moslem and found it not at all bad. Did he speak of religion?"

"Only to say there were many paths, all directed to the same end, and he advised me not to be too quick to put my religion upon the Indian, for he had one of his own that served him well."

"You have courage," Blaxton said, "to face that wilderness. The sea and the woodland . . . I love them, but I do not venture. I walk these quiet paths, stand

79

upon these headlands, pick my berries, and sometimes —rarely—I fish. For a few trinkets, an Indian will bring me fish or mussels. It is a good life and an easy one if the demands you make are not too large."

"You have your books. They are the best companions."

"Aye." He glanced at me, and I think at the moment he really liked me, although he was a distant and aloof man. "Within this room I can talk to the Hebrew prophets, to Plato and to Aristotle. It is good company I keep here."

He stood up. "Let us go to Maverick's place. You will see how well it can be done."

As we walked along, I said to him, "Then nothing can be done against the slavers?"

He glanced at me. "What slavers? Who is to testify? It is all surmise and wild imaginings. Understand, I am inclined to believe there is something in what you say. To me Pittingel is too smug, too knowing, and too sly. He seems sometimes to hold us all in contempt, yet that may be only an attitude.

"In any event, slavery is no crime, although frowned upon in many quarters. It has been with us, my friend, for several thousand years.

"And if no slavery, how is the work to be done? A man who comes to this country wishes land of his own, and he will rarely stand to a bit of work for anyone else.

"I do not approve of one man enslaving another, yet so it has always been, and the mere fact that Joseph Pittingel transports slaves into the country or to the West Indies, this will be no argument against him. He will lose favor in some homes, will find himself quietly put aside by some of our people, but to others it will mean nothing. You must face reality, my friend."

Of course, he was right. Yet, there had to be a way. I thought suddenly of those other girls.

"I knew but one of them," Blaxton said when I suggested it. "A handsome lass and pert." After a moment he added, "I feared for her. She was too filled with zest, and I am afraid—I should not say this—but I am afraid she had too little of the Lord's goodness in her."

He glanced at me. "I tried to talk to her of God, and she kept reminding me, without saying a word, that I was but a man and she knew it. She disappeared suddenly, and it was suspected she had run off with someone . . . aboard some ship or other.

"Another case of a maid where many would be inclined to say, 'Good riddance.' I would say there has been some knowing selection going on here. The mistake was when they took Carrie."

Maverick's place was a considerable fortress, with a goodly house and several guns mounted on the palisade. He had the sort of men about to defend such a place, a rough and ready lot, for he dealt in furs, and many of these were men who spent much time trapping. With so many of them and his strong place he had nothing to fear from Indians. I knew he was a respected man but one who went against the grain of the congregations because of his easy ways and tolerant views.

It was said he had been close to being expelled on several occasions, but his own forthrightness as well as the fact that his father had been a minister of some influence prevented that.

He welcomed us and put out mugs of cold cider on the table.

"They are here," he assured me, "and well. Your brother did us well by bringing a haunch of venison with him, and the maids are resting. They arrived last night, and my wife has seen to them."

"We have talked much," Blaxton said, "and I think you should hear what he has to say."

I spoke briefly, having consolidated my argument by talking with the Reverend Blaxton, and Maverick listened while drinking his cider.

"Blaxton is right, of course. It will do no good to speak against them, and it will do you much harm.

With all politeness, I must remind you that you are nobody here. Or less than nobody, coming from the wild lands to the south. Joseph Pittingel is a respected man, and feared as well. I have had few dealings with him except to use one of his ships to freight some mast timbers to England."

It was bothersome that those who had done this thing should go free of blame and lay ready to perform the same deed again, yet what could be done, I knew not.

"This lass," I said on a sudden thought, "the lass you spoke of who was taken before this? There has been no word of her?"

"None. She had a way of walking near the shore, and some said it was to give a bold eye to the sailor men, but I know naught of that. One day we saw her no more and her mother came wailing and worrying about her, and we conducted a search, but all felt she had but run off and not been taken at all."

"Such a maid—" I started to say when Maverick interrupted.

"Aye, I ken her well! A bold lass for her years, and she not yet sixteen! It would take more than a kidnapping to curb that one! I have seen her kind before this, and such women endure. They have a quality that takes them through when others might fall by the way. Bold she may have been, but there was good steel in her, too!"

"So she may be alive," I said.

"Her?" Maverick snorted. "It would take a deal to dampen her down. I confess, I liked the lass. Trouble she was, trouble for her mother from the first, and a worry to the congregation, for she flaunted herself about, ready to make eyes at any man who looked well to her, although, mind you, I think at that time 'twas all in play, not that she was not ready for something more. Had her good mother been wise, she'd have married her off—"

"It was planned," the reverend said, "but the lass would have none of it. She wanted none of the local lads but something more. I do not know what exactly, but adventure, I think."

"I think—" I spoke aloud, but it was to myself I spoke—"I think I shall go to the West India isles! I think I shall try to find this lass."

They stared at me. "To find one maid in all the Indies? You are daft. Daft, I say! And if you found her, what then? Do you think you would be permitted to speak to her? And if so, what?"

"An affidavit," I said. "A sworn statement. Or even the lass herself! Then we would have evidence that might take these men to the gallows!"

Chapter X

It was easy talk, yet the thought rankled that such things could be done and that those who did them would go unpunished. A man could say it was none of his affair, but how many would suffer until somebody did make it his business?

Maverick was patient. "You know nothing of the Indies," he said. "It is a different world than this, and it is nothing like Virginia or the Carolinas. It is a place of pirates, cutthroats, and sharp businessmen. And how would you go about finding one girl? A girl who is probably kept from sight?"

I did not know. All I knew of the Indies was hearsay, and not much of that, yet the more I thought of it, the more I decided that this I must do.

Yance was quiet, and that was unusual for him. Despite his flamboyance, Yance's thinking was sound, and he could see, even as I could, the problems involved. In the first place, there were many islands, and to which one had she gone? Had she survived the trip? Many people died aboard ship and were buried at sea, for the life was rough at best, the food poor, and many a tough sailor man failed to survive a voyage.

Jamaica, Hispaniola, Grenada, Cuba, Martinique, the names themselves were enchanting.

"You would have no chance," Reverend Blaxton assured me. "It is a fine thing you think of doing, a noble thing, but you would waste time better spent in some other way. We do not even know that she was not taken by Indians or murdered somewhere along our own shore. It would be like searching for one snowflake in the dead of winter."

"Anyway," Yance said practically, "you've got your crop back home, and Temperance will be wondering what happened to us."

"I did not mean for you to come, Yance. I meant for you to go home and let them know where I have gone."

There was a deal of talk, which, as is always true in such cases, seemed to arrive nowhere, for there is always a repeating of arguments and a rephrasing of the same ideas and much time wasted. Yet as the talk went on, I listened with half an ear and thought my own thoughts, worrying over the possibility as a dog over a bone.

When first the words came to my lips, they came almost unbidden, yet the idea would not let me abandon it. The Indies were foreign to me, and I should not be treading the familiar ground of the forest or mountains or swamp but at sea and among islands and men of different backgrounds than I, and I would be among cities, which I scarcely expected to enjoy.

Yet what if I found her? From all that had been said, I guessed there was a core of steel in the lass, that whatever else she might be, she was not one to be easily conquered by circumstance or condition.

That she was possessed of more than her share of healthy animal spirit seemed likely, and the restraints of living in a community ruled by the congregation would be irritating and confining to such a one.

Well, to suppose. If she was indeed taken by slavers to the Indies and sold there, what then? What would become of her? Many a girl might give up, accept the life, and sink to the depths, ending when cast out as no longer useful, eaten by disease, or soaked in alcohol. But I could not believe that would happen to such a girl as this one. There was strength in her; for good or bad there was strength, and that must count for something.

Suddenly the door from an inner room opened,

and Diana was there. She moved into the room like a dream of beauty and went to the fire to stir it.

"How is Carrie?" I asked.

She looked over her shoulder at me. "Sleeping, and the poor child needs it. She is exhausted."

"And you?"

"There is not the time. I have things to consider." She looked around again. "They will be coming, I think. They have had their time at Cape Ann and some other settlements."

"What do you mean by that?" Maverick asked.

"She means," Blaxton replied, "that they will have taken the time to raise the question about Diana as a witch." He watched Maverick fill his glass and then added, "Joseph Pittingel, if he is involved, is a shrewd man. He would take the time to cast rumors about, even to making a few comments of his own. 'The maids have gotten free, how else but that Diana is a witch? Also, were they *really* prisoners at all? Was this not some diabolical plot of her own? How could they vanish so utterly but by witchcraft?' He will use the very argument Sackett offered at first, from what I hear, that no Indians had been seen for some time."

"There is a place amongst us," I said. "If you like, you may come to Shooting Creek."

She hesitated only a moment and then said, "It is far, and we are known to none there."

Maverick interrupted. "Then come to Shawmut. Become our neighbors. Thomas Walford, the smith, who helped me, would surely help you. He is a rough but goodly man."

The remark irritated me, yet why should it? She would be safer close to Maverick than elsewhere. Was it because she might have accepted my offer had he kept still? I was being the fool again. It was something I was doing more easily these days.

Yance was looking at me and grinning like an ape. At least I had the good sense to say nothing, although Diana glanced once at me as if expecting some word.

Yet what could I say? It was far to Shooting Creek, and what had we to offer that was not here?

"I shall go to the Indies," I said, "and I shall find her. I shall find that girl, and somehow I will discover what is being done."

Henry had come in the door as I spoke, and he said, "If you wish, I shall come with you."

"It is no place for a free man who is black," I said, "although I'd welcome it."

"There are freedmen there," Blaxton offered. "It has been said there are several thousand that do live in Jamaica. As long as he was with you, he would be safe."

"And I can ask questions where you would get no answers," Henry said. "Some of my people lived in the hills of Jamaica and some on the other isles. They would know who I am, and they would tell us what they could."

"What if you ran into some of those you once captured?"

He shrugged. "They would be afraid. No one wishes to fight the Ashanti."

"We will go, then."

"There is no ship," Diana interposed. "None but that of Pittingel."

"There's Damariscove," Maverick suggested. "Many a vessel calls there for water or trade. Why, there was a settlement there before the Pilgrims arrived with their *Mayflower!*"

"Aye, Damariscove!" I had not remembered it. "Of course, we will go there."

"Is there need?" Diana spoke sharply. "Why should you sail off searching for some girl you have never seen? Does she sound so attractive to you?"

"It is for you," I protested, "and for others like you. This ugly business must be stopped and stopped now."

"How noble of you!" Her voice held irony, and the tone dismayed me. I stared at her, about to make some angry retort, but said nothing. That seemed to irritate her even more.

"I have not asked you to do this for me," she said, "and I would not. It is a fool's errand, going off to find a girl you know nothing of on an island you have never seen and where you'll find naught but enemies."

She turned around to look at me. "Do you believe for one minute that Joseph Pittingel or Max Bauer would *let* you go? At the first word of such a thing they would have you dead, killed in some manner. You would do better to go back to that far land from which you come and cultivate your corn!"

Her disdain for my sense was obvious, but it only made me resolve the more. "Believe what you will. I shall go."

I got to my feet, wishing to have no more words with her. Maverick was frowning at his pipe, Blaxton seemed amused by something, and Yance was smiling. What a smug lot they were! I'd be well rid of them, even Yance!

Turning to the door, I said, "Tomorrow, then, Henry. We will be off to Damariscove and a ship if we be so fortunate."

Diana turned away, ignoring me, and I stepped out into the darkness.

It was very still and damp; a fog came in from over the bay and from the sea beyond. Many a tale of the sea had I heard from my father and those of our men who had sailed with him, tales of bloody sea fights and ships captured or sunk, of Newfoundland and of the Irish coast. How long before I'd see my beloved hills again and the slopes all pink and rose with rhododendron and laurel? How long?

As a boy, I had walked the seaside when with my father. I went to the shore above Hatteras, a long and sandy shore, with a salt sea wind blowing and the salt spray in my eyes and the sea birds calling as they swooped above.

Long had I looked upon ships and dreamed of the places of their going, the far places, the mysterious places, the wild romantic names, Shanghai, Gorontalo, Rangoon, Chittagong, and Zanzibar.

Dreamed of them, yes, but of my own hills the more. I wanted only to be back there, but first to stamp out this ugly thing, for I thought of Noelle in such a plight and no one to come to her aid.

If harm were done to any whom I loved, I should come back; if it were from the dead, I should come back and lay a hand upon those who were evil.

The fog moved around me in strange curls, caressing my cheek with ghostly fingers, placing a chill kiss upon my brow with a small touch of moisture.

The palisade loomed before me, and I went to the gate. A shadow moved, and a man stood there. "I be Tom," he said, "on guard this night. Is there aught I can do for you?"

"I thought of going out," I said.

"I would not," he said. "There be unholy things i' the night and a whisper of moccasins, methinks. I'd stay within and be glad, for the wall is strong."

"Aye, you are right, and if all goes as I expect, I'll be needing rest before I go down to the sea."

"They'll be bedding for the night soon," Tom said. "The master is no late stayer these nights. Ah, I've seen the time when they made the welkin ring with their singing of songs and drinking of ale, but not with the reverend here. Besides, there's a deal of work to be done, and all must rest."

"Is there trouble with Indians at all?"

"It's been a time since. Oh, there's petty thievery and such like but no more than is expected. You can't blame them," he added. "We've so much that is new and some'at curious to them, so they be picking up this and that to look at and sometimes to carry off. They do not have the same thoughts about ownership as do we, an' 'tis but natural."

"Aye." He made sense, this man. I wished all

might be as understanding, yet it was much to expect when most newcomers thought of the Indians as savages, ignored by the good Lord unless saved.

It may have been my father's easy way with folks or perhaps my mother's way or Lila's or the teaching of Sakim, but I was not one for believing all who believed not as I to be therefore heathens. Many are the paths to righteousness, and ours, I think, is but one.

Inside they'd put down a pallet for me close by the fire, but I drew it somewhat away. I liked not to sleep too warm but cool enough to sleep lightly so my ears can hear what moves about.

All were asleep, or seemed so. I drew off my boots and looked to the charge on my pistols and then stretched upon my pallet and stared up at the dark timbers, lit by the flickering fire. It was in my mind to go south to the Indies, yet there was uneasiness on me, for I should be venturing far from lands that I knew and among men who were strangers to me and whose ways I knew not.

In the night it rained, and I awakened to hear the sound of it on the roof and in the yard outside. Lying awake, I thought of the rain falling in the forest, and I wondered where Max Bauer was and those who had been with him. Here I was safe. Yet Diana had spoken truly, for if they were slavers and discovered my intent, they would kill me or seek to kill me. Nonetheless, I knew this foul business must be ended or no maid would be safe to walk free upon the land.

Or was it simply that something deep inside me still longed for the sea, something inherited, something only half held, some unnamed yearning? What man truly understands his motives?

Yet there was something else, something of which I had heard my father speak when talking to Jeremy or the others, that where man was, there must be law, for without it man descends to less than he is, certainly less than he can become. Even on the frontier where no law had yet come, man must have order, and evil must be restrained or punished.

No man had made me my brother's keeper, but if no other moved to restrain evil, then I must do it myself.

These men had injured one whom I—I— I could not complete the idea. It was not true. It was only that—

I went to sleep.

Morning dawned, cool and damp with a wind from off the bay. Yance and I walked outside into the sea wind and stood together. "Don't worry about my crop," I said. "The birds and the squirrels will harvest for me. Tell them where I am gone and that when spring comes I shall be with them again."

"Kin, be warned. They are not easy men."

"Aye. That I know."

"Where will you go?"

"To Jamaica at first to ask about where many sailors come. I do not think there are secrets at sea even though some may believe so. At Damariscove, where I go to find a ship, I shall also ask."

"Kin, do you remember John Tilly? And Pike? They were trading to the Indies in the *Abigail,* named for our mother. And the *Eagle,* too, the craft that took mother to England. That one traded to the Indies, also."

"Aye. I remember."

Henry came to the door. "Do we go now? I am ready."

"And I. Good-by, Yance. Care for things until I return. And do not go off a-hunting. Stay close to Temperance for a bit."

"You know how to give advice," a voice said, "and do you take your own?"

It was Diana, standing alone and very still just outside the gate. I blinked at her, not quite understanding, but I held out my hand. "I will come back," I said.

"Oh, will you?" She looked straight at me, her eyes wide. "And what then, Kin Sackett? What then?"

"An end to this bad business," I said.

Her fingertips scarcely touched mine, and then she turned sharply away. What in the devil was the matter with the girl?

"Go, then," she said over her shoulder. "Go."

Chapter XI

Still lay the water over which we moved, with no sound but the ripple of our passing and the steady chunk of the oars. Fog lay thick about us and somewhere ahead an island. A long, thin, wooded island, and there was the harbor, Damariscove, settled, it was said, by a Captain Dammerill.

Yet the fisherman whose boat we hired shrugged when I said it. "Aye, it may be, but there were lads as came ashore there to dry their fish many a year before he ever caught the shadow of it."

My father, too, had spoken of this, for fishers from the Grand Banks had come here to smoke or dry their fish before heading homeward for the shores of Europe. I spoke of this, and he looked at me again.

"Did he have a name, then?"

"He did. Barnabas Sackett, it was."

He chuckled. "I ken the man. Ah, a rare one he was, too! A rare one! Tricky and sharp but strong! He made a name for himself amongst we who come from Newfoundland, for we love a daring man, and that he was."

He turned to glance my way. "You do favor him, although you're taller. D' you ken Tilly and Pike, then?

"They were his friends, and if it is to sea you are going, you'll be in luck, for there's a ship of theirs at the island now, or there was."

"Of John Tilly's?"

"Aye. The *Abigail*. She's been about a bit but

93

seaworthy. She's been taking on water and trading for fur."

My father's old ship and in port here! Suddenly I was impatient at the chunking of the oars, the slow, steady movement through the water. I had been relaxed, resting, waiting to arrive at Damariscove and thinking if I was lucky we might— I swore softly, bitterly. The ship might be gone before we arrived. Why could I not have known?

As if in answer to my impatience a small breeze blew up, and the fog began to thin. The old man went forward and hoisted the sail. Yet even so our progress was slow, too slow.

There was naught to be done but to hope she would not sail until we arrived. Henry looked around, amused by my impatience. "There will be other ships," he said.

"Aye, but yon's a special ship, and I would dearly love to sail in her, be her master whoever he may be. If he be John Tilly—"

The fog lifted, and the wind picked up a little. It was not yet midday, but Damariscove was far off. A gull dipped low above us, and I felt a queer excitement stir within me.

I was at sea! How often had I heard stories of the sea and of ships! Of my father's battles with pirates. What was the man's name? Bardle, Nick Bardle. There was another, too, but I had seen him, knew him from long ago when Yance and I had slipped aboard his ship at Jamestown and spiked his guns. A rare bit of action that and one that pleased our father, although it was done without his knowledge.

Jonathan Delve, that was the name. An evil man and one who hated our father.

Finally I dozed, rocked by the movement of the boat, and when I awakened again, it was fairly dark, and there was a darker line along the sky with a light showing low down near the sea.

"Are we there, then?"

"Yon," our boatman said. "Would ye be landed?"

"Not if the *Abigail* is close by. I'd like to board her."

"At night? They are a touchy lot aboard there and wary. I'd say you'd best be known to them if you'd board, but I'll take you alongside. And there she lies, two points abaft the beam. I'll bring her around, and we can hail her."

There was a stern light showing and an anchor light in the chains. We edged in close, and a hail came from her. "Lay off there! Lay off!"

"Is John Tilly aboard? If he is, I'd speak with him."

"The cap'n? Lay off there. Who be you?"

"The name is Sackett," I said. "I think it will have a familiar sound."

"*Sackett?*" The watchman exclaimed. "Well, I'll be!" In another tone he called out, evidently to someone else on deck. "Joel? Call the captain. Tell him we've a Sackett out here."

I saw light come into the darkness as the door yawned open; then there was a rush of feet, and a strong voice, which I knew at once, called down, "Sackett? Is it you, Barnabas?"

"It's Kin," I answered. "Kin Sackett, his eldest, and seeking passage to the Indies if it is there you'll be going."

"Come aboard, lad, come aboard!"

They dropped a ladder over, and I went up with Henry after me. My first time on a rope ladder, but I had the hang of it from words my father had spoken. The boatman had been paid, and there was naught to do but hoist our gear aboard, and little enough we had of it.

He was a strongly made man, his hair white and his beard neatly trimmed. "Ah, lad! It is good to see you! How is my old friend, your father?"

"He is gone, captain. The Senecas killed him . . .

95

finally. Black Tom Watkins was with him, and they died well."

"That he would do." He paused for a moment. "So he is gone! It is hard to believe."

"My mother is in England. She took Noelle and Brian there for their education."

"Aye. I knew of that, and I have seen them both . . . in London. It was only a short time ago."

"You *saw* them?"

"Aye. I had brought my ship up the Thames and sought them out. Your brother is a handsome lad, strongly built and something of a scholar. But your sister? She is a beauty, Kin, a beauty! I declare, lovely as your mother was. She will be even more beautiful when she becomes a woman, and she has not long to wait, believe me! Ah, what a handsome pair they are!

"Brian is a scholar. He has been reading for the law but much else besides. But there's been trouble, too, over your land in the fens. William, of whom your father often spoke and who was by all accounts an honest man, died. His nephew fell heir to his holdings and has laid claim to your father's land as well. I fear there will be trouble."

"Brian will know what to do, and if it is help he needs, we will come."

"Help is less important now than friends in positions of power. I do not know, Kin, what will happen."

We walked aft together, and in the comfort of his cabin over a pot of coffee we talked long into the night of the old days and the new, and in the end I told him what I wished to do.

"To find one girl, Kin, I doubt if it can be done, yet you are your father's son, and he was not a man to be stayed by doubt. What I can do I will do."

"There is gossip alongshore; this I know. I want to know the gossip about the ships of Joseph Pittingel and what I can discover about a man named Max

Bauer. I believe these stolen girls would be sold to outlying plantations where they could be kept unseen."

"If it is waterfront gossip you will be wanting, then Port Royal is the place. They be a packet of rascals there but friendly enough if they like you, and you'll have a good name among them."

"*I* will?"

"Aye, they'll know the name Sackett, for Barnabas made a name. Have you heard the story told of how he took the pirate ship in Newfoundland and then hung high the pirate Duval until he cooled down? Pirates favor a bold man, and your father was that, lad, he was all of that."

He glanced at Henry. "A slave?"

"A friend. He volunteered to help. He's an Ashanti."

"I know them. He will find some of his people in the islands, but most of them have taken to the hills in what is called the Cockpit County, and the wise do not go a-searching for them. There be those who call it the Land of Look Behind because you'd better or they'll be all over you. On Jamaica and elsewhere, too, they are called maroons."

"They will receive me," Henry said coolly. "I was a king among them."

"But these are long from Africa, most of them," John Tilly suggested. "Will they remember?"

"They will," Henry replied, "and if not, I shall remind them."

Fair blew the winds for Jamaica, and the good ship *Abigail,* named for my mother, proved a good sailer. Soon I was lending a hand at the sailing, learning the ropes, as the saying was, and taking a turn at the helm.

Each night we had a man or two back from the fo'c'sle to tell us what he knew of Joseph Pittingel, his ships, and of Max Bauer.

Soon a picture began to come forth, a picture of a

man both shrewd and dangerous, a man who had many friends or at least associates throughout the islands and along the coast of the mainland. A man even more formidable than we had assumed and a situation that must be handled with extreme care, for he had friends in important positions who could cast a man into jail or have him hanged.

That he was a slaver came as a surprise to many of those to whom we talked. This he had apparently kept from anyone, yet here and there a seaman would drop a word to let us realize that there were those who did know. A picture of the man became clearer, a picture of an adroit, cunning man who presented one picture to officials and to merchants and another entirely to those he considered menials.

John Tilly listened, asked a question or two, and when the last of the seamen had left the cabin, he said quietly, "This is no easy matter you have taken upon yourself, for if the man has the least suspicion of what you do, he will surely have you murdered or thrown into prison, and he will have the power, you can be sure."

"I think of Noelle. What if it had been she?"

"Aye, and the poor lasses with no man to stand by them. It must be done, lad. It must be done."

"First, to find that girl. Henry will help, for you know as well as I that there are no secrets from the slaves. He can go among them and among the maroons as I could not, for they would tell me nothing."

Several times we passed ships at sea, but they were either too far off to be seen clearly or they made haste to seek distance. It was a time when piracy was rampant, and many a ship would not hesitate to seize another if opportunity allowed.

Wet blew the wind against our faces, leaving the taste of salt upon our lips. Much was the time I spent upon deck, my body growing accustomed to the dip and roll of the vessel and the sails overhead, all strong with wind. At times the rain beat against our faces like hailstones, but I could see how a man could grow to love such a life, and how easily he could come to live upon the sea.

There was a power there, a power in the roll and swell of the waves that told a man he was but tolerated here. This was a world of fish under the sea and gulls or frigate birds above it.

Captain Tilly was a cunning man with wind and sea, knowing very well how to get the most from his ship, and we went swiftly along the coast to the south, and I never knew when we passed our old shore along the Carolina coast.

The seas grew warmer. We worked often without shirts, and the whiteness disappeared from our bodies, and they grew red, then brown, strongly tanned by tropical suns. Jamaica was a long green shore of a deeper green than found in our northern lands.

We sighted Great Plumb Point and the Pallisadoes, a long neck of land staggered here and there with trees that gave the neck of land its name, for they appeared a long broken wall to keep men out.

We held our course along shore to Little Plumb Point and passed between it and Gun Key, then rounding the point and coming at last to the well-sheltered bay.

Captain Tilly stopped beside me as I stared shoreward. Never had I seen so many houses or stores and drinking places along the waterfront. If there was one, there were at least twenty ships in the harbor, and more seemed to lie deeper within the bight of land.

No other place had I seen but Jamestown, and you could have tucked all of it into a corner of this.

"Be not trusting, lad," Tilly warned. "They are knaves aboard there and proud of it. They'll have your money, and if you say the wrong word, you will be killed out of hand. Port Royal is said to be the wickedest city on earth, the Babylon of the west, they call it.

"They be pirates and those who prey upon them and more jewels and gold than you'll see ever in London town."

We dropped our hook close in before the town, and a boat was got over the side. Tilly eyed me as I got into the boat. "To a tailor first, Kin Sackett, for in that outfit of buckskins you'll stand out like a lone tree on a headland, and every man in town will know where you go. And I've just the man for you."

"I've no great sum about me, captain," I said doubtfully. "Yonder we lived off the country, and while we've gold at Shooting Creek, I'd naught with me when we came along to Cape Ann and Shawmut."

He chuckled. "Ah, lad! Think nothing of it. I'll be your banker here. This ship was given me by your father, and all I have is by his favor. You'll be needing money, for nothing speaks but money. Money and a man's cunning or strength, for they be fighting men here, and strength is respected."

He glanced at me suddenly. "Can you handle a blade, Kin? You'll no be wearing more than a pistol in your sash. Here is the cutlass and the knife."

"Aye," I said doubtfully. "I've been well taught as a boy, for my father was a swordsman and Jeremy Ring as well and in another way Sakim, also. We fenced much as boys, but I've never fought for blood with a blade."

I caught myself at that. "Except with a knife," I said, "among the Indians. No year passed in those mountains without attacks by Indians, so we'd had our taste of that."

"Aye. I've heard of those attacks on your forts." He looked at me and shook his head. "Your father gone! 'Tis hard to believe. He was so strong, so fierce a fighting man, and he seemed like one to live forevever."

He had seemed so to me, as a child. He was a gentle but powerfully muscled man, trained in the arts of war by his father, who had been a professional soldier. He came from the fens, in the country of Hereward the Wake, and many a story did I hear of wars and struggle by land and sea.

"It is a jungle yon," Tilly warned, "and the men and women are savages. Port Royal is no place for the good or the weak. Killings happen by day and night, fights are many, and rum is the greatest evil of all."

Captain Tilly, I recalled, was not only a ship's captain but an ordained minister. It was he who had married my father and mother these many years agone. Yet minister of the gospel or not, I knew well what he spoke of Port Royal was the truth, for many a tale had I heard of the place whilst mingling with the seamen in Jamestown on our rare visits there.

With four stout seamen at the oars, we pulled for shore, Captain Tilly, Henry, and I, and soon were alongside the landing. I was first up the ladder. Beyond the rough planks of the landing was a stone-built dock and beyond that a line of dives, sailors' "rests," and the like. A drunken sailor, kerchief tied about his head and gold, diamond-studded rings in his ears, staggered past.

Tilly pointed with his thumb at a narrow street. "Up there," he said, "there be a tavern that's clean. It be called the Bristol. Go there, and tell them I sent you, and have something to eat and wait. I shall send a tailor to you."

Henry looked at me. "If it is well with you, I will be looking about for some of my people."

The narrow streets were crowded with seamen from the ships, some of them obviously piratical craft, others merchantmen of one variety or another. Looking about, it became apparent that good business could be done here had one the mind for it, for many goods, looted undoubtedly from merchant ships, were going for less than the market price. If a man could buy here, then get away with his cargo without losing it again, he might quickly become a wealthy man.

We found the Bristol, and I entered and spoke for a room, using the name of Captain Tilly; once in the room, I had hot water brought to me and bathed there. Scarcely was I finished when there was a knock at the door. Knife in hand and pants hastily drawn on, I opened the door.

A short, fat florid man with a balding head stood there; behind him was a black slave. "Master Sackett? May I enter?"

Without awaiting my reply, he walked in, followed by the slave. "Measure him," he said grandly, choosing the best chair in the room. "Measure him carefully!"

He glanced sharply at me, then at my buckskins. "We will have something for you. We work very quickly. I have," he said proudly, "forty men employed and several women. All slaves, all my own."

"I came aboard ship very quickly," I said apologetically. "There was no time to secure proper clothing."

He shrugged, waving a hand with a gesture of dismissal. "In Port Royal it is often the case. One moment a mere seaman and the next rolling in wealth. We get all kinds here and are surprised at nothing.

"You would be surprised," he added, "at the number of the gentry we receive here, many in abject poverty. Some have been shipped out as slaves or prisoners to be sold as slaves. Imprisoned for debt, most of them."

"How about women?" I suggested. "Are any of them sold as indentured servants?"

"Many! Some likely lasses, too! Some of them use themselves wisely and end doing very well for themselves. Most—" He shrugged. "Most do not. Most are mere slatterns, passed on from one to another, ending doing the most menial tasks."

He went on, chattering away, noting the measurements as the slave chanted them to him. He glanced at me several times, stripped to the waist as I was, and then said, "Have you ever engaged in pugilism? You are obviously an extraordinarily powerful man."

Then, hastily, he lifted a hand. "I do not mean to offend! Fisticuffs are often staged here and much money wagered. One of the best we had was a gentleman down on his luck. He did very well, you know. Owns a plantation of his own now."

"I am afraid I know nothing of such things," I said, "but I am flattered to be considered a fighting man. I have come here"—the idea came to me suddenly—"looking for what may be the least marketable item Port Royal may have. I mean, with so many ships being taken . . . well, there must have been some books aboard some of them. Books of history, of knowledge."

I glanced over my shoulder at him. "It was in my mind to open a school for young gentlemen in Virginia. There is nothing of the kind, and when the chance came to come here, where so many rich prizes are brought—"

He was astonished. "You come to Port Royal for *books?*" He got quickly to his feet. "I never heard of such a thing! To Port Royal, of all places! Men come here for strange reasons, but certainly none for anything . . . I am sorry, Master Sackett. It is not easy for me to grasp."

"Do not worry yourself about it," I said, "but if you hear of any such, please inform me."

He looked at me closely. "Captain Tilly said you were a young gentleman."

I waved a hand. "Of course! I came to Virginia expecting to find a plantation, but after living much in the forest and surveying much land, it seemed to me it would be better . . . better to *own* the land and let somebody else work it.

"Besides, she lives—"

" 'She'?" He smiled. "Ah, now I begin to understand."

"You understand nothing!" I said. "She has a younger brother, and there are others about. If I started a school, I could then have access to her home."

103

He chuckled. "Oh, well! I suppose it does make a kind of sense!" He got to his feet, looking over the measurements he had compiled. "Do you know? I might have clothes that would fit. I might have."

"How could that be?"

"It often happens. Clothes are ordered, then for one reason or another he who ordered them does not appear. It seems I have clothing. . . . Your shoulders are a little broader, your chest deeper, your waist . . . yes, your waist is smaller. With just a little work, a few minutes only, I could have an outfit that would suit admirably, something to make do with until your own are finished." He glanced sharply at me. "That is, if you want them."

"I shall want three complete outfits," I said. "You choose the colors that will suit me. I haven't the time."

"You trust my judgment?"

"I do. You appear to be a man of taste. Ordinarily I would not consider such a thing, but I have much to do and am but lately from the forest and am lacking in awareness of what is being worn.

"One thing only. A little on the conservative side? I am no fop."

"Of course." His vanity was pleased, I could see that, and I felt he would do me well. Yet I had other thoughts. "In such a place as this," I commented, "I expect most of the talk is of piratical ventures, looting, slaving, and the like. Do you hear anything at all of outlying plantations? I would assume life on some of them is very refined."

I was choosing my words with some care. My world in growing up had been one where English of the Elizabethan sort was well spoken, but growing older and in wilder lands, both Yance and I had become careless. Yet here I had another sort of impression to make, and Captain John Tilly was obviously a man of repute.

"On the contrary! Little that happens in the Indies is not known in Port Royal. Information, you know, is the foundation of piracy. I do not approve, but one does not voice such opinions here. I do not approve, and yet the successful pirates do not rely upon chance. They learn to know which vessels carry treasure of easily sold goods, and they seek them out."

"Are they slavers?"

He shrugged. "Very few. A slave ship can be smelled for miles, as a rule. Pirates avoid them. The cargo is difficult to handle, dangerous to carry, and offers far less profit than open piracy or privateering."

"Not even white slaves?"

Was I mistaken, or was there a subtle change in his manner? "I doubt if there are any such," he replied.

"When a man begins to deal in human beings," I commented, "it would seem to me color would be a minor consideration."

"You want three outfits, then?" He stood up and closed his book with a snap. "Come, Charles, we must be off."

He paused. "The one suit I could deliver tomorrow if it is acceptable."

"It would be a favor," I said.

He lingered as Charles left. "Slavery, of whatever color, is not a topic much discussed here. I would suggest avoiding it . . . if you will permit."

"Of course. I am a stranger, and I do not know what it is that concerns your citizens. In any event, I shall be here but a few days . . . if I can find what I want."

"The name is Jayne." He hesitated. "Augustus Jayne. If you have need of me, please call."

When he was gone, I sat down near the window. Jayne might know something and might not, yet if he did not know, I believe he suspected.

The idea of seeking books to open a school was unusual enough and harmless seeming enough to enable them to pigeonhole me as a mere eccentric. Yet in all the loot taken from vessels of all countries, there must have been books, for many ship's officers carried them, and many brought along whole libraries when going to the colonies. Also, I suspected they were the least marketable of items.

The search might allow me admittance to many places otherwise closed to a stranger, even into homes on some of the outlying plantations.

Yet two days later I had learned nothing. Henry came and went, and several times I saw him with neatly dressed black men, most of them very black indeed, several with bloodshot eyes. They were maroons, down from the hills. They carried themselves proudly and went their own way, having little to do with either whites or the other blacks.

My clothes arrived, and I dressed, then stared at myself in the mirror. Accustomed as I was to the wearing of buckskin leggings and hunting coat, all fringed to let the rain off easier, I was startled to see what a fine spectacle I had become. Pleased yet displeased by the result.

A doublet of forest green, the sleeves slashed to show the linen shirt beneath, knee breeches of a somewhat deeper green that met high boots of Spanish leather. The collar of the doublet was covered with a band of rich lace of white. As I was staring at myself and wondering whether to admire or laugh, Captain Tilly knocked at the door, then entered. He paused a minute, looking me over carefully. "You look quite the young gentleman, Kin. You are a strikingly handsome man, and that can be an advantage at times."

"Thank you, captain. I like myself better in buckskins, but if this is the style, then I shall wear it, and if any laugh, they shall answer for it."

"Aye, you being your father's son, I suspected as much, so I brought this." He lifted the sword case he had by his side. "It is a good blade, one your father left aboard ship, and I rousted it from an old chest for you. Wear it in good health."

The blade was a good one and came easily from its sheath. I stretched it, moved it, tried the balance.

"Aye! A handsome blade, although it has been years since I used one."

"You have fenced?"

"With father, as I said, and Jeremy as well, with Kane O'Hara and with Sakim. They were reputed good, so I expect I have been well taught."

"Be careful! There are fine swordsmen here and deadly fighters, although they favor the cutlass and the cut and slash method rather than parry and thrust."

A thought came to me. "My father had an old friend, one who chose not to stay in the mountains."

"Jublain? Aye, a fine man and a fighter. I wonder now what has become of him. He went back to England, then to the Low Countries, I believe. He was never one to stay still, but a rover always. I heard somewhere that he'd gone out east, to the Moslem lands."

We talked long, and then he returned to the *Abigail,* and I bedded down for the night, but I did not sleep. After a bit I got up, moved by some strange restlessness, and went again to my window. My room was in darkness, the street but dimly lit by reflected light, and a man stood on the corner across from the hotel. As I stood beside the window, I could see him but dimly, for he was in deep shadow. He stood there a moment, then crossed the street, going away. At once I knew him. Only one man was so large yet moved so easily.

Max Bauer!

Max Bauer here! Had he followed me? Or was it mere coincidence?

He had disappeared now, going away into the street below, yet I was sure he knew I was here. He might even know what room I was in.

And life was cheap here. No need to attempt murder himself, for it could be bought here for a few shillings or even a gallon of rum.

Every second, every minute, I must be on guard. I must be aware and ready.

And I was ready.

Chapter XII

Dawn found me awake and, soon after, break-fasting in my room. There was much thinking to be done. Henry would be out, and I had great confidence in his chances of gaining information, for there were no secrets from the servants and slaves. Yet I could not depend upon him alone.

Augustus Jayne, the tailor, was another possibili-ty, for tailors often visit homes, and there is little that escapes their eyes. Did he know something? Or was it merely my imagination? Certainly if a trade in white women existed, it was very much undercover, even here in this pirate port.

Looking out upon the street, I tried to find any possible lurker, anyone who might be placed there to watch for me, but saw no one who seemed to be lingering there.

Charles, the slave of Jayne. He would go most places Jayne would go, and if they traveled into the back country, he would eat with the servants of whom-ever they visited and would hear most of the back-stairs gossip. Henry could talk to Charles.

One thing I had already noticed. The maroons, although few of them were about, were regarded with awe and respect by the other blacks. Perhaps because of some innate quality, perhaps because they had es-caped, taken to the hills, and had set up their own world there.

The streets, when I emerged upon them, were crowded with bronzed and bearded seamen, some roughly clad as from the ships recently arrived, others bedecked in priceless gems and silks from the Far East. In the drinking shops they slammed handfuls of gold coins upon the table and called for rum. Often enough they were served in cups of gold or silver, sometimes set with gems, and aside from rum, easily the most popular of drinks, one might find wines from all the world there and the best of food.

They were a hardy, brutal lot, ready to use the knife or the fist, and stabbings were routine. If a dance were in progress, the music was not stopped for a killing; they simply danced around the body until that set was over. These were men who lived in the shadow of death, whether by gunshot, blade, or the gallows, a roistering lot of every nationality and race under the sun, mingling with no thought of anything but rum and women.

Moving among them, I gradually got the feel of the crowd. The women were there, also of every nationality, but mulattoes and quadroons predominated.

Suddenly I glimpsed Henry. He was standing alone near a stall that sold basketry, looking very handsome in his neat black coat and his white shirt. A girl moved through the crowd toward him, saying something, but he waved her aside. She left with an angry glance and a flounce. He waited, and I did, with the crowd moving past me.

A slim black man moved through the crowd toward Henry, but when he came near to him, he did not stop or seem to notice but walked on past, turning up an alley near the basketry stall. After a moment Henry followed.

At that moment something plucked my sleeve. It was Charles. So concentrated had I been on Henry's movements that I had not seen him approach.

"Captain? I am Charles, from Augustus Jayne. He has need of you for a fitting."

A fitting—now? I doubted it, yet I went along, following behind him to the door of his shop. It was a very strong door of oak set with iron straps and bolts.

Charles tapped; the door opened, and we entered. A huge black man was guarding the door.

Jayne was waiting for me, tape measure in his hand. As Charles usually did the measuring, this also surprised me.

As he started measuring, he talked softly. "Your name sounded a bell in my ears. I was sure I had heard it before this.

"Sackett? I said, it is an unusual name, and then I recalled a letter I had long since from England but one of a series of letters I review from time to time because of the information they contain, much of which can be profitable." He stepped back, glancing at me from the corners of his eyes. "Information is a commodity, you know, often calling for better pay than goods."

"If you have information," I said, "I will pay."

"Oh, no! I was not suggesting . . . far from it. Only that you would know that sometimes a tailor is not only a tailor. I have a friend in London who is interested in information and is often very helpful to me. It was in a letter from him that I found the name . . . Barnabas Sackett."

"My father."

"Ah? I suspected as much. My friend is Peter Tallis."

"My father spoke of him."

"He would, of course. Peter Tallis is a man of many parts and of much knowledge. He has, I believe, friends such as I in most of the ports of the world. We write letters to him and advise him as to conditions.

"You see, although the name sounded in my memory, I did not place the reason. Then it came to me. A friend to Peter Tallis is a friend to me. Or I am a friend to him."

"So?"

"I measure you in case of spies, and let me tell you, my friend, in Port Royal there are spies everywhere. You spoke of white slaves. I suspect you did not want one for yourself, knowing what I do of your father."

"You are right. I seek a certain girl who might have been sold as a slave, a kidnapped girl taken from what is called New England."

"There were several such, as well as some from New Amsterdam, from Carolina and Virginia."

"This girl was from the Cape Ann area. It would have been a year ago. More, I think. She would have been sold by—"

"Ssh! No names, please!"

"Very pretty, and—"

"Of course. Aren't they all?"

"A girl, I have heard, of independent mind and not one to scream about her lost honor unless she could gain something by screaming. From hearsay, a very courageous, somewhat unmoral young lady who did not take to the life in New England nor the strict ways of the elders. She was stolen away, but I am not altogether sure she would have objected very much."

"Ah, yes. You make it much easier, Master Sackett, much easier! For there are not many such. Most of them sink . . . or die of fever or of something . . . despair, probably."

"Not this one."

"You would save her?"

"I doubt that is the word. I would talk to her. I will do what she wishes in that respect, but I seek to put an end to this business."

"A knight errant? No white charger?"

"None. An attempt was made on a girl I . . . well, a girl whom I know."

"Does Captain Tilly know why you are here?"

"He does. And Samuel Maverick, of Shawmut, and the Reverend Blaxton."

"Maverick I know. He does business with us. A very shrewd, competent man. All right. Your credentials are good. I have heard of such a person. A very handsome, shrewd, and healthy young woman and not a slave."

"Not a slave?"

Jayne smiled smugly. "Not at all! In fact, she is

mistress of one of our fairest plantations! A woman with a will ... and as they say, where there's a will, there's a way, and she found it."

He completed his measurements, then suggested a glass of wine, and I joined him. Seated comfortably, his plump vest thrust forth importantly, he told the tale with some relish.

"Ah, yes! I like enterprise! It is what will keep our world alive when the old world has gone to seed! Enterprise! A good English trait! And our lady ... oh, yes! I do not hesitate to call her that, for if she did not deserve the name when she arrived, she certainly does now!

"What a woman! She was sold to one of our landed gentlemen, not an elderly man by any means but a lonely one. His wife had been a cold, unresponsive, greedy woman, and when she died, many of us breathed a sigh of relief for him. But he was not a man who liked living alone, and on that great estate back of the north shore, he was much alone. His house was a great old mansion, splendid place, for the man had taste.

"It was what led him to Adele."

"Adele?" I knew not the name and felt a sudden disappointment. "This cannot be she whom I—"

"Wait. There cannot be two such. As for the name, who cares about a name? Most of the population of Port Royal are using names not their own. One chooses a name if one wills, perhaps one more suited to the personality. After all, only a few inherit great names. The rest must make them for ourselves, and trust her. She will."

He paused, lighting a long cigar. I had seen them but rarely. He refilled my glass. The wine was white, of delicate flavor, and I, who drink not often, found it to my taste.

"When such slaves are sold, they are usually sold on order from the customer. They have the sale made, and they seek out the merchandise, subject to approval of the buyer. In this case the buyer died—a duel, I believe—so he was left with the merchandise."

" 'He'?"

"Only that. I say no more. The result was that he held a quiet little auction, a secluded place, only a few trustworthy and possible customers.

"The wench was bold. She appeared before them, and she looked over the lot and saw our man—her man—and looked right into his eyes. 'You,' she said. 'I want it to be you.'

"There was some bidding, of course, for she was a likely lass, but several had heard what she said and had lost interest. Our man bought her.

"He bought his clothes from me, so I had the story from his own lips, and an amazing story it was! On that first night when they arrived, he was about to order her confined when she demanded to speak with him alone.

"Once alone, she faced him boldly. 'You have a slave,' she said, 'and you may have a willing slave or wife—'

" '*Wife?*' he exclaimed.

" 'Wife,' she said, 'or slave, whichever you like, it matters not a whit to me, but treat me like a lady, and I shall respond like one. Treat me as a slave, and I will make your life a hell.'

"She gestured. 'This place needs care. It is rich and beautiful, but it needs someone who loves it ... and you. I have never kept a house like this, but I can, and for you I will. My father, while he lived, had a small business. He traded to the Indies and to England. I helped him keep his accounts. I can help with yours. You will come home tired, and I can make you comfortable. If you wish to talk, I can both talk and listen. So choose. Am I to be a slave brought to your bed when you need me, or your aide, your mistress, and your friend?' "

Jayne chuckled. "You can imagine. The man in question was a quiet sort and had not really planned

113

on buying a woman. In fact, the idea was furthest from his mind. I suspect he both wanted and needed someone desperately, and he went to see what sort of woman could be had. Now he had one, and her nerve appealed to him.

" 'You will not try to run away?' he asked.

" 'Why? Would I run from a man I wanted to buy me? Would I be so foolish? I had no home. Now you can give me one. I had no one to serve. Now I can serve you.'

"He put her in a spare bedroom, and of course she did not run away. When he came in from riding about the plantation, his robe and slippers were ready for him. Where his former wife had been cold and selfish; Adele was warm and seemed to think only of his comfort."

"But was she honest? Was not this all a sort of game?"

"That's just it. She was honest. She sincerely liked the man, as she had known she would from the start, but also she had seen the need in him and the loneliness. She had an instinct for such things.

"Within a few months he was living better than he ever had, was enjoying life for the first time, and was completely happy."

"And then?"

"He married her. Oh, he did not have to! She told him that, plainly enough, but it was his wish. And he never regretted it."

"He is dead?"

"On the contrary, he is very much alive. At this moment she probably knows more about his plantation than he does, but she seems not to. Here and there she makes a suggestion . . . only that. But he listens, and they have prospered."

Augustus Jayne sat back and smiled, eyes twinkling. " 'They are living happily ever after,' " he said.

"But what makes you think she is the one I seek?"

He chuckled, then grew serious. "The timing is right, or close to right. But that is not all. A few weeks ago I was at their place, seeing him fitted for a court dress. They were going to a ball at the governor's palace.

"He had not come in from the fields when I arrived, and she sat me down and told me she knew something about me—which her husband did not, I am sure—and that she wanted information about a certain man. About Joseph Pittingel."

I was startled. "Why? Why about him? I should think—"

"So should I have thought. That she would have had quite enough of him. But you mistake the lady. She has iron in her system, that one. Joseph Pittingel treated her with contempt. She despised him. She wanted something to use against him."

"Then she might help me!"

"What is it you want of her?"

"Evidence. A sworn statement as to what happened. I want to see the whole shameful business destroyed."

Jayne shook his head. "You will ask too much, my friend Sackett. Adele—she allows me to call her that—will not do it. She would have to reveal herself. She would have to go before a court or the governor or a notary and make a statement that would reveal all. She will not do it, not for herself but because of him. Because of the man she married.

"You see, no one knows. She is a woman of mystery, appearing from nowhere, and by the first time she appeared with him, she was his wife, completely in command of herself and her future.

"No, I am afraid not. She will not risk all for you, nor for revenge. She has other ideas in mind."

"Such as?"

"She wants the man destroyed, ruined, finished. I do not think she cares whether he is dead or alive when it is over. She wants him ruined for what he tried to do to her and for what he has done to others."

"Well, I shall just have to go see her."

Augustus Jayne smiled smugly again. "That will not be necessary. She is here . . . now."

Chapter XIII

He held aside the curtain into an inner room, and I stepped through. There was also a door, I noticed, that was hidden by the curtain. That door had remained open, and now he paused beside it. "I have much to do, and you will have much to discuss. Kin Ring Sackett, Madam Adele Legare."

He stepped out and closed the door behind him. She was not beautiful except for her eyes, which were. She was a striking young woman with a voluptuous figure. Her hair was blonde, shading toward red, and her eyes blue.

"Kin Ring Sackett. It is an unusual name. You are from Carolina."

"From the mountains, madam. You must excuse me. I fear I have few of the social graces."

"You know about me, so I will waste no time. Besides, we have no time. Max Bauer is in town, and he is at work, and that means he will have made arrangements to have you killed."

"You evidently know the man."

"I do. And do not take him lightly. You may be sure he has no intention of letting you get out of Port Royal alive unless he does what he did to a man who tried to help me."

"What did he do?"

"He was a good man. Oh, I suspect he had been bad enough in his way, but he was good to me and tried to help me."

117

She paused. "Max Bauer put out his eyes and cut out his tongue."

I was shocked, and she saw it. She shrugged. "Worse things can happen here, and in England as well. I need not tell you that, but he was a good man."

"What happened to him?"

"He lives here. He has a cottage on a hill where there is a view, and he weaves baskets, rugs. They are for sale. I have seen to it that he is cared for, but he is a proud man and chooses to earn his own way."

She turned suddenly back to me. "You look to be a strong man. Could you kill Max Bauer?"

"You mistake me, madam. I do not plan to kill him, only to put a stop to this business. I want evidence that will show Pittingel for what he is."

"Do you think that will stop them? They will simply move to some other place. Oh, it would hurt Pittingel! He likes being an important man! He likes putting on airs and strutting about! As for the name, even that doesn't belong to him. I've not been able to discover just what his name was. I know the one he had before this, but I think he borrowed that one, also.

"That is not important. The man is evil, and Max Bauer is as well. I want them destroyed."

"If I could return to Cape Ann with a sworn statement—?"

"Out of the question. For myself I do not care; for my husband I care very much. He has his position and his pride. No one here knows where I came from. I do not want them to know."

"You seem to have changed much in a year."

"A year? What is a year? All time is relative. One day may be a lifetime, a year can be forever. It is not the number of days but what goes into those days.

"I was a young girl. I was free, independent, unrestrained . . . often, I am afraid, disobedient. Suddenly I was a prisoner, and life was nothing to be accepted day by day as I had been doing. I was to be sold as a slave, and the realization was not pleasant. I had decisions to make, and quickly if I was to survive at all.

"My friend, he who was blinded because of me, warned me of what I might expect, slavery to some brute on an outlying plantation, then sold to a brothel when I became tiresome. It was plain that if I were to survive I must think."

"You became quite a woman."

"Who is in love with her husband."

I flushed. "I did not mean—"

"I know you did not. I simply wanted it understood. I will do nothing that will create difficulty for him."

"Does Bauer know where you are now? To whom you are married?"

"I think not. I was nobody to be concerned with, merely another body to be shuffled off for a price. Neither was present when I was put up for auction, and there were few present, mostly from other islands. Anyway, I look much different now. Nonetheless, I do not underrate the man."

"I had hoped to get a sworn statement from you that I could use against Pittingel."

"Impossible. What I will do is whatever I can, as long as I do not have to appear."

"Thank you." I started to turn away when a question stopped me.

"The two girls who escaped? Who were they?"

"Diana Macklin and Carrie Penney. My brother is married to Temperance Penney."

"We were friends, although her family did not approve." She smiled suddenly, amused at herself. "I was considered headstrong."

She frowned suddenly. "I liked Diana. Although we did not often talk, we were friends. I worried about her, for people were suspicious of her. She was brighter than the others and more independent."

Briefly I explained something of the situation in the time since she had left. Knowing all concerned, it was

119

easy for her to understand all that had taken place. As I talked, I found myself admiring her very much. Here was a girl who had literally lifted herself from adversity and worse simply by using her wits. Admittedly there was a good deal of luck in having such a man as Legare come to the sale, yet who could guess what else she might have contrived had it been some other?

"They know you, then? Be careful. Augustus Jayne warned me they were in Port Royal. They come here often, but I do so but rarely. You must be careful."

"And you?"

"Do not worry about me." She held out her hand, then turned toward a rear door. "We have an enemy in common, at least. Go now. I must get away from here without being seen." Again she paused. "Do not worry about me. I have friends here and protection. I cannot help you in the way you would like, but I shall not rest until they are destroyed."

She spoke quite calmly, but I needed no seer to tell me she spoke the truth. Young she might be, but she had been through the fires, and there was steel in her.

Back in the front shop there were two men now, seated cross-legged on a table, sewing. Augustus Jayne was nowhere about, and at the door my eyes swept the street.

It was crowded with sailors from the ships, pirates, and with an occasional planter from the back country or a soldier in uniform and a liberal assortment of blacks, some of them showing signs of Carib blood.

A drunken sailor, reeking of rum, staggered past, leaning for a moment against a post. In his ear was a ring, sparkling with diamonds. On the fingers of the hand nearest me he wore three others, gold and gems. He caught my glance and bared his broken teeth in what passed for a smile. "Got more where them come from! I got a-plenty!" With that he staggered on.

Looking up, I caught the eyes of a sour-looking

man with a black forelock and a scar on his cheek-
bone. The same blow must have taken the tip of his
ear, too, for it was missing. As our eyes met, he looked
quickly away. Why? His expression had been almost
guilty.

A heavy cart drawn by two oxen was coming
along the street, piled high with barrels. Suddenly I
ducked across in front of it, so close the oxen almost
broke stride, and their driver cursed me roundly. For
an instant the cart and its load barred any view of me,
and I ducked instantly into a small shop and made my
way toward the rear.

A glance back showed not one but two men dart
across the street. The man with the scar started up the
street; the other one turned down.

Only a moment and they would be back, looking
in here. I went to the back of the shop, and a man
stepped before me. "You would be wanting something?"

"To see the owner," I said, "at once!"

He hesitated, not liking me but obviously im-
pressed by my appearance. "Well . . . wait, then."

He turned and went through a curtain at the
back. Again I looked back. Nothing . . . yet.

After what seemed a long time, the clerk reap-
peared. "This way, Captain," he said.

Time, I needed time, if only a few minutes. I went
through the curtain and saw a man in square-cut
glasses looking up at me. He was a short, fat man with
a round, almost completely bald head. He had a small,
tight little mouth that I instantly distrusted, but that
was of no importance now.

"What is it?" he demanded irritably. "I've no
time for—"

"I was told," I suggested, "that you were a man
who might have something to sell." I paused just a
moment. "Something other than that claptrap out
there," I jerked my head toward the front of the
store.

He sat back in his chair and stared at me. His

eyes were cold and cruel. He was not a man with whom I should have liked to deal. "Now who could have told you *that?*" He stared at me. "I know naught of you. If you have business to do with me, there's the store out front. I thought you was somebody else when I told them to put you back to me. Now be off."

It had been only a minute. The spies, killers, whoever they were, might be out front this moment.

"There are gems," I said, "and then there are *real* gems. I look for the odd thing, the unusual thing, and I can arrange payment."

He shuffled papers on his desk. "I've naught," he said gruffly, "and there's fifty people about who might." He peered up at me from his fat-lidded eyes. "Who was it sent you to me? I'll no talk no more until you tell me."

Only one name came to mind. "Pittingel," I said, "although I doubt he'd want his name mentioned."

Slowly he put his quill down. "Pittingel? Now what would he be telling of me? What, indeed? And to whom?"

"I'm lately from the Carolinas," I said, "and before that from Mexico."

I hoped he would not ask after Mexico, for I knew nothing of the place.

"What is it you'd be wanting?"

"It is as I said. Gems . . . a big one, or two. Gold, if it is hand crafted and not melted down." I was doing what I could to keep off the street until they should have decided I was far away.

"Gems!" he shrugged. "There be enough of those about, taken from Spanish vessels." He waved a hand. "Go ask about. You'll find a pretty lot of them!"

"I look for only one or two, large stones," I added. "I have a market but only for the large ones."

Abruptly I turned away. "I waste time. This is no place. I was informed—"

"Aye," he said dryly, "and of that I would know more. Pittingel, you said? I scarce know the man, so would he send you to me? Or anybody for that matter."

"I'll go," I said. "I came to talk business—"

"And you shall," he said quietly. "Talk business, indeed! Do you take me for a fool? You're a spy! A bleeding spy!"

He snorted. "Pittingel, indeed! Aye, I know the man, but he knows little enough of me! And you to come with such a story, to me of all people! 'A large stone,' he says! Aye, is it a likely thing to come into such a place as mine, which sells sailors' truck and such, looking for gems?"

Taking another step back, I started to turn toward the curtain through which I had come. Unwittingly I had stumbled into some other affair of which I knew nothing and wished to know nothing.

"Obviously," I said, "we talk to no point. Perhaps another time—"

"Now," he said, and from under his desk he produced a formidable-looking pistol. The click of its cocking was loud in the room. "Sit down. I will have my boys in, and we shall know more about you, my young fool."

He shouted suddenly. "Harry! Tom! Here, at once!"

His pistol was gripped in his hand, but it was merely held, and he believed the threat was enough, but I kicked my chair toward him, just enough to make him jerk back from sheer instinct, and then I was through the curtains and found myself facing a burly fellow with more confidence than is usually permitted a man.

"Here, now! Just back up there! I will—!"

"Not now," I said, and kicked him on the knee-cap. He bent over, grabbing at his injured knee with a howl, and I jerked my knee into his face, then pushed him aside with the flat of my hand and went for the outer door. A slim lad with an evil face awaited me there, but he stepped aside, smiling in no friendly

123

fashion. "My time will come later," he said. "It always does!"

With that I was on the street and around the corner, across the street and around another corner. What manner of place was this Port Royal? Was there a den of thieves wherever a man looked? I had but stepped into a store—no matter.

Back at the tavern I went at once to the room and sat down upon the bench, throwing my hat upon the bed. As I did so, my eye caught a flutter from the table where sat the bowl and pitcher.

A bit of paper, held down by the bowl. I opened its one fold.

> *Madame Legare has been taken. Meet me near mouth of Rio Cobre, near Santiago de la Vega. No later than midnight.*
>
> *Henry*

For a moment I stood still, thinking. Madame Legare taken! She had escaped them once, but she would not do so again, and her husband, a good, well-meaning man, was probably not the kind to deal effectively with Bauer. Yet it was my responsibility, for it was I who had brought her to his attention.

Turning to my belongings, I dug out two pistols and loaded them and tucked both into my belt.

To leave Port Royal for Santiago de la Vega and the mouth of the Rio Cobre was simply to cross the entrance to the bay. In my mind's eye I pictured the distance.

Two miles? Or a bit more?

I would go now, at once.

Chapter XIV

The boy I found on the shore who would take me across the harbor entrance was slim and very black, his eyes large and soulful. "A shillin', suh. I does it for a shillin'."

"Make good time and keep your eyes out for trouble and there'll be another shillin'," I said.

"A shillin'," he said. "An' I see anything you should know, I tell you."

He pushed off as soon as I was seated, and we moved at once out over the dark water.

Dark water where no wind blew, and two dozen ships lay at anchor, pirate vessels most of them, some bulging with cargo freshly looted from vessels on the Spanish Main. Nor was the harbor quiet because night had come. A lighter, piled high with bales and casks, passed us. There were lights in the ships, and from a galleon, still bearing marks of fire and cannon balls, there came drunken singing. A man lurched to the rail and waved a bottle at us, inviting us for a drink. From shore there was the sound of music and drunken singing. It was a wild night in a wild port upon a wild sea with the island looming high and dark behind it.

"Lived here long?" I asked.

"No other place," he said. "I like it, suh. This is what I like, the boat, a man to take across, a shillin' comin' when you step ashore, an' sometime a cabin on the slope of the Healthshire Hills."

He was silent, and the oar chunked solemnly in

the oarlock at the stern. There was not wind enough for a sail, although beyond the ships at anchor there might be.

"I been ast to go upon a ship. More'n one time. I don't want that. I don't want no gold bought for blood. I like a quiet time with the sound of my oar or water past the hull. I like a man settin' quiet like you. I like the smells on the other side, yonder. I like it over on Galleon Bay."

For a long time he was silent, and after a bit I said, "I am from the mountains of America, far away to the north. I have a cabin there where the flowers bloom and where the mountain edges reach up to the sky. I know what you mean."

He set me ashore after a while on a sandy spit near the river, and I gave him his shilling.

"You have a family?" I asked.

I could see the whites of his eyes in the darkness and the white scarf tied about his head.

"I once had. Maman died when I was tall as her waist. Papa an' me, we put her down and marked the place. He done stayed on wi' me, but his eyes were always a-looking at the sea, and ever' time a ship sailed, I think he's heart go wi' it.

"One day I was fourteen, an' papa he say I am man now, an' I say you go, papa. You go down where the ships go because I see he's heart is with them, and he went away, and I have my boat and sometimes a shillin'."

"What name do you have?"

"Andrew, suh. I am called Andrew."

"No other name?" I saw his teeth when he smiled. "I have no need for other name. I am Andrew. It is enough. If I had another name, too, I might feel big about me, and it is not good. A boy named Andrew who has a boat. Good-by, suh."

I put the shilling in his hand, and he pushed off and went into the darkness, standing tall and quiet in his boat. I stood alone in the darkness, unmoving, until the night lost the sound of his oar.

All was black about me; a loom of jungle-covered hills and only a narrow strip of white shoreline stood close. I walked up the beach and stood to think, to decide which way I should go, but there was a soft rustling and a sound near me.

"Captain? It is Henry."

He came from the shadows. Several others moved near him, and I kept a hand on a pistol.

"It is well, Captain. They are maroons and my people."

"They have taken Adele Legare. Where are they now?"

"Not far." He laughed softly. "They do not know, but they are watched. My people are like the Indians of your country. They are quiet in the forest."

"Are they camped?"

"They move slowly, I think, as if waiting for somebody or for a time. They now are near the Salt Ponds, but I think they go to Galleon Bay. It is a good place for boats to come and not to be seen."

He led the way, and we moved swiftly. There had been a shower earlier, and the leaves dripped, yet I think it helped to obscure the sounds of our passing, and we had been going but a few minutes when a man came from the jungle. We stopped briefly while he talked to Henry; then he faded into the jungle and was gone.

"They are but minutes away." He glanced at me, as I could dimly see. "There will be fighting, I think."

"How many are they?"

"Seven now, and a light was seen on Galleon Bay, a signal, we believe." He led the way sharply downhill. The earth was muddy under foot, and several times I slipped but each time caught myself before falling.

Suddenly the water was before us, a goodly stretch of it with the darkness of land beyond. Henry touched my arm. "We walk easily here, for there is a swamp along the shore."

My boots were ill fitted for such travel, and I longed for a pair of my moccasins, which suited me better. We emerged upon solid footing, a stretch along the shore, and we walked along the sand.

Suddenly a voice spoke, "Sheer off there! Belay it! We want no visitors here!"

"But you have them, my friend," I said quietly. "You have many visitors, and we wish the young lady. You may release her now, or we will have your blood first."

"Sheer off!" There was anger in the voice and maybe a shadowing of doubt or fear.

"Are you there, madame?"

"I am," she replied.

There was the sound of a blow, and I said, "Your life shall pay for that," and we closed in around them.

A man came at me, cutlass swinging, but I fenced as my father and Jeremy had taught me. I moved back, and sure he had me, he came in swiftly. He cut sharply at me and missed; my point did not. My blade touched the point where his neck met his chest.

He fell back, coughing, and my eyes, accustomed to the darkness now, saw a man turn on Adele, and I had a pistol from my waistband and a shot.

He fell.

There was a shout from the boat coming in. "Lashan?"

The maroons were armed with cutlasses, and but two or three had muskets. They turned and fired toward the incoming boat, and there was a curse, and then the boat began to back water swiftly. I thrust my empty pistol into my waistband and held my sword ready, but the fighting was over. On the sand were dark bodies, stretched and still. A maroon moved to stop one who was crawling away. "Let him go," I said. "If he lives, he can tell them how foolish they were."

Adele came to me across the sand. "You came in time. I knew you would."

"It is Henry who deserves the thanks," I said. "May we take you home now?"

128

At least three of her captors had fled, but we did not pursue. To find them in the darkness would be difficult, and my first task was to take Madame Legare to her home.

"It is arranged for," Henry said. "We borrowed a carriage from a plantation."

"Henry, no one must know of this. I hope you did not—"

He smiled. "I did not. They do not even know their carriage is being used, and before they do know, it will be back in its place, wiped clean as if never used."

Hours later, we drove into the winding, palm-lined lane to the plantation house.

As we came near the house, a man walked out on the wide verandah. I rode on in advance.

"Master Legare?" He was a man in his thirties, not unhandsome and with a kindly but worried face.

"Yes?"

"Madame Legare was taken by pirates, slavers, or something of the sort. We have brought her home. She was not harmed."

"You are?"

"Kin Ring Sackett, of Virginia. The others," I added, "are maroons."

"Maroons?" He was startled. "But—!"

"They are our friends," I said, "and without them we could have done little."

The carriage drew up, and he ran down the steps to help her down. "You are all right?"

"All right." She smiled suddenly, her hand still resting in his. "And I am home."

"Will you come in?" He paused at the door, looking about. "Why! They are gone!"

Glancing back, I saw it was true. They had faded into the jungle and the planting as if they had never been. I had no need to ask where Henry might be. He knew, as I did, there was much to be done and that most of it must be done in Port Royal or in Santiago de la Vega.

The room into which I was shown was large and high of ceiling. Wide windows looked out over green lawns flaming with tropical flowers, whose names I knew not.

"You must rest, Captain," Legare said, "but first something to eat."

"There is little time—" I started to say, but he lifted a hand.

"Enough. We have much to talk of, you and I." He glanced at me. "You have known my wife long?"

Briefly I explained my meeting with her and why I had come to Jamaica. I added, "In the Cape Ann district Madame Legare was a friend to a girl whom I know. A girl I—"

I caught myself up short. What was I saying? I hardly knew the girl, and she knew even less of me.

A servant came in bearing a tray with coffee, eggs, ham, and a melon, of which I knew nothing.

"Adele does not wish me disturbed," Legare said, "and she knows I am a quiet man who prefers a quiet life. I have books, I read much, I oversee my plantation myself, and I engage in a bit of trade. I also"—he took up a slice of toast and broke it in his fingers—"dabble in the governing of the island.

"Often," he said, "I find it best to do what must be done without going through the usual channels. Adele is not yet familiar with my methods of operation. She does know that I prefer our life here. It is quiet, pleasant. We have a few friends and a graceful, easy life."

He put down his glass. "I understand very well how you feel and agree that something must be done. I have thought so for some time. Now—suddenly—they have brought it home to me."

"I have heard," I suggested, "that Joseph Pittingel has many friends in high places, that he moves as he wishes."

"To a point . . . only to a point. Unfortunately for him, he has never known how shallow are the roots of his power, nor has he ever been able to temper his greed. Continual success has led him to believe there can be no failure."

Legare smiled, refilling my glass with coffee. "As to that, Captain Sackett, I agree."

"I have been called 'Captain' but I have no claim to the title," I said. "I am captain of nothing."

He shrugged. "No matter. It is convenient. There are many such in the islands. It is a courtesy title as much as anything else, so grant those who use it their pleasure."

He changed the subject suddenly and began talking of trade between the islands and Carolina and the Plymouth colony. "I have been content to plant and reap, but lately I have been thinking of branching out, building a three-cornered trade between the islands, England, and Carolina. I have hesitated because it demands a trip to England to find an agent there."

A thought came to me, and I suggested, "I have a brother there who is a student of law at the Inns of Court. He is young, but he would be pleased to act for you."

"His name?"

"Brian Sackett. I hear he has established very good connections there and has already a considerable background in the law."

"Excellent! I can give him the chance, at least, and if he does well, there can be much business. The trade is growing, and I foresee much settlement in Carolina and Virginia and with it a growing demand as well as a need for a market for their produce, whatever it may be."

"My father shipped several cargoes of mast timbers and potash while he was yet alive. Furs, of course. There is gold in limited quantity and some gems—very few."

Legare got to his feet. "And you? What of you?"

"I am for the land," I said. "All of this"—I gestured about—"is well and good, but I am a man of

131

the forest and at home there. I have no great desire for wealth, and where I wish to live, there would be none to admire it.

"On the west of the blue mountains I have a cabin. I have a crop of corn which badly needs my attention now, and when this is done, I shall return. There is fruit and nuts in the forest, if one works hard enough, and there is fresh meat to have if one has the powder and lead.

"I have never wanted fine clothes or such a home. All I want of people are books. I love much to read, although a life in the wilderness leaves too little time for it. Still, by the firelight, and of an evening—"

Yet even as I spoke my thoughts were out there in the darkness. Where was Max Bauer? What now were the thoughts of Joseph Pittingel? And what had I done but frustrate them one more time, bringing us no nearer a conclusion.

They wanted me dead, and I was not dead. Not yet. Would they be out there in the dark? I thought not. They knew now of the maroons, our good friends, and they were no match for them by night.

They would await the coming of the day. They would suspect—

"I can offer you a carriage," Legare said, "to carry you back to Port Royal or whatever you prefer."

"Two hours of rest," I suggested, "and then a good horse."

"But—?"

"They will expect me to come by day, or they will expect me now. A carriage would be a death trap."

So it was arranged, and I went up to the bed they provided in a high-ceilinged room with mosquito netting all about the bed. The night was warm, but I slept well.

At an hour after midnight a black man came quietly to my bedside. "It is time, Captain. You will have coffee?"

It was waiting for me in a small, pleasant room, a

slice of melon, a thick piece of bread, and some cold meat. I ate, drank the coffee, and the black man led me down a narrow passage. "The slaves' quarters," he said apologetically. "We will not be noticed this way."

"You have spoken to Henry?"

He glanced at me. He was a tall man, quite thin, with graying hair. "I have not," he said quietly. "You have helped the mistress. It is enough."

He paused a moment. "She is very good to us," he added simply.

In the shadow of a stable a black horse waited, restive, eager to be off and away. He was saddled and bridled, and two horse pistols were in scabbards on either side of the saddle.

The black man pointed the road for me. "There is no safety anywhere," he said quietly, "but you do not seem a man who is used to safety. Ride well."

He turned away and walked to the house, not looking back. For a moment I waited, shadowed by the black bulk of the stable. There was no sound in the night. Inside the stable a horse stamped restlessly; I turned the black and rode past the corral and at the roadside paused, listening to the night.

It was very hot and still. Frogs talked in a pond somewhere not far away, and there were countless small noises, made by creatures unknown to me.

Walking the black into the trail, I started for Santiago de la Vega, some distance away.

My right hand touched a pistol, loosening it in the holster. Before we reached town, I should have need of it. This was not simply something I supposed. I *knew* it.

Chapter XV

The narrow road was a dim path through dark jungle broken here and there by open country turned from jungle to planting or grazing. The moon was rising, still unseen. The rail fences at some places took on a skeletonlike appearance.

A night hawk or some such creature flitted by overhead. Aside from the vague night noises there was no sound but the clop-clop of my horse's hoofs. Uneasily I kept turning in my saddle to look back, and my eyes searched ahead for a warning of any attack.

The jungle walled in the road on either side, no tree distinguishable from another. At last we cleared the jungle, and open fields lay on each side, all white and gray in the moonlight, yet I could not relax. Long ago I had learned the most innocent-seeming places were often the worst. My horse's ears pricked, and he broke stride a bit, then continued on. I drew both pistols and hoped my mount was familiar with shooting from the saddle.

At least he had warned me. They came suddenly from a bend in the road, one that scarcely seemed to be there, and some low-lying brush. But my horse had warned me in time, and as the first man came off the ground, I shot him.

He loomed up just at the right place for me, and I shot into his chest at no more than twenty feet. The heavy slug knocked him back, and I dropped the gun into the scabbard, swinging my horse sharply away and clapping my heels to his flanks. He was a good horse, and he leaped away in fine style. From behind me a gun bellowed, and something *whisked* past my skull. Turning in the saddle, I held the other pistol for a moment, looking down the barrel at a looming figure in the trail behind me.

When I actually squeezed off the shot, I knew not, but the big pistol leaped in my hands with an angry bellow, and the man missed a step and fell. Then I was away and holstering that gun.

How many there had been, I could not guess, but I surmised at least four. They had expected a complete surprise, but I was too much the wilderness man not to trust to my horse, and a good one he was, so I had been warned in time.

He seemed eager to run, so I let him have his head, and we went down the road at a good pace, the wind in my face and with the comforting knowledge that my two pistols were still loaded and ready if trouble came again.

After a bit I slowed to a canter, then a walk, then a canter again to let my horse have his time in cooling down. There was no sign of pursuit, so they were not mounted men. When light was gray in the eastern sky, I saw the first of the outlying huts that preceded Santiago de la Vega.

Riding by the King's House and turning into an open, paved court, I stepped down before a small inn whose sign invited travelers. A black boy took my horse, and I tipped him a shilling and suggested he feed and water the black.

" 'Tis the horse of Master Legare," he said. "I know him well, and he knows me."

It was spacious and cool inside, evidently an older house, and there were several bare tables about, and a man came along to the table where I sat and brought a tankard of rum.

"Very well," I said, "but it is food I want, and the best. But not," I added, "too heavy." For I had seen that these Spanish men and what Frenchmen there were around ate too heavily for the climate. My father had learned this from Sakim, that to remain cool it is better not to eat too much meat and food of richness.

He brought me some slices of cold meat then and some boiled eggs as well as slices of melon and plantain. I only tasted the rum, and it was not bad, but strong for my taste and too heady for a man in my position. From here on I must have my head about me, for whatever had been done until now showed little evidence of the fine hand of either Pittingel or Bauer. They had been clumsy efforts at assassination and ambush, but now they would know better, and their efforts would be more devious.

Nonetheless, all I wished for now was to have the business completed and be on my way back to Carolina and my own mountains. The air was heavy, hot and still, with a suggestion of storm. Mopping the perspiration from my face, I looked out the window.

Had I visited here at any other time, I was sure I would have enjoyed this island of Jamaica, but there was no time to see more than the lush beauty of the place and some of the people. There was only time to think of keeping alive while I tried to end the trade that was ruining the lives of innocent girls. Slavery itself must end, although it was worldwide. At this time many Europeans were enslaved in North Africa and elsewhere. Africans were enslaved here, and slavery of one kind or another existed over much of the world. Even the poor of Europe lived lives but little different from those of slaves, and in many cases they were worse off. Slaves were at least fed and clothed by their masters, and the poor of Europe had no such care.

Finishing my meal and still alone in the room, I took time to recharge the saddle pistols that I had carried into the room in their scabbards, no unusual thing for travelers in that day and time.

The proprietor came in, glanced at the pistols. "You are a friend to Master Legare?"

"I am."

His manner warmed visibly. He was a stout man with a round, pinkish face and a fringe of red hair. "A good man," he said, "and a shrewd one, although his quiet manner leads some to misunderstand him."

"You know the pistols?"

He smiled. "And the horse. I saw you ride up." He glanced meaningly at the pistols. "There has been trouble?"

"The roads are unsafe everywhere," I commented. "It was nothing."

"There have been strangers about," he advised, "some of that scum from Port Royal, I think. You had best be on your guard."

"Aye," I got to my feet. "I shall be ready."

It was but six miles from Santiago de la Vega to the little cluster of huts and a fort that stood at the mouth of the Rio Cobre. "Leave the horse and the pistols with Señor Sandoval if you wish to ride there," the innkeeper advised. "I shall see them returned."

Dropping the guns into their scabbards, I mounted and turned the black horse down the trail toward Rio Cobre. Black people passed me, great bundles or baskets on their heads; most of them gave me greeting in their quiet voices. Several obviously knew the horse, and they looked from him to me, knowing I was a friend of Legare.

Where was Henry? For hours now I had seen nothing of him. A rider passed me going in the same direction. There was something familiar about his back and shoulders, yet nothing I could place. A moment later I heard horses behind me, and glancing back, saw two men riding together who were not over fifty yards behind.

Up ahead of me were several black people walking along the road with their bundles. A carriage coming toward me drew up and stopped, and a man got down from the driver's seat and went to the horses' heads and began adjusting something.

Glancing back, I saw that the two riders were now closer, not more than thirty yards back. The rider who had passed me had stopped and was talking to somebody in the waiting carriage.

It was a lonely stretch, yet by now we could be no more than three miles, perhaps a bit less, from the Rio Cobre. Then I noticed something else that I had not seen before. Just beyond the carriage two men sat beside the road sharing a bottle. A bundle lay on the bank beside one of them.

What was the matter with me? I was getting altogether too jumpy. I eased myself in the saddle, loosening one of the pistols a bit.

As I drew up to the carriage, the man standing beside it turned to look at me, and the man on the horse did, also. Both of them were smiling. The man on the horse gestured. "Something here to interest you, Captain."

"What?" I was startled and turned to look.

Diana! Diana Macklin, her face white and strained, and in the seat beside her, Joseph Pittingel.

"I thought you should see that we had her," he said, "before you die."

It was not a time for speech or for thinking, nor could I have thought fast enough. My heels slammed into the ribs of the black horse, and I leaped him straight at the rider, who was broadside to me, blocking the way.

My black was the larger horse and was driven by the leap; smashing into the other horse, it knocked it sprawling, its rider falling free. Turning the black on his hind legs, I grabbed at the door of the carriage, and it came open.

"Out! Out, Diana!"

Men were closing in. The two on the bank had leaped to their feet, but they had to come around the fallen horse, which was kicking and struggling. The man at the horse's head turned toward me, but I leaped the black at him, and springing back to avoid the lunge, he fell.

Diana had leaped from the carriage, leaving a part of her dress in Pittingel's frantically clutching hand. As I swung the horse once more, I dropped a hand to her, and she caught it, managing a toe in the stirrup as I swung her up. We leaped the horse past them, and I grabbed a pistol, firing at the first man before me. He staggered and went back; whether hit or not, I did not know.

Down the road before me were four men, spreading out now, obviously more of Pittingel's lot. I dropped the pistol into the holster and put the black up the bank. He went up, scrambling, barely reaching the top, then over and into the trees beyond. It was a wild tangle, no place to ride a horse, so we dropped from him and squirmed through the trees. I wished only to make the shore. We ran, fell, scrambled up, and ran again.

Behind us we heard shouts and curses, the loudest of them from Pittingel himself. "Get them, damn you!" he screamed. "Get them or I'll have you flayed!"

The jungle was thick. Underfoot there was mud. It was a tangle of creepers and vines. Turning at right angles, I led the way through what seemed to be an opening. I still held the remaining horse pistol, which was unfired. We moved quickly.

There was no chance to speak to Diana, only to escape if such we could do at all. Only my reflexes, trained by much trial and danger, had saved us, and now the moment was past, we had small chance. Even as we moved, I knew this. We were close to the water now. Suddenly we emerged upon a rocky, pebble-strewn shore. Beyond the bay lay Port Royal, and several fishermen's boats lay not far off, but to my wild waves they paid little attention.

Suddenly, far off, I glimpsed one. Surely that—I waved wildly. The boat seemed to fall still in the water, then turned abruptly toward us.

Waving, I gestured him on. Diana released my hand suddenly. "Kin, they are coming. It is too late."

Four men had come from the jungle, four men who immediately spread out and started for us. A dozen yards farther along another appeared and then another.

My pistol came up, and they hesitated, then came on, and I threatened first one and then another with the pistol.

They were not fifteen yards away now, the closest of them. "Diana," I spoke softly, "you cannot help me, and your presence will make me protect two rather than just myself. Can you swim?"

"I can."

"Then swim out to him. Swim to the boat. It is Andrew, and I know him."

"All right."

She wasted no time in pleas or farewells but went down to the water's edge and stripped off her outer gown. Then she walked into the water.

There was a shout of rage from one of the men, and they started to run. Instantly I fired at the nearest. He threw up his arms and fell to the rocks. Throwing the pistol to make them dodge, I drew one of my own from my waistband. This they had not suspected, and they halted suddenly. They were close enough for me not to miss, and they knew it.

One of them drew a pistol, also. I suspected their orders had been to take us alive if possible but not to permit us to escape in any event.

Behind me I could hear the chunking of the oar. I had two pistols of my own now that Legare's heavy horse pistols were gone, but I also had a sword.

Taking a step back on the slippery rocks, I drew the second pistol, holding one in either hand. The man with the pistol hesitated no longer but lifted his to take careful aim. That was all very well, but we who lived in the forest and must ever be ready for attack by the red men often had no time for such things. I shot from where my gun was held, and the man dropped his pistol and went to a knee. He started to grope for the fallen gun, and I fired again. Then, thrusting both guns back into my waistband, I drew my sword and backed into the water.

None of the others seemed to be armed with

firearms. The water raised about me, and I heard a voice say, "Here, Captain, behind you."

The boat was there, and Diana, very wet, was already aboard. I climbed in over the gunwale and dropped to the bottom. Instantly Andrew pushed us away, and I sat up slowly.

"One shillin', suh," Andrew suggested, "I will need to have a shillin'."

Chapter XVI

And now suddenly all changed.

Legare came into the room as I ate breakfast, and Henry was with him. My gesture invited them to join us, and they did so. In many places in the islands the presence of a black at the table would not have been permitted, but in the pirate city of Port Royal there were no distinctions as to race.

"Adele has spoken to me of your need for some kind of a statement," he said. "She thought only of protecting my good name, but there is more at stake here, and despite her wish to protect me, my good name rests on no such shaky foundation. I married Adele, and she is my lady, and that is enough. If more is wanted, there is a field of honor where I can bring those who question my judgment.

"Now—" He drew from his pocket a rolled sheet of parchment. "A statement sworn to before a notary. This is her story. Names are named here, that of Joseph Pittingel among them. If you need more, I shall myself come to Cape Ann or Shawmut or wherever and make my statement."

"Thank you. I am sure this will be sufficient." At that moment there was a tap at the door. "You are in time to meet Diana Macklin, who was taken for the second time by Pittingel's men."

Opening the door, I admitted Diana and a maid I had hastily secured for her through the good offices of Augustus Jayne.

Legare bowed over her hand. "Adele has spoken

of you," he said. "May I express my regrets for all that has happened? With the statement he now has, Kin Sackett may soon put an end to all this."

She turned quickly to me. "Please! Can we go home? My father was wounded when they took me, and I have no idea if he is alive or dead."

"We will go. My friend John Tilly will be in port tomorrow, returning from the outer islands. At least, so he has planned."

"You are sure you will not need me?" Legare asked.

"I think not," I said. "And I am sure Adele will."

He smiled quickly, shyly for a man who had proved to be so unexpectedly bold and swift in action. "She is my first and greatest happiness."

"And you?" I looked over at Henry. "You are among your people now. Will you stay here?"

He shook his head. "My place is with you if you will have me along. These people are of my race and my blood, but I have always been a man alone. I like the way you fight and the way you think. Mayhap our roads are the same."

"If you wish it," I agreed. He was a good man and a strong man, and wherever I would go, such would be needed.

Legare extended his hand. "Enough, then. They know me in Port Royal, and what you need, you may have if you will but speak. I cannot thank you enough."

When they were gone, and Diana and I were alone but for the maid, I said, "Have you eaten? I had just begun."

"I waited for you. I thought . . . well, I thought you might not wish to eat alone."

I held a chair for her. "I hope," I said, "never to eat alone again."

Her face was faintly pink, and she looked up to meet my eyes, hers twinkling a little. "That might be taken as a proposal."

"I hope it is," I said seriously, "because I would not be very good at such a thing. I'm afraid I'd be clumsy. You see, I know very little of women. Ours is a lovely land but a lonely one and a hard one, and such a life leaves very little time for thinking of women or learning about them."

We sat long over breakfast and talked of many things, none of them important, I fear, but each one a means of learning about each other. Yet as we talked, I could not help but remember Joseph Pittingel and Max Bauer. They were both about, both free, and there was no authority in Port Royal to take exception to what they had done. I must be on my guard, for they must kill me to survive themselves, and they would now wish to kill Diana.

John Tilly might arrive within the next few hours, but much as Pittingel worried me, I had no wish to remain penned up in this room. Outside there was much to see in this wild, unruly, rich, and bloody town. And I had a wish to see it for myself.

There was much else to see, including the Walks, a well-known drive along some rocky cliffs that I had promised myself to see. Yet a worry lay upon me, for I knew that Max Bauer was somewhere about, and I knew only one or two of his men by sight.

Diana wished to do some shopping, and the maid Jayne had sent would accompany her. I must needs go to the waterfront to inquire after John Tilly and the *Abigail*.

The maid, whose name was Bett, had gone out and bought a few things for Diana. As she had served ladies before, she knew well enough what was needed, but Diana wished to choose clothes for herself, beyond her immediate needs.

While they prepared themselves for the shopping, I went down to the lower floor and looked out upon the street. It was crowded as usual, but I saw a tall, slim black man loitering near the door. He looked familiar, and I gestured to him. He had the look of a maroon, and I was sure he had been placed there by Henry.

He came into the room when I gestured to him. "Can you get two or three stout fellows to be around while Mistress Macklin goes among the shops? Our enemies are still about."

He smiled. "Henry speak to us, suh. They may go where they wish. We will be all about."

"Good! I have much to do along the shore."

He gave me a sidelong glance. "It is no good place to be, suh. It is bad-man place."

"I must go."

"Ships come, ships go. Who know what happen, suh? Sometimes man go. Never again see. You take short steps, suh."

Upon these streets all men wore arms, and I would not be without mine. To learn of the *Abigail* was my first wish, but I will not deny it was in my mind to see Port Royal with my own eyes, for this was ever my way, to see, to know, to learn. To go from place to place and taste the food and wine of the country, to look about, to *see*.

We who walk the woodland paths know that although all men look, not many see. It is not only to keep the eyes open but to see what is there and to understand. Jamestown I knew but little else. I had seen no towns, although my father and Jeremy talked much of London and Bristol, and Kane O'Hara was forever speaking of Dublin and Cork. This was the first town of my experience that was wider than a village.

When I had donned fresh garments, I looked upon myself in the glass and admitted myself pleased. Not with myself, for I was, as always, a tall, tanned young man with the wide shoulders hard work had earned for me and a shock of curly black hair. My face was wedge shaped, cheekbones high; my eyes were green. The outfit I wore fitted me well, and that was the important thing. I looked the gentleman without any of the flash and color of the pirates I'd seen. Not that I did not look upon their clothes with some envy but would have been embarrassed to wear the like myself.

Thinking of that, I chuckled at the thought of Yance. He would have outdone the flashiest of the pirates, for he was a lover of color in his clothes, although we'd little enough chance for anything of the kind, living as we did. I felt regret for him now. He'd have loved this wild, unruly, pirate town, its dark streets, its motley population, its crowds, tinkle of glasses and clink of coins, a town of blood, gold, gems, and lust, and all of it clad in silk and leather, often enough soiled, sometimes stained with blood, for the pirates I'd seen were rarely overclean.

It was a shouting, swearing, wine-guzzling, rum-swilling town with more powder than brains and every hand ready to grasp a blade. Murder was a small thing. A man might be stabbed and killed on a dance floor, and not a man would stop for his body, nor would the music cease to play. They'd merely dance around him.

Every night bodies were found in the streets, and no man inquired whose they were or how they came to be there. It was every man for himself, and the devil take the hindmost.

The black man who was one of those who would guard Diana was waiting at the door. He looked around at me. "Have you a knife?" he asked.

"I have a sword," I said, "and a pair of pistols when it comes to that."

"It is no place for either, although you may use them." From his waistband he drew a knife and scabbard. "Take this." I observed two more in that same waistband. "It is a good blade. At close quarters, in a dark place, it is better than a sword."

He handed it to me, and I tossed it up and caught it deftly by the hilt, wishing to get the feel of its weight and balance. It was a lovely thing, a two-edged blade and long, with a point like a needle.

"I am grateful," I said. "It is a lovely thing."

He flashed white teeth at me in a quick smile. "Ah, yes, suh! Lovely, indeed."

With the knife in my sash I went down the street to the waterfront where the long ships lay.

Sails furled, dripping a little from a quick shower, creaking as they rode the tide, fine, long, lovely ships, like things alive, made for speed and all lined with guns. I remembered the time long since when Yance and I had slipped aboard the pirate ship of Jonathan Delve, that old enemy of my father, and spiked his guns as the ship lay in the river at Jamestown.

The docks and beach, for many ships unloaded on the shore, were stacked with barrels and bales, mostly covered with spare sails or tarpaulins to shield them from the rain. Men moved among them, working, buying, selling, drinking. Here and there I paused to listen to idle talk, and having the gift of tongues, I recognized words in several languages. We at Shooting Creek in my father's time had men from all the world, Sakim, who spoke any language you might wish, and my father, who did a bit in several, and my mother, too, who had sailed with her father on his trading ship, sailed to India, the Malabar Coast, the Red Sea, and the far coast of Cathay. I knew a lot of words, few languages well, but the sense of many.

Yet all was not gold and excitement here. I noted a number of men missing legs or arms or hands, men with patches over an eye, with fingers missing, with faces twisted by scars. These were the casualties of piracy and the sea, those who did not go down to Davy Jones's locker or fiddler's green, who did not walk the plank or dance from a yardarm but who had been so maimed that they went no more to sea, although many an injured man did if he was a known gunner or the like. A good gunner was literally worth his weight in gold.

I stopped by one such, who sat on a bollard looking at the ships. "A fair evening to you," I said.

He was a stalwart, sun-browned man of forty-odd years, looking hard as a knot of oak but minus a leg and a hand. His eyes were glassy blue and uncomfortable to look upon, and I trusted him not even though he had but one hand.

"It may be," he said grimly. "I've no seen the bottom of a glass yet."

"You may see the bottom of several," I said, "if you've news of the *Abigail*."

"Ah? The *Abigail,* is it? I don't know your lay, nor can I make you out by the cut of your jib, but I'd say a canny man would have nothing for the *Abigail*. That's a cool lot aboard there."

"They are," I said, "and friends of mine. They are due to come into port, and I'd like to know when, for I am to sail with them."

"Sail? Aye, there's a good word! Once I swore I'd never off to sea again, but now that I cannot find a berth, I'd give an eye to be aboard a good ship now, with a prize in the offing. But they've no place for me." He held up the stump of an arm. "Look, man! Eleven year at sea and never more than a scratch or two, and then one ball from a Long Tom and flying wood, and I am torn to bits."

"You're lucky you made it," I replied. "Many do not."

"It depends on the view." He looked out over the water, then spat viciously into it. "I am a proud man, and one who worked hard and who fought well, damned well. Now all is gone and only to wait for dying."

"Nonsense!" I said irritably. "You've one hand and two eyes, and you look to have been a sharp man. Such a man should find something he can do, can make, can be. If you quit at this, it's because you've no guts in you."

He glared. "It is easy to talk. You're a whole man."

"Easy it is," I agreed, "but in your spot I'd not quit. There's always something."

From my pocket I took a gold coin. I showed it to him. "If I gave you a shilling," I said, "you'd buy a drink or several, but if I give you this, you could live a month on it if you did not drink. It will give you time to look about and use your head for something besides hanging those gold rings on."

"Who do you want killed?" he asked, glancing at the coin.

"I want an eye kept out for the *Abigail* and any report of her, and when it comes, take the word to Augustus Jayne. He will pass it to me. My name is Kin Sackett—"

"*Sackett?* Aye, I know that name! I knew a bloody tough man by the name once, a long time back. Saw him whip our skipper in the street. Whipped him well, he did, and easy as that. His name was Barnabas Sackett."

"My father," I said.

"Aye, you've the look of him, though taller, I think. Well, I should have sailed with him but didn't. The *Abigail,* is it? All right, I'll keep a weather eye out for her."

He reached a hand for the gold coin, and I slapped it in his palm. "I'd have done it for the shilling," he added. "I'm that hard up."

"I know you would have," I said, "but look about, see what you can find. There's many a berth ashore for a man who kens the sea. So find it."

So I walked away from him along the shore, and it was not until then that I realized it was almost dark. Shadows had found their way into the streets and lingered there, waiting the chance to rush out and engulf even the alongshore.

It was time I was getting back, but a sound of music drew me, and I went up the shore toward a place where the sailors were, and in the door I lingered, looking on at their gambling and carousing. A burly, bearded man grasped my arm. "Come! A drink! A glass of rum for old times' sake!"

"Old times?" I smiled at him. "What old times? I never saw you before."

His grin revealed a missing tooth. "So? Who

cares? It is for old times we both have had, old times
we should have had! Come! A drink?"

He thrust his way through the crowd, and
amused, yet reluctant, I followed. It was a noisy, not
unfriendly crowd, and many seemed to know him, for
they shouted invitations at him. Resolutely he shook
his head and went on until we found a table in a
corner.

"Rum? It is a raw, bold drink. Not bad, either, if
aged. But we will have something else, you and I, for I
know you now whether you know me or not. I know
you, lad, and it is a bit of the German you will have, a
delicate wine from Moselle."

"You can get it here?"

He looked over his shoulder at me from under
bushy brows, beginning to gray. "Aye, you can have
that and whatever you wish. It's me whose standing for
it, too, get that in your head."

It was a bare plank table, and the benches on
either side were crudely made. It was a rough place,
thrown roughly together for a rough trade. A big man
brought a bottle to the table, but my host waved it
away. "White wine from Moselle, a good wine, a
delicate wine."

"For you," the waiter said grudgingly, "although
we've little enough on hand."

When the waiter had gone, he looked across the
table at me. For the first time I looked at him, to really
see him.

He would be thirty pounds heavier than me and
four inches shorter, but little of the weight would be
fat. His beard was dark and streaked with a bit of
gray. His face was brown, wide and strong, with contemptuous, amused eyes, as if all he saw about him
was ironically amusing. His hands were thick and powerful, hands that had done a lot of work and some
fighting, too.

"Put it down that we're two ships that pass and
show our flags and each goes on his way. I like the
way you carry yourself, lad, and I'm not one to drink

alone nor talk to myself, although God knows it is all there's been a time or two."

He looked at me sharply. "You're no seafaring man, although you could be. Are you here for long?"

"A day or two more," I said.

I'd chosen the seat in the corner, and he sat opposite, but neither had a back to the room, for we sat in a sort of corner off the main room.

"Where are you for, then?"

"Plymouth. It's a place on the coast of what was once part of Virginia. They be calling it New England now, or they are starting to."

"Aye, I know the place. A psalm-singing lot, isn't it?"

"That's the latecomers. The first ones were an easier folk." The wine bottle was cold and the wine niccly chilled. He filled my glass, then his. "Yet it is not my country. I live in the mountains in the west of Carolina."

He shrugged. "Names! I have heard them used but know nothing of the land. How do you live?"

"We hunt. There is much wild game. We plant crops. It is a wild, beautiful land."

"Savages?"

"Aye, if you wish to call them so. They have their own way of life, which is good for them. I could live it, although I should miss books."

"Ah! There speaks a man of my own heart! I sensed it in you." He lifted his glass. "You would not guess, but twenty-odd years ago I studied at Cambridge and was nearly always at the head of them all. I was destined for the church."

"What then?"

He shrugged again. "What? A woman. I was young, and she was older but not wiser. We were discovered together. . . . Nothing had happened, worse luck, for we were not believed, and her husband set some ruffians on me to kill me."

He finished his glass and filled it again. "I was alone when they came, but I was strong, and they

151

believed me a harmless student, and I killed two of them with my blade and had to fly. And here, after more than twenty years, I am."

He looked at me across his glass, eyes twinkling with that same ironic amusement. "You should know my name. Or at least the one by which I am known. It is Rafe Bogardus."

"A good name. Mine is Kin Ring Sackett."

He smiled. "It is too bad, you know. You are a man I could like."

"Too bad?"

"Aye, and if I did not need the money, I'd not do it. I really wouldn't."

"Do what? I am afraid I do not know what you are talking about."

"No? You of all people should know, Kin Sackett, because you see, I have been paid to kill you."

I was astonished. "To kill me?"

"To kill you. Here . . . tonight."

Chapter XVII

It was my turn to laugh. "Finish your wine," I said.

His eyes were cool, suddenly wary. "You think I shall be drunken?"

"Of course not! But you so obviously enjoy it, I think you should have your fill of it before *you* die."

The laughter went from his eyes, and he measured me coolly, carefully. "Sackett, it has been said that I am the greatest swordsman in Port Royal, perhaps the greatest in Europe."

"I do not doubt it, but you are not now in Europe, nor are all the great swordsmen in Port Royal. After all"—I gestured widely—"they are mostly rabble. They cut and slash. What do they know?"

"And in Carolina?"

"Swordsmen are rare. We live by the musket and pistol there."

"So?"

"We shall see. And a pity, too, for you are a rare companion, and I was looking forward to talking to you of books and writing men, of magicians and satyrs, of gods and heroes. You spoke of a family?"

He dismissed them with a gesture. "That is long ago. They have forgotten me."

"Then I shall not have to worry."

"Worry?" He was scowling now.

"About sending word to them that you are dead, nor disposing of your belongings—if you have any."

"You are a fool," he said irritably. "You speak like a child."

But half my glass was gone, so I lifted it to my lips, tasted the wine, and put the glass down, and I took my time. No doubt he was a superb swordsman. No doubt he was confident. There were few good swordsmen in Virginia, Carolina, or Plymouth in these days, for men who were swordsmen had not yet begun to come across the sea. There were fighting men like Capt. John Smith, only he had returned to England. No doubt Bogardus, if that was his name, felt sure of winning.

I had rarely fought with a sword, yet from earliest childhood my father had trained me as his father had trained him, and I had the added advantage of working as a boy with Jublain, Jeremy Ring, and, above all, with Sakim. Not only was the Moslem a superb swordsman, but his style was entirely different from that of Europe. Therein, I hoped, would lie my advantage, if such it was, for he would be unprepared, I hoped, for that style of fencing.

But that I must conceal at first. I must seem orthodox and careful, defending myself as best I could and allowing him to believe I was more clumsy than skillful, then suddenly to try a trick upon him unused in the West.

The difficulty might be that at some time he had served in the Moslem countries and knew all that I knew. It was a risk I must take. Even if he knew, he might not expect such moves from me.

"Do you do this sort of thing often?" I asked. "I mean, do you kill men for money?"

"Why else? I am not such a fool as to kill them for amusement or just to be killing. It is simply I have found it more restful than piracy and an easier means to a living. If it is conscience you are thinking of, I have none. Men enter the world to die. I merely expedite matters."

"Or have them expedited for you."

He shrugged. "So far I live."

"Shall we order something to eat? If you are to die, I would not have it said you were hungry when you went out."

We ordered a meal, and I sat back in my chair and looked at him. He seemed undisturbed, but this I did not believe, for I was accepting the situation with more ease than he could have expected. He had thought to surprise me, and he had, yet my recovery had been swift and complete, and I was much less disturbed than he must have expected.

Now I was proposing that we dine, and he must have been puzzled by my reaction.

"You see," I continued, "your comment that you intend to kill me can be nothing but mildly interesting. Since I was a child, those of my family have been constantly threatened with death. I was born on a buffalo robe in the heat of an Indian battle with a swordsman standing above my mother to defend her during her labor.

"Since that day I have never known one in which my life was not in danger. Naturally you cannot expect me to be alarmed by your statement that you intend to kill me. Actually it greatly simplifies matters."

He scowled at me. I expect he had believed his calm statement would frighten or alarm me, and my manner irritated him. "Simplifies? What do you mean by that?"

The wine was good. I was no judge of such things, lacking experience, but to me it tasted well. "It is obvious, I should think. Here I have been attacked a number of times and from all sides, unexpectedly and in numbers. Now I no longer have to concern myself with that. Now I know my attacker. I know where the attack will come from and by whom. It makes it very easy."

"You will die nonetheless."

I laughed. "Who can say? You know what you can do, and that is very helpful. You are no doubt skilled, or you would not have survived, but I, too, have survived, and I think in a harsher world than yours."

"We will fight with swords. It is my weapon."

"Shall we? If this is to be a duel, then I am the challenged party and have the choice of weapons."

He glared at me. "I have chosen the weapons. When I kill you, it will be with a sword."

Our food was served, but Rafe Bogardus seemed in no mood to talk. On the other hand, something had loosened my tongue, though normally I talked little. Now, here, I talked over much, perhaps because I could see that it got on his nerves.

"Have you ever fought Indians, Bogardus? They are remarkably good. Not so muscular as some of us but wiry and supple, very quick to move and deadly at close-in combat with tomahawk or knife. They have no discipline, fighting much as they will, each man on his own, so they are rarely a match for us in sustained combat, but for the sudden attack, the quick raid, they are remarkable."

"You talk too much." He stared at me with no liking. "It will be a pleasure to kill you."

Finishing my meal, I pushed back the trencher and emptied what remained of the wine. "Then let's have at it, shall we?" I believed I had him off balance a mite and meant to keep him so. "I have no more time to dally." I stood up abruptly and with a gesture swept the dishes into his lap. The crash made people look up, and he sprang to his feet cursing, but I slammed the table against him, pinning him to the wall. Reaching across with my left hand, I took him by the throat and smashed his head hard against the wall. "You talk of killing! Why, you paltry fool! I am inclined to—"

My sudden shoving of the heavy table against him had caught him unawares, and my left hand, powerful from much swinging of an axe, held him tight to the wall. With my right I drew my knife and held the point of it under his nostril. "I've a notion to let you have about four inches of this up your nose," I said, "but you're hardly worth it."

We had spectators then, a room full of them. I turned my head slightly. "He's been paid to kill me," I said conversationally, "and I don't think he can do it. I am going to turn him loose now, for, after all, he took the money, and he must make his try."

"Kill him," somebody said. "Have done with it. I know the man, and you'll never have him by the throat again."

"He shall have his chance to run or fight," I said, and I flicked his nostril only with the very point of the blade, but it drew blood, which trickled slowly down his lip and his chin. Then I stepped back and dropped the knife into its scabbard.

Rafe Bogardus shoved back the table. The way he moved showed the strength of the man. Surprisingly he was calm.

"All right, you have had your bit of amusement. Now I shall kill you."

"Like I said," the same voice said, "you should have killed him while you had him trapped. Never give them a second chance."

Men pulled back from us, and their women, too. The light had a reddish glow, and there were shadows beyond the tables and chairs. The room, despite its size, was crowded. The atmosphere was hot and close, smelling of the crowded, often unwashed bodies. There was also the smell of rum and tobacco smoke.

Bogardus drew his sword. He was very cool now, and had I ever doubted his ability, I could not do so at this moment, for he held himself with an absolute certainty, sure that he could make his kill.

He discarded his coat, and I did likewise. I drew my own blade with less confidence. The only fighting I had done with a sword had been in these past few days, and little enough that was. My father had been said to have been a swordsman of uncommon skill and the others, also. I had good teachers, *but were they really that good?*

What possible standard of comparison could I have?

Grimly the thought came to mind. In the next few minutes I would know.

He saluted me. "Now, Sackett, you die!"

He lunged swiftly, and I parried his blade. I think it surprised him, for he may have planned to end it all with that first thrust.

He was more cautious then, discovering that I knew a little, at least. He began to fence, working toward me, pushing me back, deliberately testing me, and I had the good sense to be clumsy, or was it actually that I was awkward? What skill I had I must hold in keeping, and I must fend off his attacks while watching for my chance, nor must I appear to be defending myself with skill.

He was strong. I could feel it in his blade, and he had the delicate touch of the master. He lunged again, and a quick skip back was all that saved me. As it was, the point of his blade ripped my shirt. I heard a gasp from some onlooker, and someone else said, in the almost total silence, "Good, isn't he?"

Aye, he was good. I discovered that quickly enough and was hard put to defend myself, having no need to feign awkwardness with the speed and skill of his attack. Had it not been for the few fights of the past days, I might have failed, but often it takes little time to recall old skills, and I had fenced hour upon hour with my teachers.

The art of the sword had developed greatly in the past few years, but as in all such things, it had come to be highly stylized. The weapon was controlled largely with the fingers; the cuts were made with the first few inches of the blade. The endeavor was to make light, slicing cuts and not to overpower with great slashing cuts. He was swift, sure, and very strong. My own efforts were largely to stave off his attack, and somehow I managed it.

Sweat began to bead on my brow, but as I warmed, I felt the old skills returning. He was better than Jeremy Ring, I thought, perhaps as good as Jublain, but not, I believed, as good as my father had been. Sakim? Ah, Sakim was another sort of man, and his style of fencing was much different.

My style was not orthodox, and I could see that disturbed him while it gave him added confidence, for to him it meant only that I did not know what I was doing or knew it not well enough.

The room was hot, the air close. He pressed me hard, striving to work me into a corner, which would impair my movements, for my speed afoot had surprised him. He thrust; I parried and slid my blade along his. He leaped back just in time, or I might have knicked his wrist. He shot me a sudden sharp glance and made a cut to my cheek that I parried with difficulty. He kicked a small bench toward my feet, and as I sprang out of the way, he lunged, his sword point tearing my shirt at the waist.

We fought savagely then, all pretense thrown aside; it was thrust, parry, head and flank cuts, and he drew first blood with a sudden thrust to the head that opened a thin red cut on my cheek. An instant later, and his point found my ribs, just an inch below the heart but wide of it. He grinned wolfishly. "Soon!" he exclaimed. "Soon you shall be dead!"

He pressed hard, and I fell back, working desperately to ward off his continual attacks. He dropped his blade a little, an invitation I declined to accept, but instantly he moved in with a dazzling series of movements that had the spectators cheering. A thrust followed by cuts to the arm, right cheek, head, and chest. How I parried them I will never know, but as he drew back, momentarily overextended, I thrust suddenly and sharply for his throat. The thrust was high and a hair wide of the mark. It ripped the ruffle at his collar but merely scratched his neck.

He was dangerous, too dangerous. I was in serious trouble and knew it. The man was good, very good. He made a riposte to the head following a parry of my thrust.

He was intent now, ready for the kill. Each fencer tends to favor certain moves, those that are easy for him, to the exclusion of others, and a skillful man with a blade will soon determine which of these his opponent is apt to use. Knowing this, I had deliberately been responding to certain moves of his with the accepted counter. Yet to continue to do so would be to let myself be killed, and the trap, if trap it was, could be used but once. His responses were quick and easy, and at any moment now, having learned what he believed I would do to each move of his, he must be ready.

So far I had been lucky. My face was streaming with perspiration. Twice he glanced at my eyes. Was he trying to find fear there? Believe me, there was enough of that, for the man was good, and it had been long since I had fenced enough to matter.

Around us men crowded, gold gleaming from their ears. One huge bearded man had a heavy gold necklace that must have come from looted Inca treasure. They watched, intent, and I was conscious of them only as a backdrop to what happened here. The gleaming blades, the movement in and out, the circling, the darting steel, as in some weird ballet of death where I was at once the participant and the observer. The tricks I knew seemed to find no place here, for the man left no chance. For all his strength, he moved lightly, easily, and with confidence. My arm would grow weary; my strength would go.

He was smiling now, his eyes bright with purpose. He feinted a head cut and then thrust at my ribs. My parry was quick, but I was too far from him for a good thrust at the body, so with a flick of the wrist I cut him along the inner sword arm with the back of the blade.

It sliced, and deep. I saw him wince, saw him start to step back, and attacked instantly. His parry was slow.

There was blood on his sleeve now. Somebody gasped and pointed. There was a splash of blood on the floor. I feinted for the head; he tried to parry, and I thrust hard for the ribs. He stepped back quickly, and I moved in.

He was a swordsman. Even now, his arm badly cut, he fought beautifully. Yet there was death in his face. I could see it, and he knew it. I feinted, held my thrust, then, on the instant, followed through. His parry was started too soon; my point slipped past it, and his recovery was slow. The blade slid ever so neatly along his ribs, through the hide and between the bones, and withdrew almost as if there had been nothing but a shadow there.

Bogardus missed a step, his whole side now stained with blood, red blood in a widening blotch on the side of his shirt.

My point lowered a little. "I have no wish to kill you."

"I am dead. Finish what you have begun."

"Have done. You have chosen a poor profession. If you live, choose another."

"I took money to kill you."

"Keep the money. You tried."

Taking up my coat with my left hand, I turned my back on him and went into the crowd, and with my naked blade still in my hand it opened before me.

When I was on the street again, I looked carefully about. This was no time to be careless, but of one thing I was sure. My sightseeing in Jamaica as well as my business were over.

Tomorrow I would find John Tilly, and tomorrow I would take Diana Macklin home.

Chapter XVIII

Strong blew the wind, dark the angry clouds, vivid the lightning. Upon the deck, near the mainmast shrouds I stood, one hand upon them to steady me, my eyes out upon the sea, its dark, huge waves lifting like great upthrusts of black glass, ragged along the breaking edge. My father had gone to sea in his time, but I had no love for it. He had bred a landsman, whether he preferred it or not.

There was a challenge in the storm, a magnificence in the power of the sea, and I rode the deck like a gull upon the wind and confessed inside me that while afraid, I was also drunk with it. Salt spray stung my face; my tongue licked it, tasted it, loved it. She put her bows down and took a great sea over them, and the water came thundering back, the decks awash, the scuppers sucking and gasping.

John Tilly came down upon the deck and stood beside me. " 'Tis a raw night, lad, a raw night! We be sailing north with the coast out yonder, and many a proud ship gone down in weather no worse than this!"

"I'll be glad when I'm ashore," I told him frankly. "I want my feet upon solid earth."

"Aye!" he said grimly. "So think we all. We think ofttimes in the night that once the storm is over and the storm gone, we will go ashore and stay there. We'll tell ourselves that in the night watches, but when the day has come, and our money is spent ashore, then we go seeking a berth again, and off to sea it is."

"I am a man of the hills and forest."

"It may be so. Your father made a good seafaring man, though, and belike you could do the same, given time. You are a strong one and active, and you've a cool head about you. I saw that ashore there."

"Ashore?"

"In the fight with Bogardus. Ah, lad, I feared for you! I've seen him with a blade before, but you had him bested—"

"My father taught me, and the others."

"It showed. I could see your father's hand there, but you've the greater reach and height. He never beat a better man than Bogardus. But you did not kill him."

"I have no wish to kill. A man's life is a precious thing, though he waste it. A life is greater than gold and better than all else, so who am I to take it unless need be?"

"He intended to take yours."

"He has not my thoughts, nor my wishes nor my desires, and if he lives, life may bring him wisdom. Who knows? It is a good thing to live, to walk out upon such a deck as this and feel the wind, to walk in the forest on a moonlit night or out upon some great plateau and look westward—"

"You, too?"

"What do you mean?"

"Ah, you are your father's son! He looked to the westward, too! To his far blue mountains. But was it the mountains? Or was it that something beyond? We need such men, lad, men who can look to the beyond, to ever strive for something out there beyond the stars. It is man's destiny, I think, to go forward, ever forward. We are of the breed, you and I, the breed who venture always toward what lies out there—westward, onward, everward."

We were silent then, riding the deck as it tipped and slanted. She was a good ship, even as she had been in my father's time, and she bore a good name.

"I wonder if I shall ever see her again?"

"Who, lad?"

"My mother. She went to England, you know, so that Noelle would not grow up in the forest among wild men. My father sorely missed her."

"Aye, he did that. But she was wise, lad, wiser than all, and you'll be proud of the lass when you see her. A fine lady she is, although but a girl yet, and Brian! What a gentleman! They tell me at the Inns of Court that he has a rare way with words."

"It is the Welsh in him. When did they not?"

"And Jeremy, lad? And Lila? Fare they well?"

"How else? Athough it be months since I have seen them. When I go south again, I shall go calling. Jeremy is a fine woodsman now and an owner of wide lands, and Lila serves no longer but is mistress of her own estate."

"What of the lass below there?" Tilly asked. "She has eyes for you, lad."

I felt wary and uncomfortable. "It may be. We have talked a bit."

"She's a fine lass, a brave, tall girl. You'd be wise to take her, lad, if that is the way you both feel. I deem there's been trouble behind you?"

"She comes from Cape Ann . . . on the coast of what they are calling New England. They thought her a witch there, and she was twice taken by slavers, the last time through sheer vengeance, dropping down of a sudden, knocking her father about and carrying her off. It was Pittingel. He wished me to see her with him, for to kill is not enough. He wanted me to suffer in my mind as well."

"And now?"

"To her father again if he lives. What else will come we shall talk of then, but if I take her home with me, it is a far travel for a lass, far through woods and the places where savages are."

"She'll stand to it. There's a likely craft, lad, and one to sail any sea. You can see it in the clear eyes of her and the way she carries her head. Give me always a woman with pride, and pride of being a woman. She's such a one."

We talked then of ships and the sea and of the old ways of men upon the water, of how men measured the altitude of a star by the span of a wrist or a hand outstretched before them and how they guided themselves by the flight of birds, the fish they saw, and the way water curls around an island or a cape and shows itself as a special current in the sea. "Terns will fly far out to sea and rest upon the water when they wish, but the herring gulls never get more than seventy-five or eighty miles from land, and at eventide they fly toward shore to roost. When you see them winging all one way toward evening, there's land there, son, land. It has saved many a seafaring man, knowing that. Men steered by the flight of birds and found their way by the stars for these thousand years or more."

At last I went to my bunk, but once stretched upon it, I lay long awake. Was Diana indeed the girl for me? Or was I, too, to have that westward feeling?

Jubal Sackett had it. Where was he? How far westward had he gone? Did he live yet, that brother of mine? Or did his body lie in the rich black earth beneath the trees out there near the great river of which he spoke?

We Sacketts wandered far upon the face of the world. Was there something in us truly that moved us ever westward? Did we fulfill some strange destiny? Some drive decreed by God, the wind or the tides that move across the world? Why Jubal, of us all? Why not Brian, who had gone again east? Yet I knew within me that Brian's way was westward, too. *Knew?* Was it the gift of which our father had spoken? The gift of second sight we sometimes had?

My father lay buried in the hills that he sought, but he died bravely there and no doubt rested well. The red men who killed him knew where his body lay, and sometimes they came there and left gifts of meat upon the grave, offerings to a brave man gone, a man who fought well and died well.

Where, in its time, would my body lie?

Westward, a voice told me, off to the *westward.*

So be it. Only that I lived well and strongly before that time came and left my sons to walk the trails my foot would never tread. For it is given that no man can do it all, that each must carry the future forward a few years and then pass the message on to him who follows.

There must be fine strong boys and goodly women to do what remained to be done, and Diana? Who else to be the mother of them? And the woman to walk beside me on the hills where the rhododendron grew?

Soon.

The dark shore lay off there, somewhere beyond the black wings of night; it lay there, that long white beach upon which I played as a boy. And somewhere, not far from here, was that place of which I had heard, that place upon the open sea where may lie the gates to another world. My father in his time had seen them, or was it a trick of the sun upon the sea? A mirage, perhaps? Who could know. For now we sailed off the Carolina coast. Bermuda lay off to the northeast.

When my eyes opened again, there was a shaft of sunlight falling across the deck, a shaft of sunlight that moved slowly and easily with a gentle roll of the ship. The storm had gone.

Rising from my bed, I looked out—a fair day and a fine breeze blowing.

John Tilly was on the quarterdeck when I went out to get a smell of the wind. He seemed preoccupied, so I asked no questions. Several times he glanced aloft as if expecting some signal from the lookout at the masthead.

A cabin boy came up the ladder to the quarterdeck. "The lady, maister," he said, "she asks if you would break fast wi' her?"

"I will be along at once." I turned to Tilly. "Captain? Will you join us?"

He threw me a quick, impatient glance. "No, eat without me. I shall be busy here."

Diana was at the table when I came into the

cabin, and I had never seen her look more lovely. John Tilly had gone into his stores and found some captured clothing taken in one of the constant sea battles. Attacked by pirates, they had proved too stiff a foe and had taken the pirate ship as prize.

There was sunlight through the stern light, and we sat long over our food, talking of many things. The cabin boy served us chocolate, the drink from Mexico of which we had heard much. Yet even as we talked, I was disturbed by Tilly's manner. Usually the most gracious of men, he had been abrupt and obviously worried.

The weather was fine. Did he sense a change? And the lookout aloft? What would he—

An enemy ship? Pirates?

Joseph Pittingel had ships, several of them. And we had evidence enough of his hatred. Had that lookout seen something? Or had John Tilly himself?

When our meal was finished, I got up. "Diana, change into something—anything—I do not think our troubles are over."

She wasted no time asking for explanations. Too often in emergencies had I seen people who took the time to ask "Why" not live long enough to receive an answer.

As for myself, I went to my chest and took my two pistols and charged them anew. Then I laid out my sword and thrust a knife into my waistband. What was happening I knew not, but it was best to be prepared, to stand ready for whatever.

Off to the westward would be the Virginia or Maryland coast, how far I did not know and had best learn. Ours was a good vessel, manned by sturdy men, but the best vessel and the best men can meet their match.

When I appeared on deck, the lookout was talking to Captain Tilly. Avoiding them, I walked to the rail and looked all about. I was perfectly aware that the distance one can see from a ship's deck was limited indeed, not nearly so far as one would believe. At fifteen feet above the water I could see perhaps four and a half miles, and the lookout from the topmast could see no more than ten.

John Tilly left the lookout to return aloft and walked across the deck to me. He noted the arms. "You do well to go armed," he said quietly. "I believe we shall have trouble."

"The lookout has seen a ship?"

"No, and that worries me, for there was one close to us in the night."

"You are sure? What could have become of him?"

"Ah, that is what bothers me, Master Kin. What, indeed? And why?

"It lacked but an hour or so of dawn when I was awakened. I came on deck, and Tom Carboy—he is my mate—pointed out to me a black shadow of something against the sea. It was some distance off, and by the time I reached the deck, indistinct. I could not make her out, only that there was something.

"Carboy is a good, steady man. He had been watching ahead, for the gale was still blowing, although it had begun to ease somewhat, and some bad cross-seas were running. This is the devil's own stretch of water, you know, and there are currents that create a very mixed-up sea in some storms. He was alert to what happened, to see her ease into those big seas and not take them on the beam.

"He had his eyes glued to those big ones, and his helmsman was ready to meet them across the bow when he happened to turn around and look astern. It seemed it had been only minutes since he had done so, but there was a ship coming up, overhauling him rapidly, a ship without lights.

"He called me, but something must have alarmed the dark vessel because it seemed to fall back, and by the time I reached the deck, it could not be identified."

"I do not believe in ghost ships," I said, "although in these waters—"

"I do not believe in them, either. Yet why a ship showing no lights? Why did she fall back?"

"Where is she now?"

"My lookout can see nothing. Once, when he went aloft for the first time and just after daylight, he thought he glimpsed a topm'st."

"Then if it is a ship, she may be following us? Hanging back, over the horizon, waiting?"

"That is what I fear. She waits until the darkness of another night, then overtakes us for a sudden surprise attack."

"A pirate?"

"It may be, or your old friend Pittingel following you still. The *Abigail* is a good sailer and by most accounts a fast ship, but she is nowhere near as speedy as some of the pirate vessels. Joseph Pittingel has one—the *Vestal*—that is very fast."

Again I glanced astern. If she lay back there, twelve or thirteen miles off, she would need three hours to close in, perhaps four. Yet as soon as it became dark, she could begin to move closer, and we would not see her until she was just a short distance off, within cannon shot or nearly so. I liked it not and said so.

"Is there no way we can evade her? Sail toward shore, for example?"

He shrugged. "It might be, but we draw too close in, and we might get caught against a lee shore, and no sailor wishes to sail too close in because of the hazards."

We stood silent then, each busy with what thoughts he had. Suddenly the bright sea had become a menacing place where danger lurked just beyond the horizon.

"We shall try," Tilly said at last, "but 'tis a bad shore yonder, and many a fair ship has been trapped there. He would not fall back unless he was sure of his speed."

"Why did he not attack this morning?"

169

Tilly shrugged. "It was late. By the time he over-took us, day would be breaking, for as he moved toward us, we were moving away. His chance for surprise was gone."

Throughout the day we sailed, yet we did more. We cleared the deck for action and made ready the guns. She had fewer guns than in my father's time, for the weight of them deprived her of cargo.

Tilly kept a man aloft, but he saw nothing, re-ported nothing. Dusk came, and we made ready. Dark-ness came at last, and Tilly sent word forward to extinguish all lights. I went below. "Diana? Trouble comes. The light must go out."

"It is a bother," she protested. "I was remaking a dress." She put out the light and in the darkness said, "I shall fix the curtains, then mayhap a little light?"

"None," I warned her. "None at all. There is a dark ship yonder that will attack, we think, this night. We will move in toward shore, and anything may happen, so be ready."

She was silent for a long moment. "What shore is it, Kin? Where are we now?"

It irritated me that I had not thought to ask Tilly, for it was always important to have a location, and I could only surmise it was somewhere north of that coast of which I knew a little. Perhaps north of the mouth of the Chesapeake Bay.

After saying as much and warning her we might be in a boat erelong and to dress warmly, taking whatever she might need that could be easily carried, I went on deck.

It was cold and windy there. The sails pulled well, and we were tacking across the wind, working in toward shore, and well I knew how a mariner dreaded sailing along a shore at any time, let alone at night. When landsmen write of such things, they always tell of the first mariners hugging the shore, which is utter non-sense and something no seaman in his right mind would do. The open sea has fewer dangers.

John Tilly loomed near me. "She's back there and

closing in. I saw a mast draw a black thread across a star."

"It might have been a bird."

"Might have been, but it was not."

"Is not Maryland somewhere about here?" I asked.

"It is, and a coast of which I know little. Always along here I am well at sea and wanting only more sea room. Yet I hear there are islets and reefs, offshore winds. Who knows?"

No darker night had I seen and no blacker a sea. The wind held steady, and the *Abigail* was sailing well. I walked to the taffrail, standing over where Diana must be, and looked astern.

Nothing.

Only the night, only the darkness, only the wind and the sea. Occasionally a star showed among scudding clouds. And then, suddenly, she was there coming up alongside like a black ghost from a black and glassy sea. She was at our stern, her bowsprit dangerously near, and I saw a huge man with a black beard making ready to swing a grapnel. They would board us then.

He swung the grapnel, and I shot him. I never recalled drawing my pistol, only the flare of the gun and the startled look of the man as the ball took him in the chest. He fell forward, his grapnel going wild, and then she was alongside us, and her men were swarming over.

Somewhere I heard Tilly shout, and from our guns there was a belch of flame. I saw a section of bulwark go flying, heard a man scream, and then all was flames and fighting. I fired again, my second gun; it was knocked from my fist, and I smashed the man in the mouth and drew a knife, plunging it deep in his side.

Then I had a sword out, shifting the knife to the other hand, Italian style, and I went among them, cutting, slashing, thrusting. Men were all about me, and it was a wild corner of hell we were in.

A man went down beneath my feet grasping wildly at my legs, and I kicked free and fought clear of the mass. Tilly had rallied some of his men around him, and they were encircled by attackers. Yet the broadside had done its work, delayed though it had been, for flames were leaping up from fires aboard their ship, and I could see men dancing about fighting the fire that suddenly leaped to the sails, which went up in a great billow of flame like an explosion from a powder magazine.

Flaming bits of canvas fell, and one man, his clothing afire, leaped over into the dark, rolling sea. One glimpse I had of him, musket raised to fire when the sail caught and the flame leaped up at him like a great hand with a dozen fingers. I saw his eyes distended with horror, and then the flame was all about him, and he plunged from the topmast into the sea, screaming all the way.

Desperately I fought my way to the ladder and down it to the door that opened from the great cabin to the deck.

It swung wide, and I plunged through. A man opposed me, a man with rings in his ears and broken teeth, a man who swung a cutlass at my head. I parried the blow and went in with the dagger, and it took him in the ribs. His foul breath was an instant in my face, and then he slid down me to the deck, and I stepped over him into the cabin.

Diana stood there, her back to the bulkhead, tall, lovely, and perfectly still. Eyes wide, she faced a man whose back was to me, but I recognized him instantly. It was Joseph Pittingel.

"So now," he said to her, "I shall kill you!"

"First try to kill the man behind you," she told him coolly. "I think him too much for you."

"Such a paltry trick!" he sneered. "I think—"

Then something in her eyes did make him turn, and he reacted instantly. Foolishly I had expected him to speak, to warn, to threaten, to beg, I know not.

He lunged, sword in hand, and the blade might have taken my life but for the pistol I had thrust empty into my belt. The blade struck it, and before he could move again, my own blade had smashed his aside. He thrust wildly at me, eyes bulging with hatred and fury. My fingers turned the blade off mine, and I held my blade up and ready. He came at me again, then stopped suddenly, and turning his sword, raised it to slash sideways at Diana!

She stood, back to the bulkhead, nothing between her and the swinging sword edge. I struck swiftly up between arm and body, and my blade caught him only in time, cutting deep into the muscles that held arm to shoulder.

His blade flew from his fingers, narrowly missing Diana, and fell with a clatter to the deck.

He turned on me, blood streaming down his half-severed arm.

Ignoring him, I held out my hand. "Diana? Shall we go now?"

Chapter XIX

We reached the deck, and Tilly was there and a half-dozen others he had rallied about him. The fighting was over, and a body rolled in the scuppers; another hung limply on a bulwark, and even as I looked it slid off the bulwark and lay sprawled upon the wet deck.

The black ship was blacker still and far down in the water, her decks awash.

She lay there, a cable's length away, and we could see a few men about the deck.

"How is it, John?" I asked Tilly.

"Bad—bad," he said. "She's been hulled, I think, and will go down."

Our deck had an ugly feel to it, a heavy, sullen feel that I liked not. "Will she make the shore?" I suggested. "If we could get some sail on her—?"

"Aye, I was thinkin' o' that. Would you take the chance? It would be safer than the boats, and at least we can have a go at it."

He started to give the orders, but the crew were already moving.

"What of them?" I asked.

He glanced toward the sinking *Vestal*, if that was indeed who she was. "They've the same chance we have, and they came looking for it. Let them bide."

Leaving Diana on the quarterdeck, I went along forward, picking things up and making her shipshape. The two bodies left on the deck were only that, the life gone from them, so I dumped both overside.

I found a pistol upon the deck and thrust it behind my waistband. We were moving, and the man at the wheel had put the helm over.

We were taking on water, and it was a wild chance we took to make for the shore. What if we hung up on a sandbar off the coast? Yet there was a chance to save both crew and ship as well as the cargo, and the ship was the *Abigail*, almost a part of our family.

Yet she had a sullen feel to her, and I liked it not. "Stand by," I told Diana. "I must know where you are if the worst comes. We'll make the shore together."

"Or drown," she said.

"We'll make the shore," I said, "for I am wishful of taking you to my cabin in the mountains yonder, the far blue mountains, as my father called them. And we'll make it, too. I will need sons to seed the plains with men and build a country there, a place with homes."

She could carry but little sail, but we moved, and somewhere off to the westward was land, a lee shore but a shore.

Once the canvas was set, there was little we could do except to wait. Slowly the remaining sailors came on deck, each with a small parcel of his belongings.

"Make the boat ready," Tilly suggested. "Store her with food and water, what bedding we will need, and arms as well as powder."

"You expect more trouble?" one of the men asked.

Tilly glanced at him. "To be prepared, that is the price of existence, lad. Help them pack the boat now."

He took the wheel himself as we neared shore. The sky was faintly gray behind us, but the dim, low line of the shore offered nothing, promised nothing.

Of the sinking *Vestal*, we saw nothing. It was likely she might sink where she was, but she might float as well, might float for some time.

Suddenly I bethought myself of Pittingel. The man was below in the cabin, whether dead or dying, I did not know. Yet when I went below, sword in hand, he was gone.

There was much blood upon the deck, and there was blood on the sill of the stern light. He had dropped into the sea, when or where I did not know, or even whether he had done so of choice or been dropped by somebody.

Gone. It made me uneasy to think he might still live. Yet he had been badly cut, if not fatally. That he had lost much blood was obvious, yet his disappearance left us with one less thing to worry about at the moment, and the moment was all important.

For me the shore loomed near and vastly to be desired, for as fine a seaman as my father may have been, I knew that I was not. In time I might have become one, but there was to be no such time if I could help it. My destiny lay in the mountains of my own homeland, and the shore yonder was the first step. Once ashore, I could go anywhere. At sea I was at best uncomfortable.

Fortune seemed to be with us now that our vessel was sinking beneath us, for the wind had lessened, and the waves were nothing to speak of. Slowly but steadily we moved toward the coast. Now we could hear the beat of it upon the long, sandy shore. It was a familiar sound, for it was upon such a barrier of sand that I had played as a child, on the Carolina sounds.

"There's enough sea to carry us in. She'll hit hard enough to wedge herself in the sand."

"It is my fault, John," I said. "Had I not come to you, none of this would have happened."

He brushed my comment away with a gesture. "Your father gave me this ship. Owned a piece of it, actually, although I never had a chance to give him his share. She's a good vessel, and I'd like to save her."

"We can try," I offered.

He considered that. He was a thoughtful, careful man, and to lose his ship hurt him hard. He eased her speed by taking in some canvas, not that she was making any speed to speak of, but he kept on just enough to give her a little help with the steering.

There were no toppling combers, no welcoming crowds, no fanfare of trumpets when we came in to the shore. The sea had quieted still more, and the dawn had turned the sand from dull gray to pale flesh color, and we came in easy like bobbing flotsam on the tide, and we bumped our bow into the sand and stayed there.

We had the boat over and got some men ashore, and with a sigh of relief, I was first to put a foot on land. On land I was my own man again, subject to no vagaries of wind or sea. Yonder was the forest, here was the shore, and both were matters I understood. Somewhere far off, beyond the sand and the trees, there would be mountains, the blue mountains of home.

We unloaded what we could on the shore and at my advice moved back into the forest's edge where we not only would have fuel but would be less easily seen and our numbers estimated. Then we got a line ashore tied about a buried log or "deadman."

The cook made a meal over a fire of my building. I loaded a musket and my two pistols, and leaving all close by the fire, I scouted a bit. We had landed on a narrow barrier island, but the mainland was but a short distance away. I found tracks of deer and glimpsed some wild turkeys but did not shoot. We had food enough for the time; and it was of no use to warn anyone who might be within hearing of our presence. I went back and sat on the sand with my back against a great driftwood log and watched the fire.

John Tilly and some of his men were going over the vessel.

"Hulled twice," Tilly said, "and she took on a bit of water, but if the weather holds, we can pump her out and float her again."

"I am a fair hand with working wood," I said, "and a better hand at what needs a strong back, so I'll stand a trick at the pumps."

We talked it over, weighing this and that in conversation as we ate. Nor would we wait until dawn, for who knew what might develop with the weather.

"And the *Vestal?*" I said. "Do you think she sank?"

"I do, but Hans—he's a fo'c'sle hand—said he saw them get a boat or two free of her. So we'd best keep a sharp lookout."

"Aye." We could see the beach for a good stretch in either direction, but there were woods behind us. Yet I fancied myself in the woods and feared naught but an Indian.

"If they get her afloat again," Diana said, "what will you do?"

"Turn inland," I said. "It is a far piece to where my home lies and almost as far to Shooting Creek, but we'll be for it.

"John?" I spoke suddenly, remembering. "There's an island in a bay not far from here where a man named Claiborne has a station. He does a bit of trade, has a pinnace or two. You might sell him some of your cargo if all is not spoiled or trade for furs. He's a good man. Cantankerous but good."

"Aye. I know the name."

Several of the crew were already at work on the hull; others were already manning the pumps. Leaving Diana to get together what clothes she could, for Tilly had told her to take whatever she found that was useful, I went to the pumps. Any kind of physical work was always a pleasure. I was strong and enjoyed using my strength, and the pumps were a simple matter that left one time to think.

For hours we pumped, and the water flowed from the hull in a steady stream. By nightfall we had lowered the level considerably, and one of the holes in the hull had been repaired. Other men, while not busy at the pumps, went about repairing damage to lines and rigging that had been incurred during the brief fight.

We had lost four men: two had fallen over the side, and two had been struck down on deck. How many the *Vestal* lost we had no idea. Our sudden broadside as they came up to use their grappling irons had been totally unexpected.

The day remained quiet and the sea calm. The sunlight was bright, not too warm, and the work went forward swiftly. In the late afternoon I went ashore and gathered fuel for the night, taking the time to scout around while doing so. The long stretch of beach and shore was empty, nor could I see any smoke or sign of life to the shoreward.

None knew better than I that while thousands of square miles of land went unoccupied and unused except by the casual hunter, Indian war parties were constantly coming and going through the country. If we escaped a visit, we would be fortunate indeed.

Over the campfire we sat together. John Tilly spoke of floating his ship on the morrow, then asked of our plans.

"I am ashore," I said, "and it is my world. I think we will go inland from here."

"It is a long way." Tilly glanced at Diana. "Are you prepared for such a walk?"

"Where he goes, I shall go." She smiled. "I have walked much, Captain. At Cape Ann there were no horses nor carriages."

"There will be savages. You understand that?"

"I do."

Henry had come up close to the fire. I had seen but little of him these past days aboard ship, for he had stayed much by himself, leaving Diana and me to talk when we could. It was a thoughtfulness I appreciated.

He spoke now. "And if you wish, I shall go with you."

"We wish it, Henry," I said. "You will like my mountain country."

He shrugged. "I have no home now. There is no use returning across the sea, for much would have changed, and I have changed, also. If you will have my company, I will come with you."

"There is one thing that yet must be done, John. As you did for my father, so I would have you do for us."

He raised a quizzical eyebrow. "Marry you? Aye, I will do it, lad, and be glad. She's a fine lass."

Tom Carboy had also come up to the fire, leaving behind the work on the ship to drink a bowl of broth. "If the lass will have me, I would be glad to stand in her father's place, to give her away."

She looked up at him very seriously. "Tom, had I no father of my own, I'd be glad to claim you for mine. Would you stand for him?"

The old sailor looked around, suddenly shy. "I would, miss, I would indeed."

"Tomorrow, then?" Tilly suggested. "At the nooning, to give all a chance to make ready."

I went for a walk along the shore. Was this the right way for me? Something inside me said it was so, yet I did not know. I had small experience with women and knew little of their ways except what I had observed when Lila and my mother were about, to say nothing of Noelle, young though she was, and the wives of Kane O'Hara and some others whom I'd seen. Yet being a husband could be no more difficult than some other things I'd done.

The shore was quiet, with only the rustle of the surf along the sand and the mewing of the gulls. I sat on a driftwood log and watched the water roll in and saw the moon rise over the sea.

She would be well received amongst us, and Temperance, Yance's wife, was her old friend. It was a good thing, a very good thing.

The sky was cloudless. It would be a good day on the morrow, a good day. We would launch the *Abigail* again, with luck, and Diana and I would be married.

There was a faint sound in the sand behind me, and I came swiftly to my feet, taking two quick steps forward before turning, a hand on a pistol.

Three Indians stood there in the moonlight, their

hands by their sides. Each carried a spear, each a bow and quiver of arrows slung over a shoulder.

The nearest one, a broad man with a deep chest, spoke. The tongue was familiar.

"You are Catawba?" I asked in his tongue.

Immediately they were excited, and all began to talk until the first man lifted a hand for silence. "You speak our words. How is this that you, a white man, speak to us in our tongue?"

"I have a friend," I said, "who was the friend of my father before I was born. His name was Wa-ga-su. Many Catawba have fought beside us."

"Wa-ga-su strong man, great warrior. I know."

"You are far from home," I said. "What can I do for you?"

"Eat," he said. "We are much hungry."

"Come," I said, "and walk beside me that they will know you for a friend."

Surely fortune was with me, for now we should have company on our long trek to Shooting Creek, for our way was also the way of the Catawba.

Chapter XX

The way of our return to the home of my people must be devious, for the Catawba had enemies, as did we. Yet I was told by the Catawba there had been no raids since the death of my father, that the Seneca bided their time. "They will come," he said, "for they will wish to know if the sons are as strong as the father."

"Let them rest beside their fires, in the lodges they have built," I said. "We wish to kill no more of them."

The Catawba added sticks to the small fire. "The old men know that times change, and they would be content with peace, but what of the young men who wish to test themselves? How better than against the sons of Barnabas?"

In the morning we would float the *Abigail,* and the Catawba would help. They were six strong young men, for although but three had come to the fire, three others had remained behind until it was known how they would be received. Had they known I was a son of Barnabas, they would all have come at once, for had not the Catawba always been the friend of the white man? And did not the sons of Barnabas know this?

"Many white men do not know the Catawba are friendly, and to them all Indians look alike, so be careful whom you approach."

The Catawba smiled cheerfully. "So we came to one man alone. If one man is unfriendly, he is easier to kill than many."

They looked at Diana. "She is your woman?"

"Tomorrow she becomes my woman. You have come in time."

"What do they say?" Diana asked.

My smile was wide when I told her the question and my answer. She flushed. "You have not asked *me!*"

"But I did ask!"

"Not when we would marry. It cannot be tomorrow. I am not ready."

"John Tilly," I explained, "is not only a ship's master but an ordained minister. As such, he married my mother and father, and he can marry us.

"Tomorrow we will float his ship. He cannot linger on this coast. It would be foolhardy to trust the weather another day, and as it is, he has been unbelievably fortunate. Only a little wind could pile sand up behind her so she might never be floated.

"I regret that we must hurry, but unless you wish to go into the forest traveling with a man and unmarried to him, then I think it would be wise if tomorrow was the day."

"Oh, you do, do you? Have you thought that I may have changed my mind?"

"If you have," I said, growing irritated, "now is the time. Captain Tilly will take you home. He is planning to stop by Shawmut, and he would be glad to take you there."

One of the Indians asked a question, and I replied. They stared at her with admiration and many grunts and exclamations. "What is that all about?" Diana demanded.

"They wanted to know how many blankets I traded for you."

"Blankets? For *me?*"

Chuckling, I told her, "I said I traded five muskets, one hundred pounds of lead, a keg of powder, and ten blankets for you."

"That's a lie!" she objected. "You have done noth—"

183

"Ssh!" I admonished. "What I told them is an enormous price. I told them you were the daughter of a great chief, a wise man, and that you were a wise woman, a plant woman, and a medicine woman. That makes you very important by their standards."

"And not by yours?"

"Of course! I wish them to respect you, and to do that I must speak a language they understand. Now they think of you as a princess."

Long before daylight we gathered on the beach to attempt the floating of the *Abigail*. She had been pumped free of the water she had taken on, and some of her cargo had been landed on the beach. The sand had not begun to pile up behind her, and with a line run out to a boat and twelve good men at the oars, we went to work. Yet it was midmorning before we worked her free of the sand and got her fairly afloat. And it was nearly dusk before her cargo was reshipped and she could set her sails. While she lay off the shore, Diana and I, standing upon the beach, were wed.

It was a scene I shall never forget. The long sweep of the glistening sands, the vast marches of the ocean nearby, the low stunted growth inland, and about us the small group of British sailors and Catawbas.

When all was over, John Tilly held out his hand to Diana, but she ignored it and kissed him lightly on the cheek. A moment we lingered, saying a few last words, with a last-minute message from Diana to her father, whom we soon hoped to see, and then they shoved off and were taken aboard.

We waited only a moment longer to be certain she cleared, but her sails filled, and she bore away to the open sea. We walked inland then, going toward the place where the Catawbas had left their canoe, and only once did we look back. Only her topmasts were visible against the red afterglow of the sunset.

Diana was quiet, as well she might be. She had trusted herself to a man of whom she knew, after all, very little and to six Indians of whom she knew nothing.

Their canoe was large, a birch-bark canoe such as the Hurons make, far better than the heavier dugout canoes of the Iroquois. That it was a captured canoe, I had no doubt.

The inland waters were calm, and we made good time, moving up a bay called the Sinepuxent. The Catawbas, great wanderers and warriors, now wished to be home. We swept to the head of the bay, had a brief glimpse of the open sea again, and then moved across a wider bay and into the mouth of a river.

We made camp there under the loblolly pines and some scattered hardwoods, and one of the Catawbas killed a deer that had come down to the river to drink in the late dusk.

At daybreak we went up the river until it became so shallow we had to walk in the water and pull the canoe behind us. The river flowed from a swamp called the Pocomoke, and we crossed the swamp moving west and south, then up another stream, a long portage, and gradually we worked our way westward. We saw much game but few signs of Indians.

Coming at last to a wide bay, we followed it down until we entered the mouth of another river.

Diana and I talked but little, and the Indians spoke only a word here and there, alert for all the sounds of the forest or swamp. From time to time I took my turn at the paddle, for I had long been familiar with canoe travel.

From the *Abigail* I had come well armed, with a musket, two pistols, powder, and ball. We had also brought a good stock of food from the ship so that little time would be lost in hunting.

Our first destination was the trading station of the man named Claiborne in the upper part of the bay, or so I had heard. This was the place where I had suggested Captain Tilly might sell or trade a part of his cargo, but I doubted that he had made such a decision, being eager to get on to the north and hence to New-foundland.

At the Claiborne station I was sure I could obtain knowledge of what was happening in the country about and what supplies we might further require. The Catawbas knew of the station but had not been there.

Those first days, despite the swamp and its mosquitoes, had been idyllic. The weather was fair, the water smooth, and our progress steady. All about us the land gave evidence of fertility, but it was largely uninhabited. Several times we saw distant smoke, as from campfires or perhaps a village, and once, far off, we saw a canoe with three Indians. As we were the larger number, they shied off and vanished into an inlet on the eastern shore.

To deny such country to the impoverished of England was criminal, and when I thought of the crowded, sweaty, ragged people of the European cities of whom my father, Jeremy, and Kane had told me, I knew this must indeed be their promised land.

Surely the two peoples had much to learn from each other, yet even as I thought of this, I shrank from it, for I could see no common ground of meeting. The exchange of ideas and methods offered much, but I had dealt with Indians enough to know that our ways and theirs were poles apart. It would be no easy thing to bring them together.

We moved along at a goodly speed, slowing our pace as we neared the southern tip of Kent Island, wishing not to surprise them into hostilities, for they knew not who we were.

On the shore we saw several men armed with muskets and with them a few Indians. I lifted a hand, waving to them, and we came on in, moving slowly so they might see who we were.

The fort, if such it might be called, sat back from the shore on a slight rise of ground. The great gate was closed; only a smaller door that would admit the passage of but one man at a time stood open.

A thickset man with a wide, florid face came

down to the small-boat landing they had built into the water. He stared at us curiously, obviously surprised to see a white girl amongst us.

"Claiborne?" I asked.

"I am Deal Webster," the man said, "a trader here. William Claiborne is not here at the moment."

"We would trade," I said, "and buy supplies. I am Kin Ring Sackett, of Carolina, and this be my wife. She is newly from Cape Ann."

"Come ashore! Come ashore!" he said cheerfully. "You be welcome here, and seldom it is we have visitors." He glanced at the Catawbas. "I do not know your Indians."

"They be Catawbas, from Carolina, and friends to all white men."

"Ah? Yes, I have heard them spoken of. Fighting men, I hear."

"If need be," I replied cautiously, "but they come now in peace, escorting me to my home in the mountains."

I stepped ashore and offered my hand to Diana, who followed me, stepping easily to the small landing. The Catawbas drew their canoe up on the shore near the small pier, disdaining to even glance at the Indians who stood about.

Those Indians needed no introduction to the Catawba, I knew, for their fame was wide.

Webster took us to a cabin built against the outer palisade and utilizing its logs for a back wall. It was a pleasant room, with a fire blazing on the wide hearth and a general air of comfort and well-being. Seated at a table, a servant brought us food, well-cooked venison and some pieces of fish of a kind I knew not. The bread was fresh and warm, and there was butter, real butter.

"We have two cows," he explained proudly, "and the only ones anywhere about. William Claiborne brought them in, and they do well upon the grass near the fort, yet we must keep them close, for there are Indians out there who would kill them for meat."

He seated himself opposite us with a tankard of ale. "You wish to trade? I saw some furs—?"

"They belong to the Indians. I shall have to pay in gold," I said.

"Ah, well!" he smiled. "You will have no trouble in that respect! Gold is a rare thing." He looked at me carefully. "Know you Lord Baltimore?"

"I do not."

"We have trouble," Webster said. "William Claiborne recognizes only the government of Virginia, and Baltimore insists we sit upon his land and will have us out of here."

"I know nothing of such things," I said. "We live far from government and have our own, such as we need."

We talked long and ate well, and in the end bought what we needed of powder and shot as well as what food we would need for our travels.

"Inland there," Webster asked, "where you live. What do you there for powder and shot?"

"We make our own. There are lead mines in the mountains, and we have heard of others farther to the west. Our powder, too, we make. We have skilled men amongst us, and we have found deposits of iron ore as well."

"No gold?"

I shrugged. "Such a little it is scarcely worth the time, yet we hear of great mines of copper far to the north, and I suspect there is much wealth of which no man knows."

At daybreak we again were afloat; our canoe not proving sufficient for us, we had purchased another from Deal Webster, leaving four persons and what supplies we had purchased from Webster to each canoe.

Down the bay we went to the mouth of the Rappahannock. But on the first day we but crossed from Kent Point to the mainland shore and down to a wide bay where Webster had assured us there was much herring to be taken. We camped there near the mouth of a creek and gave up a day to fishing and smoking the fish.

Once, as we paddled offshore, nearing the mouth of a great river, we beheld a sail off to the east of us, some small craft sailing up the bay toward Kent Island. Yet it was far off, and we lay low in the water and against the shore, so they saw us not. Yet the sight of that sail left me uneasy, for there were all manner of men about, pirates and such, and many who walked a borderline between piracy and trading, ready to loot and kill where it could be done with safety to themselves.

It was with relief that we came to the mouth of the Rappahannock. Once upon the river, our days became idyllic. We had smoked fish and venison, we traded with some Indians for additional corn, and we had what supplies we brought from Kent and the *Abigail*.

We had only to be wary, for no man or woman traveled in safety where war parties roamed as they did upon these rivers. Yet we met none. Our days were spent moving up the river and to the mouth of the Rapidan and thence westward along that river.

From Wa-ga-su I had learned much of the Catawba tongue, and traveling with the six warriors, I soon learned more. Diana learned quickly. She had a quick, active intelligence and an interest in all things. Here and there she collected herbs that might be of use, and the Indians showed her others that they themselves used.

Reserved though she was, she had a natural, easy manner with all people and talked to these Indians as though they were her brothers. Most tribes, I knew, had a tradition among them of certain special women, endowed with unusual gifts of leadership or wisdom. Among the Cherokee these were usually referred to as the Beloved Woman, or some such term, and many times their prestige was such as to overrule the tribal council. I could see our Catawbas were accepting Diana in that way. Part of it was her quality of stillness and inner repose, for whatever happened, she maintained her poise. As the days went by, I began to see this girl I had married was even more than I had suspected and in every way.

Yet absorbed as I was in my bride, I began to see there was increased wariness on the part of our Catawbas. They spoke no word, but from time to time all would lift their paddles from the water and listen. One such time I took up my musket and looked to its charging.

"Is something wrong?" Diana whispered.

"Aye. Unless I mistake them, there is trouble about. We must be silent now."

They dipped their paddles more carefully, moving with deep, powerful strokes, and I looked carefully about, scanning the river itself, the trees, and even the occasional glimpse of the blue ridge of mountains that lay before us and toward which we moved.

The water itself held my attention, for many a floating object could speak of what lay before us. I saw nothing, heard nothing. If sixth sense I had, like my father before me, it was not in working order just then.

When it came my turn to take the paddle, the Catawbas shook their heads and gestured to the musket. They preferred me armed and ready with the musket than using a paddle I must put down before I could fire.

We had come, in these past days, higher and higher toward the blue distant mountains, just as blue now but no longer so distant. The current ran stronger, but the river had grown more narrow, and there had been times, for one or another reason, when we had to take the canoes from the water and carry them about some obstruction.

It was such a place to which we now came. Several large logs or trees had fallen into the water, blocking a part of the stream. Around the end of these logs the water rushed with tremendous force, far too strong a current for three men with paddles.

The Catawbas wasted no time in debate. He who was in the lead canoe promptly turned the canoe sharply to the left and into the mouth of a small creek. He led the way up the creek to where it widened in a sort of swamp. Taking the canoe in toward the shore, he gestured for all to land.

"No more canoe," one of them said to me. "We walk."

Swiftly the canoes were taken into the swamp and hidden by vines; others, including myself, worked to assort the goods we carried into packs, Diana taking a somewhat smaller one without hesitation.

One of the Catawbas slipped away into the woods, going back toward the Rapidan. The rest of us started out, walking swiftly along the flank of the mountain, taking a dim trail southward.

No attention was given to he who had left us, the Catawbas taking it for granted he would take care of himself and catch up when he could. It was apparent that he had gone to have a look down the river to see who, if anyone, might be following us.

On that subject I had my own thoughts, private though they were. What Diana thought, I knew not, nor did I ask.

One name hung in the back of my mind, the name of a man who knew how to hate, a man who would not be frustrated, our enemy always.

Max Bauer.

Chapter XXI

We hastened on into the gathering dusk and at last came to a hollow among great trees where boulders lay about and there was a spring from which a small branch flowed.

The place was shadowed and gloomy when we entered, and the fire we made was small, for hasty cooking. Among themselves the Catawbas muttered, and I knew from a word I caught it was of their brother they spoke.

"What is it?" Diana whispered.

"The other one has not come. They talk of it now."

She was silent. We ate then and put out the fire. About us the dark columns of the trees lost their shape in the shadows, and only overhead could we see the black fringe of leaves against the starlit sky. A wind stirred. In the aisles of the forest, leaves skittered, and cool was the wind from off the high ridges.

Three Catawbas slept, and two remained awake. After a time I, too, slept, yet for minutes only, awakening with eyes coming wide and ears stretched to hear the slightest sound.

At dawn we awakened, chewed on jerked venison, and moved swiftly away. There was no sign of him who had left us.

"He is dead," one said when I spoke of him. "If he has not come, he is dead."

"You wish to go back? We will go, also."

"No. There is another time. There is always another time."

We crossed over the mountains at Swift Run Gap and descended into a lovely valley beyond and turned south once more. Diana, although the hard travel left her tired, made no word of complaint, yet I was worried, fearing for her but hating to be driven by whoever it was who came behind us. If the young Catawba had been killed, the blood feud was mine as well as theirs, for he had been acting for us. It was all very well to say they would have come this way, and all might have happened, anyway, yet I liked it not. Had Diana not been with us, I would myself have turned back to see who our enemies were and to take toll of them.

Yet there was wariness in me, too, for if the Catawba had been killed, someone among them was a woodsman, and one skillful indeed. To hunt down and kill a Catawba warrior was no small thing; of course, even the best made mistakes.

We held close to the mountains, traveling in the forest when possible.

On the last morning I came upon a tree that I myself had blazed upon a trail my feet had often trod. "We will be home soon," I said to Diana, and she put her hand on mine, touching it lightly.

The trail opened upon a meadow where fresh-cut hay was stacked and beyond it a cornfield. Melons lay on the ground among the rows of corn. This would be a good harvest.

We saw the palisade before us, low upon its knoll near the creek. The gate stood open, and two men faced us, shading their eyes to see us. I lifted a hand, and there was an answering wave.

The first to reach me was Yance.

"Where you been, lad?" he asked, smiling. Glancing at Diana, his smile widened. "I told Temp you'd be bringin' a lass with you, but not who it was. She's been devilin' me for a name, but I haven't told her a thing!"

"There's somebody behind us, Yance. Somebody who wants us real bad. He's killed one of our Catawba friends, or must have."

"It is a bad time, Kin. Two of our men are down sick with chills and fever. Will they be many or few?"

"Few, I think, but not easy men."

He grinned widely, cheerfully. "When have they ever been easy? We were born to hard times and hard men, Kin, and I am thinking we are hard men ourselves." He glanced at the Catawbas. "Where did you come by them?"

So I told him as we walked, and he listened, nodding from time to time. He shook his head. "You took a long chance going to the islands, Kin. A long chance."

"White women are not so many, Yance, and they are noticed. Yet without Henry I could not have done it."

"He is a good man and welcome amongst us." He nodded toward the settlement. "They know you are coming, and they have prepared a feast for the prodigal."

"Me? A prodigal? It should be more likely you."

They were waiting for us, and Temperance ran forward when she saw Diana. "Oh, Di! You're my sister now! If I could have chosen, it would have been you."

"Come within," Lila said quietly. "There is food upon the table, and you be hungry folk."

My eyes went to her, this woman who had once served my mother and had married one of my father's best friends. The size of her never ceased to astonish me, for she was nearly as tall and broad as I, who am larger than most. There was a little gray in her hair now, and it pained me to see it. Yet she was older than my mother.

My mother, would I ever see her again?

She was gone across the sea to England with Noelle and Brian, but I remembered her well.

Jeremy came up from the field, his hand hard

from the work there but his smile as bright as ever. "It has been too long, lad. You must stay now."

This man had stood over me when I was being born during a battle with the Senecas, guarding my mother during her labor. He had been my father's friend and had left England with him, a down-at-heel gentleman, a wandering swordsman, and a farmer now but holding broad acres with excellent crops and a good trade in furs with friendly Indians.

"I have brought trouble," I said, and explained.

"The men are coming from the fields," Jeremy said.

They started within where the food was upon the table, but I lingered to look about. There was a place where some of the logs were blackened near the ground, a place where fire started by Indians had seared the logs before being put out. My father and his men had come into this country when no white man was nearer than the coast and had remained here until he went beyond the mountains scouting for fresh land. For this was our way, bred into us, and we knew it well, always to go beyond the mountains to open new lands.

Within all was bright and cheerful—sunlight through the windows upon burnished copper pots and the dull shine of pewter. The floors were spotless as always and the windows hung with curtains. Muskets stood in their racks near the walls, and the heavy shutters were thrown back now but could be drawn quickly shut.

A strongly built man with a shock of flaxen hair pushed back from the table. "I go to the wall," he said.

When he had gone, Jeremy said, "He is Schaumberg, a German. He heard of us and came looking, one man and his woman with a baby son. They came through the forest alone."

"He belongs here, then," I said. "He is a good man?"

"He works hard, and he is handy with tools. He seems to fear nothing."

"It is better," I replied, "to fear a little. One is cautious then."

"Aye, but he is a careful man."

One by one they slipped away to the walls, and when I looked again at the rack of muskets, it was half empty. I started to rise. "Sit you," Lila said. "There will be time enough when the fighting begins, if fighting there is to be."

She filled my glass again and stood across the table from me. "I like her. Does she have family?"

"A father. A good man. He should be amongst us. He would make a teacher," I added, "and we will need such."

We talked long then and of many things. Yance came in and sat beside us. When I asked about our enemies, he shrugged. "We have seen nothing, but they are there. A fawn was crossing our field where they always cross, and suddenly it turned sharp away and trotted back almost the way it came."

"If it is Max Bauer," I said, "he will want victory without cost. He will wait, or he will find a way."

I turned my head to Yance. "I want him," I said. "I want the man myself."

Yance shrugged. "Let it happen, Kin. If he comes my way or Jeremy's, so be it."

My hackles rose at the thought of him. There were few men I disliked, none that I hated but him. But this went beyond hate, for we were two male creatures of strength who saw in the other an enemy. No matter how we met, we should sooner or later have fought. It was in our natures, deeply laid, and he knew it as well as I. We ached to get together; we longed for the moment.

The man was a monster of cruelty, a savage man but cold and mean in his savagery. I had hated no Indian whom I fought. Warfare was their way of life, and they fought because it was their way. They were splendid men, most of them, and although they had slain my father, he himself would have felt no hatred for them. They were men, opposed to him but men, and warriors. They fought, but there was respect there, also.

It was not so with Max Bauer and myself. We must fight, and one must destroy the other, and each was aware.

Lila needed no urging to keep me from the walls, for it was in my mind that he would not attack. He would come, he would look, he would go all about us in the forest, and then he would try to find some way he could hurt or injure me or mine before he killed me. He was that sort of man, and he knew that death can be an end to suffering. He wanted me dead but only after I had suffered all a man can suffer. It was his advantage, perhaps, that he wished to kill and I did not. I wanted to fight him, to destroy what he was, to break him. I did not care about killing.

Jeremy came back and sat down opposite me. "Kin," he said, "since the death of your father, you are the accepted leader here, but we have troubles coming that you have not, perhaps, considered.

"The settlements along the Virginia coast are growing. People are moving into the Carolinas. This you know."

"I do."

"This land we occupy is ours only by right of settlement, which in the courts of England would be no right at all. Think you not that we should take steps to establish a claim to our land?"

"But how? My father dared make no such claim. He was flying from the queen's justice, a wanted man. Falsely charged though he was. We have held our land for many years now."

"Be wise, Kin. Explore the chances. Perhaps you might write to Brian? Or to Peter Tallis? Believe me, we can wait no longer."

What he said was, of course, true. Although I

would not say anything of that to Jeremy, I had been worrying over just that very thing and worrying even more since I saw men moving out from Cape Ann and Plymouth, looking for land. The troubles of Claiborne over Kent Island had been explained to me, for although Claiborne had settled there, Lord Baltimore's grant took in all Claiborne occupied, and he might be thrown off at any time. So it could be with us.

I worried not for myself or for Yance. There was always the frontier for us. Yet my father had brought men with him, and those men held land because of his urging. Some of those men, Jeremy Ring included, had become well off from the trade and the produce of their land, yet they might lose the land itself if something was not done.

"I shall write to Peter Tallis," I said, "and to Brian as well."

There was a packet of letters awaiting me and a press of business that needed my attention, for our plantations had grown and their demands upon my time as well. Glancing over the receipts and payments, I could see our small colony was doing very well indeed, but soon it would come to the attention of the tax collectors and of His Majesty's officials, who were ever greedy for themselves as well as for the Crown.

In the months that I had been gone in the mountains as well as to Jamaica three shiploads of mast timbers had been sent down the river and loaded aboard sailing ships. Thirty-two bales of furs had been sent, seventy tons of potash, fourteen buffalo hides, twenty fine maple logs for the making of furniture.

Our enemies awaited us in the forest, but each thing in its time, and the time for our enemies would come when they attacked or made some move against us. In the meantime I would trust to Jeremy and those others and would be about my business here.

It had never been easy for me to write a letter. I was a man of the forest or of the plow. I could kill a deer for meat, fell a tree, or break ground for a field. I could hew timbers, build walls and houses, but a letter was a painstaking thing that required putting thoughts into words.

First I wrote to Peter Tallis. My father had told us much of him. From a booth in St. Paul's Walk where he dealt in information and all manner of things that could be done with inside information or knowledge of where lay the powers, he had become a wealthy and respected merchant. He was the middleman, the man to whom one could go if one wished to approach a minister or anyone in a position of power. If there was merchandise to be sold by some stranger or foreigner, Tallis was the man who could tell the best market, the best price. He was our friend in London, our agent as well.

Explaining our situation, of which he was no doubt aware, I also expressed my wish to establish legal title to our lands. Brian was in London, undoubtedly seeing Peter Tallis, and together they could develop a solution. That my father had been a fugitive from the queen's men posed a problem.

Next I wrote to Brian. As a student at the Inns of Court, he would understand better than I the legal complexities of our situation and those who depended upon us. Of Yance's marriage he knew. I now told him of mine. At the same time I told him of Legare and his need for a representative in London.

How strange are the fortunes of men! My father, a strong young man with ambition, had found on the Devil's Dyke a rotted wallet in which were several ancient gold coins. Their sale had given him his start in life and led to his coming to America. Yet they had also brought much trouble, for the queen's officers, inspired by his enemies, believed my father had found King John's treasure, the lost Crown jewels of England, among which there had been some old coins of gold. The find and the fact that my father lived in the fens not far from the Wash where the treasure had been lost was all that was needed. My father had been seized, questioned, and imprisoned. Despairing of making anyone believe his story, he had escaped from Newgate prison and fled to America.*

Our plantations now did well. Our trade with Indians prospered. Each year more and more people came to America, and we knew a time would come when they would press hard upon us, so already Yance and I had gone beyond the mountains and had explored lands there, building our two cabins and planting crops where only Indians had been before. Or so we originally supposed. Now, from discoveries there, we knew that others had been before us.

My hand was tiring from the unfamiliar writing, so I placed the quill upon the table and sat back and stared off into nothing, thinking.

Our father was gone, killed by the Seneca along with his good friend Tom Watkins. My mother was in England with Brian and Noelle. And Jubal? What of Jubal, my strange, lonely, wandering brother?

For years now there had been no word of him. Each season I watched the trails, hoping he would come again to see us, if for a few days only.

He was ever the lonely wanderer, ever the remote one, loving us all and being loved, yet a solitary man who loved the wild lands more. He had gone westward, and he had returned from time to time with tales of a great river out there, greater than any we knew, and of wide, fertile lands where there was much game. And then he had come no more.

Yance came to the door. "Kin? Better come to the wall. There's somebody out there with a white flag."

---

*As related in *Sackett's Land* (Bantam Books, March 1975) and *To The Far Blue Mountains* (Bantam Books, June 1977).

Chapter XXII

Outside the sun was warm and pleasant. It felt good to be back in buckskins and moccasins again. Pausing a moment, I took a long look around and about, and as far as I could see, we were ready. The men had come in from the fields, and those on the outlying farms would have closed up shutters and barred doors by now.

Since I was hoe handle high, I had been taught to be ready, and so with all of us. A body never knew when the Indians would be coming down upon us, especially the Senecas, who had selected us for their foes. I won't say enemies because we had nothing to fight about except to make war or protect ourselves. The Senecas lived a far piece away to the north, and it took them days to get where we were. As long as I could remember, they had been coming.

Mounting the ladder to the walk along the inside of the wall, I looked out over the palisade, and there was the white flag.

Turning, I looked at the back wall, but Jeremy Ring was there, and Jeremy wasn't about to be taken by surprise. There was always a chance that under cover of talk they would try to close in on us.

We had sickness amongst us, so we were short-handed on the walls, but there were six of us up there, and at the first shot the womenfolk would be out to reload for us, and we had two dozen spare muskets, all of which could be kept loaded and ready for use.

"If you wish to talk," I shouted, "come out in the

open! But no more than one of you or we start shooting!"

What Bauer had in mind, I had no idea, but by this time he had scouted our position with care. Our fort was well situated, but scattered up the valley were a dozen other cabins occupied by members of our little colony, often enough by families. Each was prepared to defend itself, and each was built in such a way as to receive support from at least one other cabin. In other words, when attacking one cabin, the attackers must in most cases expose themselves to fire from another.

Yet I doubted if he had any true estimate of our strength, nor had I any of his. Whether he had a half-dozen men or many more I had no way of knowing. We ourselves must do some scouting.

It was Lashan who came forward.

He strode into the open and stood there, feet well apart, hands on hips. He wore a cutlass and a brace of pistols but carried a musket as well.

"You folks in there!" he called. "You give us Sackett and that Macklin girl and we won't burn you out. If you don't surrender them, we'll kill you, every one!"

"Diana Macklin is now my wife," I replied, "and we have no intention of surrendering anything. As for you, I would suggest you start back to the coast while you still have supplies enough to feed you."

No doubt he had brought his men along with a promise of loot and had never expected to face an established fortress surrounded by what would be to them a trackless wilderness. It seemed the odds were with us, yet I was wary. Max Bauer might hate me enough to follow and kill, but he was a canny man with an eye to enriching himself always.

Nor was an attack by him to be compared to an attack by Indians. Max Bauer would know something of siege warfare and might many times have attacked such positions as ours. Indians, on the other hand, had not learned how to attack fortified positions. No doubt time would change that.

Clouds hung low around the Nantahala Mountains to the east, and the nearer slope of Chunky Gal Mountain was dark with foreboding.

"Going to storm," I commented idly to Yance.

"Threatenin'," he agreed. He shifted his musket. "What you reckon they'll do?"

Lashan was still there, standing in the same way, and somebody might have been talking to him from the trees. He called out sharply. "You got an hour. You best make the most of it."

"Stalling," I said. "They've something in mind."

It was very still. Then, back over the Nantahalas, I heard a mutter of thunder. Rains could be mighty sudden here, sometimes a regular cloudburst. They had better find shelter for themselves.

Bauer knew, of course, that I had not yet been to Shawmut or Plymouth with whatever evidence I had obtained. He also knew that once I put such evidence before the authorities there, such as they were, his profitable trade was ended. The trade in young white girls was a specialized trade, yet it involved no costly transportation across the ocean, only rare losses at sea, and top prices. No doubt some of his trade had been with the Indians for captives they had taken, but once the word was out, all ports would be closed to him, and he would be a fugitive.

My first intent had been to get Diana to a place of safety. The trip overland to Plymouth could be a fast one, and Samuel Maverick would put his influence behind the evidence I had. The bare fact that such things had happened was enough to destroy the chances of it happening again.

So Max Bauer, both for his own safety and the continuance of his lucrative trade, must eliminate me.

Somehow or other he must lure me from the fort to be killed or destroy the fort itself with me inside.

Lightning flashed back over Chunky Gal Mountain, and thunder grumbled in the canyons. A few spatters of rain fell.

"They aren't likely to try anything now," Yance commented. "Get their powder wet."

"I was thinking about my cabin," I said, "and my corn crop. Be a while before we get back out that way."

"Likely." We were both huddling under the eaves of the blockhouse, watching the forest. "I've been thinking," Yance said, "of that long valley the Cherokees told us about. This here"—he covered the area with a gesture—"is all right, but that sounded mighty nice."

"That's the trouble, Yance. There will always be a place somewhere that sounds nice. Some of us should stay and build here."

He chuckled. "But not you an' me? Nor Jubal. Wonder where ol' Jube is about now? Yonder by his great river?"

The rain fell hard. "Get yourself something to eat, Yance. I'll stand watch."

The rain had drawn a veil over the Nantahalas and over Piney Top, and it was falling now on the Tusquitees and in the dark canyon of the Nantahala River where the Indians said they had killed the great horned serpent they called *ulstitlu* and taken the gem from between his eyes.

It was a deep, narrow, dark canyon where the sun reached only at midday. The Cherokees said that was the meaning of Nantahala, "the Land of the Noonday Sun."

Jeremy Ring came and stood beside me and watched the steel mesh of the rain.

"I miss your father," he said suddenly. "Barnabas has been gone for several years, but his stamp is upon everything. He was an extraordinary man."

"He made big tracks," I agreed.

"You will do as much, Kin. I have no doubt."

I told him about Jamaica then and of my fight with Bogardus. Swordsman that he was, he must have every detail, and we refought the battle, move by

204

move. Yet as we talked, we scanned the edge of the forest all around.

"I must go again to Shawmut," I told him. "I must take the statement I have from Adele Legare as well as the letters I have written to Brian and to Peter Tallis. You are right. We must wait no longer about establishing a legal claim to our lands."

"We must consider alternatives, too," he said. "Although I should hate to give this up, it may be necessary."

"Aye, but there are lands to the westward. Good lands. Yance and I have seen them."

"The place you have now? Is that good?"

"It is not the best. It is too high up. It is only beautiful, with just a little corn land. Down below in the flat lands is where we must have land. The soil is rich and deep."

"Do not wait too long."

"It will be a hundred years before men get over there unless it is the French. Jubal saw Frenchmen over there, and they claim it all."

"Settlers?"

"Trappers and hunters like us. I do not think the Indians would let anyone settle. There has been much fighting there, and some parts of it they shy from. They say it is haunted ground."

After a while I went below to my own place, and Diana was there. The table was set, and she was standing before the fireplace, a long spoon in her hand.

"I wonder," I said, putting my hands on her shoulders, "how I was so lucky."

"You married a witch," she said, smiling.

"Why not? We did not have a witch. Every community should have one. I wish you would put a spell on Max Bauer and make him disappear."

She dished up a bowl of stew and put it before me. "Eat," she said. "I do not think he will wait until the storm is over."

"His powder will be wet."

"His blades will not, and if they are, it will not matter. Do not take him lightly, Kin."

She sat down across from me. "I worry about father."

"We will know soon. When this is over"—I gestured toward the outside where Bauer was—"we will go north and bring him down to join us."

We talked long while I waited for sounds from outside that did not come. At last I went again to the wall to allow Yance to eat.

The clouds were lowering, and there were occasional drizzles of rain. There was no sign of movement from the forest, and I expected none. He would wait. Perhaps Max Bauer had decided upon his course of action, but if he was the woodsman he seemed to be, he could live, at least for a while, on the forest around him. He would know that we had crops. We had much work to do outside, and we would weaken ourselves in scattering out to attend to it. Or so he hoped.

Yet the game would lie quiet while it rained, and to come upon anything worth hunting, he would have to startle it into movement. Nor would the immediate forest offer much. We knew that, for we now hunted far afield despite the fact that we had tried not to disturb the game close by, wanting to allow the deer to range freely until some emergency. Buffalo had become scarcer with each year in the areas east of the mountains.

Kane O'Hara came along the walk to me as soon as I returned. "I don't like it," he said irritably. "We've work to do. We're losing time."

"There's no help for it," I said. "He knows our situation, and he will use it. He wants us to become careless."

"We've fought too many Senecas for that."

"That worries me, too." I watched the woods as I spoke, my eyes straying along the tree front. "Suppose he manages to meet them and set up a joint attack?"

"What kind of a man is he?"

"Big, very strong, very tough, a good woodsman, and a shrewd, dangerous man. He wants me and he wants Diana, but he wants all we have here that is portable. By this time he knows our strength, and he knows we've done a lot of trapping. He will know we have bales of furs here, and we have women."

Kane stared gloomily over the wall. "This looks like our best crop," he commented. "It should not be neglected now."

After a pause, he asked, "How's that country out west? Where you and Yance have located?"

"Beautiful, but the soil is average. We could do better down in the bottoms, but you know how it is with Yance an' me. We like to be high up and where there's game. In the bottoms along the creeks there are meadows where the grass grows knee-high to a man on horseback."

"I'd like to see that," Kane said enviously. "How far does it go, Kin? Is there no end to it?"

"There's always an end. At the Pacific sea, more'n likely."

It was very still. The rumbling of thunder was occasional but distant. The rain had become a fine, soft rain, and the air smelled fresh and cool. In the forest no leaf moved, nor was there a sound or any sign of smoke unless a faint blueness in the air to the eastward might be smoke.

A stealthy attack by night was likely when some of my men must sleep. No more than two could be on the walls at once and must not follow prescribed patrols but must be careful to set no pattern Bauer might recognize. Yet there was no way we could, with only two men, keep a proper watch. Fortresses and walls have forever distressed me. I am not inclined to defense, for it is better to be the attacker. We had women, children, and goods to defend, so we had no choice, yet I would have preferred being out there in the forest.

The thought held my attention. What was it father had advised? "Attack, always attack. Whether you have one man or fifty, there is always a way of attacking. No matter how many his men, the enemy must be attacked."

Of course. But how?

"Tonight," I said, "I may go into the forest."

"Aye," O'Hara agreed. "It has been on my mind, but we can ill afford to lose a man, and especially you."

The crops could not wait, nor could my letters to Peter Tallis and Brian, for the more I considered our situation, the more it disturbed me. Our approximate location was known to some in Jamestown, although none of them had been so far inland. They also knew we were shipping bales of furs; occasionally gems were sold by us, and we were self-sufficient. It could be no more than a matter of a short time until settlers came around us, and some one of them might have the power to get a grant from the queen, even of our lands. We had no legal right to them, only that of first settlement and occupation.

It was the experience of William Claiborne that came to haunt me, too. He held lands, traded in furs, and was doing very well until Lord Baltimore's grant took in even the island on which he resided.

Kane walked on around the wall, and Diana came from the house bringing fresh coffee. It tasted good, and we stood together under the eaves.

"I have brought trouble upon you," she said. "Were it not for me—"

"I will not have it," I said. "You have no reason for blame. What happened has happened. Now we must do what we can."

We walked along the wall together and from time to time stopped to study the forest out there. Since I was a small boy, I had watched that forest for enemies or for game, and I knew its every mood and shading, how the sunlight fell through the leaves and where the shadows gathered. It held no mysteries for me but much of memory. I had played there as a child with Yance, Jubal, and Brian, later with Noelle. We had climbed its trees, picked berries there, and played hide-and-seek under its branches.

My father had ever been a pillar of security. He was always *there*, ever kind, ever considerate, always strong. He had a temper, and I had seen it from time to time, but we all relied on him, not only we children but the adults as well.

Now it must be I who was strong. I must be the one to hold our little community together, to provide reassurance. That was why I could no longer wait for an attack, for Bauer was too shrewd a man. He would contrive some ruse, some stratagem, some trick.

"Never let an enemy get set," my father had said. "Attack, worry, keep him off balance. Never let him move from a secure position or give him time to move his pieces on the chessboard."

It was never a part of my thinking to shelter women from the truth. I had learned from my father to trust their judgment. "Tonight," I told Diana, "I am going out there."

"But what can you *do?*"

"I won't know until I see, but I must do something."

"What about Yance?"

"Yes." I knew what she meant. "Yance might be better than I. He is very wily. But the responsibility is mine. For whatever reason they are here, it was I whom they followed. Although he is attacking all of us, he is my enemy, and it must be up to me to do something about it."

"But what can one man do?"

"I don't know," I admitted. "I must just go out there and see."

Oddly enough, I wanted to go. Lurking behind walls was uncomfortable for me, for I was a man of the forest and the mountains. To let an enemy have the time to choose when and how he would attack had never been my way, and now that I had resolved to go out there, I was enormously relieved.

"You'd better rest, then," she said. "I'll get Yance."

She went down the ladder, and I waited while the rain softly fell; under the low clouds the forest was a darker, deeper green, a richer green.

There was no way to plan for what lay before me; only when I was out there and found their camp could I decide what would be best to do. Out there in the forest at night, yet it was a forest I knew well from the slopes of Chunky Gal and the Nantahalas to Piney Top and the Tusquitees, from Compass Creek to the Gap and Muskrat Branch. And even far beyond from the Chilowees to the Blue Ridge I had roamed and hunted, fished the streams, and lived off the fruit of the land.

I had fought the Senecas there, too, the warriors of the northern lands, the snakelike, wily, crafty, and very brave Senecas.

Tonight I would go.

Tonight.

Chapter XXIII

Then the rain fell no longer, but the forest dripped. Heavy were the leaves with rain, soft the grass beneath the moccasins. The narrow door opened; wraithlike, I slipped through and stood against the wall. Silent in the darkness, listening.

Black and still was the night. Water dripped from the branches, and I crossed the open acres about the fort and went into the trees. Among them, my body close along a slim dark tree, I waited again and listened. I did not know where lay their camp, but this night I thought they would have a fire, burning low now.

Only slightly blew the wind, a baby's breath of wind, but I moved across it, my nostrils ready for the slightest smell of smoke.

Nothing.

How many watched the fort? Or had they all withdrawn to rest? My hand felt for a leaf, which was wet, and I put the wet fingers to my nose, for a wet nose smells better. A smell of rotting vegetation, for I was near the bank of a creek where there was a bit of marshy ground.

The tree beside which I stood was a chestnut. My touch upon the bark told me that, but this mountainside, as all through the hills, was covered with a variety of trees: chestnut, oaks of several kinds, tulip trees, red maple, sourwood, and many others. Some I knew by the smell, all by the touch. Careful to make no sound, I worked my way into the forest, working

211

my way deeper and swinging in a rough half circle, always alert for that telltale whiff of smoke.

It did not come.

Before me the forest thinned. Only a few yards farther was the trail that led along the west side of Piney Top to Tusquitee Creek. Pausing, I listened. My ears heard nothing; my nostrils found no smell of smoke, only the faint sweetish smell of crushed magnolia, not unusual, for there were many about, and their leaves often fell and were crushed underfoot. None of our people had been out, however.

It was probably nothing. I waited, and then I heard faint stirrings. How far off? Carefully I worked my way through the forest. The sounds had ceased. Ahead of me was thick brush. Wary, I avoided it.

With the rain, wild animals and most birds had taken shelter, so I could rely upon none of them to give me warning of a foreign presence. Yet as boys we had been taught by the Catawba to develop our sixth sense and to be always aware. We would take turns at staring at one of us until he turned suddenly, becoming aware of our attention. By continual practice we had become as sensitive to this as any wild animal.

Often our father, when in the woods with us, would suddenly stop and ask that we describe some area just passed or the tracks of animals or insects we had just glimpsed in the dust of the track. With time our awareness had grown until we missed very little.

In the wilderness attention to detail was the price of survival.

Abruptly I paused. A faint smell of wet buckskins and wood smoke. I held perfectly still, then turned my head this way and that to hear the better and to catch any vague smells. Primitive man, I suspected, used his nostrils quite as much as his eye or ear, but civilization, with its multitude of odors, soon distracts the attention until the brain no longer registers them on the awareness. It was different living in the wilds.

Careful to permit no leaves to brush my shoulders, I worked my way through the brush and trees, pausing often to listen. It was a murmur of voices I heard and then the stronger smell of wood smoke; a moment later, the glimpse of fire.

At that moment I stood very still, alert to every sound. Now I was close. I had found them, but what was to be my next move, I did not know. At least one of them, Max Bauer himself, was a skilled woodsman, not to be trifled with. I wanted to see, to hear, to estimate their numbers, but not to be heard myself.

After a moment I edged closer, not over a few feet, and could see into their camp. I took care not to look directly at Bauer, although I could see him, or at Lashan, who was lying at one side.

"Not at daybreak," Bauer was saying. "Indians often attack then, but after daybreak when they have decided there will be no attack and they have relaxed. Some will be eating, some will be beginning their day's work. Not more than one, probably, on the walls. Lashan, you are good with a lance. Can you get that guard for me? Kill him instantly?"

"I can. At thirty feet, which is the closest I can get, it will be easy."

"Then kill him. I want him *dead*. If we cannot strike when the gate is open, we will go over the walls. Toss loops over the tops of the poles, and up you go, but I want at least a dozen men going up at once. The surprise will be complete. No looting and no women until every man is dead, you understand? Any man who does otherwise answers to me."

Lashan suddenly got to his feet. "Max? There's somebody out there!"

Turning swiftly, I slid through the brush and hit a path on the run. So far I thought I had made no sound, but behind me I heard a shout.

"All of you! Out there! Get him! Alive, if you can, but *get him!*"

Down the path I fled, knowing not where it led except that the general direction was toward Compass Creek. Turning from the path, I slid through a gap in the trees and ran desperately. Pulling up sharply, I heard a rustliing in the brush before me. Turning, I ran on, but slower, not knowing where to next expect an enemy.

A narrow, natural avenue through the trees opened. The clouds had broken, and there was a faint light. Dimly I could see, and I plunged on. If they took me now, it meant not only death but that they would use me, somehow, to force an opening of the gates.

Turning sharply right, I ran up a track that ran along a creek bed. The Tusquitee, I thought. The sky had clouded over again. Turning again, I started up a steep, rocky slope. I was hurrying, wanting to get back, to warn them of the impending attack. I saw an opening and plunged into it. Suddenly there was a sickening feeling of collapsing earth; a bank gave way, and I fell.

A sickening sense of failure and fear. I brought up with a terrific jolt, my skull rapped a rock, and that was all.

A groan, and a groan stifled. A feeling of chill, a sense of being wet, and a dull throbbing in my skull. My eyes opened on a gray world, low gray clouds, a grayish-black bank of mud rising above me and the crumbled edge over which I had fallen. It was not much of a fall, and I had landed in soft earth and water at the creek's edge. If only my skull had not rapped against that rock.

Heaving myself to a sitting position, I sat there while my head buzzed. It was daylight. What hour I knew not. Our enemies had not found me, or I should be either dead or a prisoner.

Shakily I got to my feet. The trail where I had been running was obviously long unused and had been undercut by the creek at high water. My head ached frightfully, and my neck was stiff. One knee had been bruised, also.

Looking around, I judged that the creek beside which I had fallen lay somewhere on the north slope of Piney Top, and to get back to the fort by the quickest route would be over the top of the ridge, roughly a climb of some two thousand feet, the last thousand feet very steep indeed.

Carefully I looked all around. The place where I had fallen was a small creek bed littered with stones and logs and scattered debris from the mountains above. The creek was only a couple of feet wide, a few inches deep. It was thickly walled with timber and brush right to the edge of the bank, and the mountain rose abruptly just beyond a curve in the stream bed.

There was no sound but that of a mockingbird singing in a tree a short distance off. I turned and started toward the mountain and almost fell. My knee was hurt worse than I had believed. My eyes swept the ground for a stick to be used for help in walking. Seeing nothing of the right sort, I staggered on, rounding the bend to find a broken branch about six feet long and an inch to two inches thick lying at the stream's edge. Taking it, I started on.

It was slow going. My head throbbed at every step, and my knee was stiff. It hurt when I walked, but there was no help for it.

Was I too late? Had Bauer made his attack? In an agony of fear, I pushed on, working my way through the laurel and up the slope. It was slow, painful work, with my leg so stiff it was awkward to walk. Yet at last I came to a low saddle with Piney Top on my right.

Grasping a branch for support, I stared through the leaves at the valley of Shooting Creek.

The fort was still there. Slow smoke rose from its chimneys, and all was still. From where I stood, no scene could have seemed more peaceful with the slow smoke rising and the sound of the creek stilled by distance. The fields lay easy under the sun, an island of cultivation in the vastness of the wilderness around.

Nothing yet. Or had it all been done? Had the fort been taken, our people slain? I could not believe it. Surely there would be some sign, some evidence of it, and there was none. But I was still far away, at least two miles in crow-flight distance but more than three miles on the ground and the way I must go. Not less than an hour, perhaps more.

Painfully I hobbled on, seeking the best route down the mountain. My knee had swollen, binding my pant leg as it stretched the buckskin.

To return was all I now thought. My venture had been for nothing. I had hoped to find some way, some means for creating havoc among them. I had done nothing but get myself hurt, and the news that they meant to attack would come too late to be of help now.

The mountainside was steep and the forest thick. It was at least two thousand feet of descent, but carefully I eased through the laurel and stopped under a huge old maple, lightning struck in some bygone time. Listening, I heard nothing. Soon the noise of the creek would make it doubly hard, for they did not call it Shooting Creek for nothing.

There was much fallen wood here, dead branches from the tree, and some great slabs of bark. A signal fire? It would only serve to let Bauer and his crew know where I was, and my own people might misread the signal and think me in trouble. They might try to reach me and so expose more of our strength to disaster.

What I did I had to do alone. And I had to trust to Yance and Jeremy, to Kane O'Hara and the others, to keep the fort. My task now was somehow to get down the mountain and into the fort.

Ferns grew waist high about me, and there was a tangle underfoot that I managed badly with my game leg. The continued silence from below worried me. There was no sound, no shot. Nothing.

What could have happened? When I stopped again, it was in a clump of yellow birches growing around an outcropping of rock. Sitting down on a rock, I took my knife and cut a thin slit in my legging to ease the swelling and constriction. It helped.

Wary, I studied the mountainside below me and

tried to see into the trees beyond the creek, but I saw nothing. A wood thrush skimmed past me and lighted on a branch almost over my head, regarding me with curiosity.

The clouds seemed to have broken, and here and there sunlight streamed through. Rising, I started again to limp my way through the forest. My move to somehow attack Bauer and his men had come to nothing, and I would be lucky to get back alive, all because of that fall into the gully.

Already the day was fading, and with darkness my chances of getting to the fort were greater, my chances of getting in much less. My fears grew. What had happened?

So far as I could see, and my vantage point permitted me to see into the enclosure, I saw no movement either in the yard or on the walls. Yet at the distance it was unlikely I could make out the figure of a man unless he was moving, and then only the movement would be visible.

Taking up my staff, I worked my way down the slope, traveling diagonally along it through the timber and brush. By the time I neared the bottom, shadows were long in the narrow valley.

Our fort lay no more than three hundred yards away now and scarcely half that distance from the edge of the trees, yet that was where Bauer's men would be if they had not begun their attack.

My leg throbbed, as did my head, although that ache had dulled as the day went by. Yet even my leg had loosened up some due to the constant movement and the release of constriction by slitting my legging.

Longingly I looked toward the fort. There were no lights. I told myself it was too early, yet it would be dark in the cabins, and there should be lights if anyone were alive to light them.

The valley around the fort was empty. Nothing stirred, nor was there any suggestion of movement.

Now was a time when I could use the help of the *Nunnehi,* the immortals that dwell beneath the mountains and rivers of this strange, wild land. The Cherokees spoke of them, whispered of them rather, with many a glance over the shoulder and into the shadows, for none knew when they might be about.

Suppose the fort had been deserted? That Yance had led the others into the forest? Yet that made no sense, as we had too much at stake in that small fort, all our families; our stored grain, jerked meat, whatever we had gained by our hard years on the frontier, were there or in the scattered cabins.

Yance was a shrewd one. Deliberately he might be playing possum, watching for a chance to make a strike that would destroy Bauer and all that he stood for.

Aware that I had been in one place too long, I moved, easing my way through the tangle of brush and trees near the clearing.

A faint whisper of movement alerted me. Knife in hand, I looked all about. Something was moving nearby. Some crawling sound. Drawing back, I put my back against the trunk of a huge old maple and waited.

Waited, knife in hand.

Chapter XXIV

My body was flattened against the maple, a big old tree at least three feet through, so my back was well covered. I gripped the staff in my left hand, but the knife I carried low, cutting edge up.

Whoever was coming was a woodsman. I knew that by the way he moved. Something stirred in the leaves not three feet away. A sudden lunge and I could have the blade into him, but I was never one to start shooting or cutting on something I didn't see. There are would-be hunters who will blaze away at anything that moves, but I must see and identify.

He was rising from the ground, and I knew he sensed my presence. He knew something or someone was close by; it is a feeling one gets.

I took a careful step forward with my left foot, putting the end of the staff firmly on the ground, ready to cut upward with the knife.

A hand, then the rough outline of a head. Starting forward, I suddenly froze in place. I knew that—!

"Yance?" I breathed the word.

He came through the leaves as though materializing from them. He was grinning widely. I could not see his eyes, but his white teeth showed his smile.

"Worried about you, lad. Where've you been?"

"Waiting for you," I replied softly. "What's happened?"

"Jeremy's holding the fort. We're hoping to get them out in the open. Get them to thinkin' maybe we've slipped away. No fires, no lights, everything quiet and ready.

"Me an' the Catawbas, we didn't take to bein' cooped up, so we slipped out. We're all here, holdin' fast. If they rush the fort, we'll take them from behind, and I think they're fixin' to."

He moved closer. "You all right?"

"I took a fall."

We waited together, listening. It was good to have Yance there beside me, for we had been a team since we'd been old enough to travel together.

"How's Diana?"

"Worried about you. She's got herself a couple of pistols hard by, an' she's ready." He turned to look at me. "You picked a good one, Kin. She'll do."

It was dark now, but the clouds were broken, and here and there we could see a scattering of stars. The air had grown suddenly cool. I sheathed my knife for the moment, drying my hands on the front of my buckskin shirt. The night was very still, and we waited, listening, our ears seeking out the unnatural, unexpected sounds, but there were none. It reassured me that the Catawbas were out and around, for they were good men and great warriors.

We could but dimly see the stark black line of the fort against the sky and the huge old trees that lay just beyond it. From where we now lay the fort was only slightly more than a hundred yards away, the ground open. Only on the north side had we allowed the trees to grow close to the fort, as the half-dozen trees left standing there provided shade during the hotter months.

It was quiet. Yance put his lips close to my ear. "Kin? I'm scared. Something's wrong!"

My eyes were on the line of the wall against the sky. A breeze stirred the branches in the chestnut trees beyond the wall. I could see the branches move slightly against the sky.

Suddenly I swore bitterly. The branches moved! *But there was no breeze!*

"Yance! They're coming over the wall!"

And then I was running. My injured leg forgotten, I lunged from the ground and ran for the fort, Yance only a step behind me.

As we ran, we saw several men round the corner of the fort just as the gate swung wide. "In here!"

There was a shot from inside the fort, then a scream and another shot. Men were crowding at the gate, and Yance and I reached it on the run.

A burly bearded man, pistol in hand, turned to shout. At that moment there was a flash of light from inside, a pistol that missed fire, and I caught a fleeting glimpse of his shocked expression as he recognized me, and at that same instant I ripped him, low and upward. He let out a gasping cry, and I shoved him back, grabbing for his pistol with my left hand. He let go of it, falling back, and then I was past him and in the gate.

Yance was at my shoulder. "Sackett here!" I yelled not wanting them to shoot into us, and I heard Jeremy's answering shout.

How many there were of them I never knew. It was cut and shoot. I fired my pistol, then threw it at a head that loomed before me and had the satisfaction of seeing it bounce off a skull.

Yance was down, then up. A wicked blow, a glancing one, opened a gash in my skull. My head rang with the blow, but I kept my feet.

Pulling back, I looked wildly around, seeking Bauer, but he was nowhere in sight. The door to my house stood open, and I sprang past the fighting and ran to it.

"I wish he was here," Bauer was saying, "to see you die."

He held a pistol in his hand, and he was facing Diana. "I am here, Max," I said, and he turned sharply.

He was not one to dally but was ready for instant action. His eyes caught me as his ears registered my voice, and as he turned, he fired.

Yet his shot was too quick; anticipating it, I had

221

lunged to his right. I felt the heat of the blast and the fiery sting of powder grains on my cheek.

He turned sharply as I lunged at him and struck down with the pistol barrel. Missing my skull, the blow came down across the top of my shoulder, and only the thick muscles there kept me from a broken bone. As it was, my right arm was stricken numb for the moment, and the knife dropped from my hand.

He came at me then, a small smile on his lips, for he was sure he had me. The look in his eyes was almost amused. He had his knife low and ready, the pistol in the other hand now. Warily I backed away, watching my chance.

The room was large for the time and place, but the fireplace, where lay fire tongs and poker, was across the big table from me and hopelessly out of reach.

There was no nonsense about him now. He was coming in for the kill, and I had only my bare hands with which to face him. He worked me into a corner, and there was no chance to elude him, although I had brought him away from Diana.

One thing I knew. Somehow I had to kill him, for if he killed me, Diana would die in the next moment. From outside there was a confused sound of fighting, shouts, and the clash of arms. There were several shots. They needed me out there, too.

Bauer took a wicked slash at my stomach, which I evaded by a leap backward that brought me up hard against the wall. He lunged with the knife, but I sidestepped away along the wall and got into the open again. I feinted a rush, but he merely smiled. He moved quickly, cutting left and right. He ripped a gash in my hunting jacket and scratched my arm. The numbness was almost gone now. I backed away again, and he came on and thrust hard.

Slapping his knife hand aside with my left hand, I grasped his wrist with my right and threw my left leg across in front of him and spilled him over that leg to the floor. Desperately I tried to wrench the knife from him, but his grip was strong. We rolled over on the floor, and I was up first. He was too strong and too heavy on the floor. To fight him, I had to be on my feet.

He came up fast, and my kick missed his head. My heel hit solidly against his shoulder, but he only missed a step and came on.

He slashed at me, and I hit him across the mouth, throwing a kick at his kneecap that missed, and then he was on me. I went down before his attack, and then he was atop me and holding my throat with one hand and coming down with the knife. Somewhere he had lost his grip upon his pistol.

The knife came down hard, and I twisted my head only in time. The knife hit the floor, and I hit him with my fist with a blow that turned his head and momentarily stunned him.

Throwing him off, I leaped to my feet, and he came up, knife in hand. Diana suddenly called "Kin!" and tossed me the poker from the fireplace.

I caught it deftly. It was two and a half feet long with a point and a hook, also sharply pointed. Holding it ready, I moved in. He leaped at me with the knife, and I thrust hard with the point of the poker. It caught him coming in, and the point went in all of two inches low on his right side.

He jerked back, but twisting the poker, I caught the hook in his clothing and jerked hard. His shirt ripped, and the hook tore a bloody gash—not deep—across his belly.

From outside the noise of fighting had ceased. His smile was cool. "It is too late now," he said. "My men have won. Give her to me and that letter and you shall go free and we'll not burn your fort. After all, there are other women."

My poker held ready, I made no reply. His knife was not a small one but a fifteen-inch blade, thick and heavy. Blood was staining his shirt from the wound on his right side, and there was an angry streak of blood along the thin cut on his belly.

The poker, for all its usefulness, was unwieldy,

and if his wounds bothered him, there was no evidence of it. He was an unusually strong, agile man and obviously was no stranger to hand-to-hand fighting.

Suddenly Diana screamed, *"Kin!"*

Lashan was in the doorway, pistol in hand. As my eyes caught him, his pistol was lifting to take dead aim at me. I could not hesitate nor even take the time to think, I simply tossed up the poker, caught it by the middle, and threw it as a spear.

The poker struck him even as he fired, deflecting his shot by only a hair. The ball struck behind me, and I saw Lashan fall, and the next instant Bauer was on me, thrusting and stabbing. Whether he had hit me, I did not know, but his blade was bloody. Back hard against the wall, I grabbed his head by both ears and jerked his face down as I butted up with my skull. I felt his nose crunch, and then I shoved him off and swung a right fist at the point of his jaw. It caught him off balance, and he fell backward to the floor.

He had lost his grip on the knife, but he lunged up from the floor and came at me. I struck straight and hard to his already broken nose. Both of us were bloody, but neither had time to realize whether we were hurt or not. I struck him again, and he grabbed at my throat with both hands.

Stepping aside, I hit him again. He closed with me and got a hand up, clawing for my eyes. Twisting my head, I got my shoulder under his chin and jerked up hard. Again I shook him off. He was weaving now, exhausted as I was, but I gave him no chance. I struck hard with my right, and as he staggered, I knocked him back against the doorjamb.

Lashan was up, his face bloody from where the thrown poker had struck him, but before he could join Bauer against me, Yance loomed in the door. Lashan turned, and Yance, gripping a pistol, shot him.

He fell backward, turning as he fell, and Bauer broke off the fight and plunged past Yance through the open door. The gate yawned opposite.

Some of his men lay dead; others were fleeing

across the open ground toward the forest. He was running toward the gate, blood flying from his wounds, when Diana tossed my knife. I grasped it by the point and threw—

The knife struck him in the middle of the back, and he took on last leap forward, then sprawled on the ground just outside the gate.

For a long moment I simply stood there, staring at his fallen body, hands hanging empty at my sides. There was no more fighting. Our Catawbas had scattered into the woods, and I knew there would be no stragglers reaching the coast, not even to report what had happened. I could only stand, exhausted and empty, staring at the man who had brought so much trouble to so many. That he was dead I had no doubt, for my knife must have severed his spine, and it had been thrown hard.

A bad man but a damned good fighting man. Almost too good.

"Kin?" It was Diana. "Come, you're hurt. Let me see to you."

Dumbly I let her lead me inside and to a seat. Now, of a sudden, I began to hurt. My bruised leg, oddly enough, hurt the most.

Outside I could hear the mumble of talk as our people cleared up, carried away the bodies of the dead, and once more closed our gates against the world.

Yance came in. He looked at me, worried. "You all right there, big Injun?"

"All right. How about the others?"

"Wounds—mostly scratches. We were lucky. And waiting for them."

Lila came in and watched Diana's skillful fingers. "You're like your pa," she said. "You fight well."

"And Jeremy," I said.

One of the candles had been knocked over during the fighting but had luckily gone out. Lila lighted it again, adding more light to the room. Outside, the lighted bundles of brush that had given light in the yard were slowly burning down.

225

Leaning my head against the back of the chair, I closed my eyes. Diana was putting something cooling on the places where I had been cut and stabbed. She was using some concoction made from herbs that she kept ready for such things, and Lila was beside her.

Apparently I had been stabbed at least twice and had several bad scratches, yet at the moment I wanted only to rest.

Yance and Jeremy came in. Then, as they talked, Kane O'Hara joined them. Three men, they said, had been killed from Bauer's party. There might have been more who got away into the shelter of the forest. If so, I did not envy them, for the Catawbas were great hunters, and we had long been their friends. The most hospitable of people to friends, against enemies they were ruthless.

"We will go for your father," I said, "or send someone."

"I know," Diana replied. "Don't think of it now. Just get some rest."

My eyes closed again. Something was cooking at the fireplace, and it smelled good. Warm, friendly smells were all about me.

Tired as I was, I did not want to sleep. I wanted simply to enjoy.

I was home again.

ABOUT THE AUTHOR

LOUIS L'AMOUR, born Louis Dearborn L'Amour, is of French-Irish descent. Although Mr. L'Amour claims his writing began as a "spur-of-the-moment thing," prompted by friends who relished his verbal tales of the West, he comes by his talent honestly. A frontiersman by heritage (his grandfather was scalped by the Sioux), and a universal man by experience, Louis L'Amour lives the life of his fictional heroes. Since leaving his native Jamestown, North Dakota, at the age of fifteen, he's been a longshoreman, lumberjack, elephant handler, hay shocker, flume builder, fruit picker, and an officer on tank destroyers during World War II. And he's written four hundred short stories and over fifty books (including a volume of poetry).

Mr. L'Amour has lectured widely, traveled the West thoroughly, studied archaeology, compiled biographies of over one thousand Western gunfighters, and read prodigiously (his library holds more than two thousand volumes). And he's watched thirty-one of his westerns as movies. He's circled the world on a freighter, mined in the West, sailed a dhow on the Red Sea, been shipwrecked in the West Indies, stranded in the Mojave Desert. He's won fifty-one of fifty-nine fights as a professional boxer and pinch-hit for Dorothy Kilgallen when she was on vacation from her column. Since 1816, thirty-three members of his family have been writers. And, he says, "I could sit in the middle of Sunset Boulevard and write with my typewriter on my knees; temperamental I am not."

Mr. L'Amour is re-creating an 1865 Western town, christened Shalako, where the borders of Utah, Arizona, New Mexico, and Colorado meet. Historically authentic from whistle to well, it will be a live, operating town, as well as a movie location and tourist attraction.

Mr. L'Amour now lives in Los Angeles with his wife Kathy, who helps with the enormous amount of research he does for his books. Soon, Mr. L'Amour hopes, the children (Beau and Angelique) will be helping too.

Now Available!
The Complete Sackett Family Saga in a Boxed Set

THE SACKETT NOVELS
OF LOUIS L'AMOUR

$29.95   **(01300-9)**

Now, for the first time, the 15 novels of the Sackett family have been collected in four handsome large-size volumes with a beautifully designed gift box. Each volume has a special introduction by L'Amour.

These best-selling L'Amour novels tell the story of the American frontier as seen through the eyes of one bold family, the Sacketts. From generation to generation, the Sacketts conquered the frontier from the wild forests of the East to the dust cattle trails of the Great Plains to the far mountains of the West. Tough and proud, the Sacketts explored the wilderness, settled the towns, established the laws, building a mighty Western tradition of strength and courage.

You can enjoy all these exciting frontier stories of the Sacketts by ordering your boxed set today. And remember, this boxed set is the perfect gift for a L'Amour fan.

Use this handy coupon for ordering:

BANTAM'S #1
ALL-TIME BESTSELLING AUTHOR
AMERICA'S FAVORITE WESTERN WRITER

☐	14931	THE STRONG SHALL LIVE	$2.25
☐	14977	BENDIGO SHAFTER	$2.50
☐	13881	THE KEY-LOCK MAN	$1.95
☐	13719	RADIGAN	$1.95
☐	13609	WAR PARTY	$1.95
☐	13882	KIOWA TRAIL	$1.95
☐	20460	THE BURNING HILLS	$2.25
☐	14762	SHALAKO	$2.25
☐	14881	KILRONE	$2.25
☐	20139	THE RIDER OF LOST CREEK	$2.25
☐	13798	CALLAGHEN	$1.95
☐	20180	THE QUICK AND THE DEAD	$2.25
☐	14219	OVER ON THE DRY SIDE	$1.95
☐	20473	DOWN THE LONG HILLS	$2.25
☐	20219	WESTWARD THE TIDE	$2.25
☐	14227	KID RODELO	$1.95
☐	20468	BROKEN GUN	$2.25
☐	13898	WHERE THE LONG GRASS BLOWS	$1.95
☐	14411	HOW THE WEST WAS WON	$1.95

Buy them at your local bookstore or use this handy coupon for ordering:

Bantam Books, Inc., Dept. LL2, 414 East Golf Road, Des Plaines, Ill. 60016

Please send me the books I have checked above. I am enclosing $_____ (please add $1.00 to cover postage and handling). Send check or money order —no cash or C.O.D.'s please.

Mr/Mrs/Miss_____

Address_____

City_____ State/Zip_____

LL2—7/81

Please allow four to six weeks for delivery. This offer expires 1/82.